sit-down comedy

sit-down comedy

edited by malcolm hardee and john fleming

EBURY
PRESS

1 3 5 7 9 10 8 6 4 2

First published 2003 by Ebury Press,
an imprint of Random House,
20 Vauxhall Bridge Road, London SW1V 2SA
www.randomhouse.co.uk

The Random House Group Limited supports The Forest Stewardship
Council (FSC®), the leading international forest certification organisation.
Our books carrying the FSC label are printed on FSC® certified paper.
FSC is the only forest certification scheme endorsed by the leading
environmental organisations, including Greenpeace. Our
paper procurement policy can be found at
www.randomhouse.co.uk/environment

Addresses for companies within The Random House Group Limited can be found at:
www.randomhouse.co.uk/offices.htm

The Random House Group Limited Reg. No. 954009

www.randomhouse.co.uk

Printed and bound in Great Britain by Clays Ltd, St Ives PLC

A CIP catalogue record for this book
is available from the British Library.

Cover design by Jon Gray
Interior by seagulls

ISBN 0091889243

FSC
www.fsc.org

MIX
Paper | Supporting
responsible forestry
FSC® C018179

contents

Forever remembered by the public for performing the naked Balloon Dance on TV show OTT as a member of The Greatest Show on Legs, Malcolm is an iconic legend to alternative comedians: a former agent, manager and confidant to many of the successful acts of the last 25 years. His Tunnel Club in Greenwich gave early career boosts to everyone from Harry Enfield to Jo Brand and Harry Hill while his award-winning Up The Creek club continues to discover new talent. His autobiography I Stole Freddie Mercury's Birthday Cake has become a collectors' item.

malcolm hardee

There are only two things you can do when you come out of prison and you want immediate employment. You can either be a minicab driver or you can go into showbusiness. When I came out of Exeter Prison three days after Jubilee Day in 1977, I did both.

I became a minicab driver and I joined The Greatest Show on Legs which, at that time, was a Punch & Judy show – it later developed into one of the forerunners of what became known as alternative comedy.

I went back into prison in 1979 for a short stretch and, when I re-emerged, I put all my eggs in the comedy basket because it was becoming a burgeoning thing and places like the Comedy Store were opening up. The result was that, over the years, I have met, worked with, booked, managed or agented for all the contributors to this book.

I've known **John Dowie** even longer than I've known Arthur Smith. I remember a gig with John in the 1970s when I was still doing the Punch & Judy show and he was hopping around from leg to leg at someone's party. John was doing stand-up even before the Comedy Store and Tony Allen and all that lot. But he was always more of a poet. He sort of left stand-up comedy and moved down to Brighton and has linked up with an old friend of mine, Neil Innes of the Bonzo Dog Doo Dah Band, who I never really played with except I did a couple of times.

Arthur Smith I met at the Edinburgh Fringe in 1981 when he was part of the National Revue Company, an official-sounding name for a bunch of four chancers. I swear that Arthur is actually the bastard son of Sid James. He's never confirmed or denied this, but I do know Sid James put himself about a lot. He and I have been appearing at the Edinburgh Festival for years but, so far, we've never appeared there together because we're too similar. We're both drinkers and womanisers and there's never been enough to go round. Though, now he's given up drinking due to health problems, there might be. I owe him £2,000 plus £175 when I was forced to break the window in his front door, but that's another story.

In 1984, I started the Tunnel Club at the south end of the Dartford Tunnel under the River Thames and **John Hegley** performed there on the opening week. He has been performing on the circuit for as long as anyone can remember. At one time, he was in the Brown Paper Bag Brothers which comprised him and a man called Otiz Canneloni. They were both called John on-stage and both carried brown paper bags. They said things like, "My bag's better than your bag," and tried to outdo each other on the bag front. Quite funny. He's very good. I don't like poetry at all, but his poetry's more like stand-up. He has managed to make verse a comic art form.

As the Tunnel Club developed, I started being agent to some of the acts, including **Jenny Eclair** who is an old friend. I haven't shagged her. I thought about it once, but Jo Brand was free at the time. Apparently, I'm her favourite comic. I don't know why. She lives about five miles from my ship in south London and never comes to see me. But, when I was living in quite a nice house, she did her *Jenny Eclair Squats* series for Channel 5 and brought a television crew with guests round to my house and we had a bit of a drink-up and then they went away and they cleaned it up very nicely before they went. Afterwards, she told me I had made all the other guests feel very nervous because they were all journalists pretending to be a bit hard and I was 'a proper big fat old lag'. She said it made her laugh like a drain.

In her early days, she perhaps didn't always judge her audiences correctly. She was performing at the Elephant Fair in Cornwall in the 1980s. She was filling in for the anarchistic Vicious Boys, whose audience comprised the great unwashed. I was the compere and introduced her with: "The Vicious Boys can't make it, but here's the next best thing – Jenny Eclair!" She came on dressed immaculately in a sophisticated cocktail dress and her opening line was: "You know the problems you can have with a Hostess trolley at a dinner party?" I'd like to say she won the audience round, but she didn't.

Jim Tavaré had trouble too. He used to come down to the Tunnel and do open spots. He was initially known as James Kerouac (as in the writer) although his name really is Jim Tavaré – related to the famous cricketer Chris Tavaré. It was at the Tunnel he received what became a famous heckle. He walked on stage and said, "Hello. I'm a schizophrenic," and immediately someone shouted out: "Well, you can *both* fuck off, then!" Jim used to die a death week after week after week at the Tunnel until, one week, he turned up and did exactly the same jokes while holding a double bass. He's never gone down badly since. He's now a favourite of Prince Charles and does shows in front of the crowned heads of Europe.

Another Tunnel performer was **Hattie Hayridge**. She was definitely there and I think I used to help her out in the early days when she was starting, but I can't remember. I think I may have been drunk. I know Hattie did Tunnel spots three or four times. Once, they started chanting: "Burn the Witch!" but she got away with it. She's not as quiet as she looks – some bloke threw an egg at her one night and she went over and punched him. She always comes to my birthday parties. I bumped into her in Bournemouth one Christmas. She was walking along with her mother. I remember that well.

I met **Linda Smith** around the same time as Hattie. She was quite a radical feminist in the early days and I vividly remember her at a meeting where Ivor Dembina tried to get a comics' union together and Linda said women should be equally represented on the bill: whenever there was a bill of four people, there should be two women and two men. I said, "Well you should have the proportion of people who're over 50 on each bill then." Despite this, she's always been surprisingly nice to me. It might have something to do with the fact that she says none of that story is true.

When I showed her what I'd written, Linda couldn't stop laughing: "Well, at least it doesn't say I was molesting donkeys, Malcolm, but none of it's even half-true." She says she never went to any of Ivor's meetings because she lived in Sheffield at the time; she was never a radical feminist and never went for that 'equal representation' stuff. "You must've been drunk," she told me. "Maybe you've got me confused with Jeff Green."

Even **Dave Thompson** says my memory's a bit unreliable. *Time Out* called Dave 'The weirdest dude on the face of the earth', and I have to admit he is a *bit* weird. He came along to perform at the Tunnel with his girlfriend Charmian Hughes who billed herself, for some reason, as Teatro De Existentiale. The audience at the Tunnel didn't like overtly arty performers. Charmian went on stage wearing a tutu and died a most horrible death. The audience was very unsympathetic, to say the least; she came off after a very short time. I then introduced Dave with the lines, "Well, you've been very cruel to her, however the next act is very good ... and he's her boyfriend." After about three minutes of Dave's act, somebody shouted out: "Malcolm! Don't let them have children!"

Yet another contributor who had a hard time at the Tunnel was **Stephen Frost**. I remember when he and Mark Arden were performing as the Oblivion Boys. They were quite big because they were on TV in *The Young Ones* and other shows, but they were dying a death one night at the Tunnel and people were throwing beer glasses at them (which was a tradition at the Tunnel Club). I went on stage with Stephen to try and help out, but the audience still threw things. Stephen, Arthur Smith and I have lasted the course at the Edinburgh Fringe. Stephen's been around. He's been on Arthur Smith's tour of Edinburgh. He's been up lamp posts naked.

Owen O'Neill is another stalwart of both the Fringe and the Tunnel Club. He used to be an alcoholic and in the early days his poetry was gripping. Having given up the drink for a number of years, he now lives at peace with himself in Hounslow. This peace, of course, is shattered by the fact that he lives directly under Heathrow's flight path. He recently revealed he wants me to marry him because, now I'm the captain of my own ship, I'm allowed to carry out marriage ceremonies. He's trying to persuade his betrothed – well, they've lived together years and they've got a kid. The piece that he has written for *Sit-Down Comedy* is one of my favourites and I don't owe him any money. He appeared not only at the Tunnel but also, like most of the contributors, at my next club Up The Creek which I opened in Greenwich in 1991.

I met **Boothby Graffoe** during the recording of a TV programme unimaginatively called *Stand Up* and invited him to perform at Up The Creek. I've got millions of stories about Boothby, quite a few unprintable, because I actually shared a flat with him for a while. He leaves his wife every year and, on this occasion, I'd just split with mine too. Until he stayed with me, I didn't realise how much of a night person he is. In the winter, he never got up until about four o'clock in the afternoon, so he never saw daylight. He just used to go out and work like a demon at night then stay up on his computer writing – always writing things. He's a very underrated comic and should be up there with all the ones who *are* up there, wherever up there is. He's always a success at Up The Creek, as is **Tim Vine**, whose one-liners the patrons like a lot.

Tim's a very strange man. When they were building the Millennium Dome, they wanted to have the skull of a stand-up comic in the Body Zone and this skull would tell two minutes of jokes on a loop. They phoned me up and I went to see this extraordinary man who gave me £500 just for advice; he wore an Armani suit but no shoes. I recommended that they should use Tim Vine because he is very much a one-liner merchant but I also said, "If you really want one-liners, Tommy Cooper would be your best. But he's dead, of course." So they phoned up a Tommy Cooper impersonator and paid Tommy Cooper's estate an enormous amount of money to tell his jokes. But then they needed laughter, so they went to Up The Creek, recorded some audiences laughing and paid me another £500.

"It's not going to work," I told them, "because laughter from other people's gags won't be in rhythm with the Tommy Cooper jokes you've got." And I was right. They phoned up, panicking, and asked me, "Can you go into a studio for two hours and tell the Tommy Cooper jokes and we'll get the laughter off that." So I went into a studio with my mate Chris Luby and they paid me even more money plus they paid an audience of sixty people £50 each to sit outside the studio with headphones on and laugh at our version of Tommy Cooper's old jokes. We couldn't see the audience; they couldn't see us. If you went to the Body Zone in the Dome, you'll have heard this Tommy Cooper impersonator and lots of strange laughter. It should have been Tim Vine with real laughter and he would have been funnier. He's a master of the one-liner and has strange relations. The presenter Jeremy Vine is his brother and David Vine's a cousin. He's a Christian and plays the organ in church, so very rarely works on Sunday.

Ed Byrne is one of our Irish friends from across the water – he lives in North London. I think I might have given him his first

British gig at Up The Creek, but I can't remember. I may have been drunk again. He's probably had more women than me and Arthur Smith put together and some of them didn't even realise he was a comedian until afterwards. He's a fine performer and it's a pity they made *Father Ted* before he was around on the circuit. I'm sure he'd have had a major part.

Stewart Lee is one of your Oxford University lot and seems to know more about me than I know about him. I think his story in this book is very closely based on me. He wrote a lovely review of my autobiography *I Stole Freddie Mercury's Birthday Cake* for the *Sunday Times*. I see him every year at the Glastonbury Festival. Every year, I say to him: "You know what, Stewart, I remember this when it was all fields," and every year he laughs, which is very kind of him.

He's matey with **Simon Munnery**, who is what people would call a comic genius sometimes and he actually is a genius. He's been rated at genius level on the old Mensa scale and all that. He was at Cambridge University and was all set up to be a nuclear physicist. That was going to be his life. But, instead, he found the world of comedy, drink and drugs. That's how he's ended up like he is. He's better as a comic. Physics would have driven him mad and he'd probably have ended up bombing everyone by now. Better to get his anger out in comedy rather than making bombs.

Stewart and Simon are Oxbridge. The East End element in this book is represented by Jeff Innocent and Ricky Grover.

Jeff Innocent is a relative newcomer to the comedy scene. When he realised that a university education didn't work for a Cockney and that he couldn't sing, he tried his hand at stand-up with great success. His sartorial elegance is matched by his observations on the rich and varied lives of the old East Enders. It's about time he either had a regular part in *EastEnders* or hosted a quiz or game show where contestants get beaten up for giving the wrong answer. He could also step into the shoes of the late Arthur Mullard, which reminds me of a gag I used to tell, where I produced a wooden duck on stage, cut it in half with a saw, held the two halves aloft and said: "Alf-a mallard!" Doesn't really work on paper.

Anyway, that takes us to **Ricky Grover**, perhaps my favourite stand-up, particularly as his character Bulla is really just Ricky with a string vest. He's come on the scene fairly recently and he did his first gigs at Up The Creek. He used to be a boxer as well as other things. I took him up to the Edinburgh Fringe and he knocked out comedian Ian Cognito. He's a very nice man, but you wouldn't want to mess with him.

Finally, the youngest – or, at least, the youngest-looking – of the contributors is **Dominic Holland**. I've booked him at various clubs and he seems a very nice young man. If you were a girl, you could take him home to your parents and they'd love him. He's a *What if...* comedian. A *Have you ever noticed...* comedian. He's a very funny observational comedian but doesn't take his clothes off on stage or climb naked up lamp posts, so he's not like me. He's a very good writer and has turned to writing books of late; I hear his novel *Only in America* is a belter.

The thing about this *Sit-Down Comedy* book you're about to read is ... well, it's actually not quite the book we expected. But, if you commission people with original minds to write anything they fancy in any style in any genre, you're bound to get something unexpected. What we got was a series of very well-written tales of beheadings, psychopaths, robbers, tramps, bombs in toilets, some gentle poetic fantasy and one piece that I think even owes a debt to Samuel Beckett. It's occasionally very funny, but not the superficial laugh-a-minute gagathon we all thought we were going to get. It's better than that. Fortunately, the publisher liked it, still laughed at lots of bits and gave us the money. So here it is. Oy oy!

Born in 1968, Stewart came to prominence as part of the comedy duo Lee and Herring, who had two BBC2 series: Fist of Fun *and* This Morning with Richard Not Judy. *His debut novel* The Perfect Fool *was published to great acclaim in 2001. His radio work includes* Lionel Nimrod's Inexplicable World *and* On The Hour *for which he won a Writers' Guild Award and a* Radio Times *Comedy Award. He is also rock critic for the* Sunday Times. *He directed and co-wrote the libretto for* Jerry Springer – The Opera.

stewart lee

i'll only go if you throw glass

They say you play Bangor University Student Union twice in your career. I'll be there in an hour, for the second time. I had run out of money. There was nothing on the horizon, at least nothing for me, nothing I could call mine. Respective heads of TV comedy depts had played musical chairs again. The ones that liked me missed their seats and sighed and waited for sackings or suicides. I grew pallid in Stoke Newington and bled into the toilet bowl. After six months lost in the NHS system, I cashed my last cheque for a consultation with a showbiz physician. He prodded my liver and banned me from drinking. So here was I, sober and dry, returning to the stand-up circuit to die, scrabbling for loose change, and at my age. But I had a trade, see, something to fall back on, like a plumber or an electrician. And I was going again, just a little ashamed, to Bangor University Student Union.

Bangor was the worst stand-up gig on the National Comedy Network. It took pride in its hostility and so, like the entire city of Glasgow, was regarded with suspicion. "If you don't do the required time," explained the Entertainments Officer, complicit in the scheme, "your fee will be reduced according to how short your set has been." Yes, last time I was in Bangor teenage drunks threw plastic glasses. Experiences like this had crushed my faith in the masses.

"I'll only go if you throw glass," I said, wittily, from the stage, and security guards dodged the shards to enter the melee. It was a good line, and it was funny, but it wasn't one of mine, and they still docked my money.

I'll only go if you throw glass, was an old standard from an old stand-up, Malcolm Tracey. And Malcolm Tracey was coming. To Bangor. With me.

Now he sits in the car un-speaking, reading pornography and smoking, with Scott Walker quietly exploding on his personal stereo. He will not shut the window. And it is starting to snow. I don't think you can begin to understand what Malcy's presence means to me, at this strange stage in what I call my so-called career. I'll try and explain.

Five hours earlier, at the top of a council block in Finchley, I rang the bell and waited to be met by Mrs Tracey. The door swung in and there she stood, pinch-faced, small and shrewish, an apron tied around her waist and a rolling pin in hand, as if assembled to express some absurd ideal of everything I'd feared. "Who are you and what do you want?" she hissed through lipstick lips. "I'm Tim and I have come," I said, "to pick up Malcy, your only son. I am going to Bangor to perform. And he's coming too as my support." "You don't look old enough," she said, and took my hand and stroked my hair. And studying my sick-thin face, she laughed and led me in. From the kitchen she called out, "It's a young man called Tim." Malcy grunted from a box room, a fifty-year-old teenage boy. I looked over my shoulder and glimpsed him through a door, going about his business, crouched upon the floor. A black suit shape beside the bed, scratching at his balding head, he stuffed debris into a bag and searched for cigarettes.

Malcy's mother sat me down and chattered as she worked. Something about tranquillisers and did I want some grub? Not that service station muck, but something she would rustle up. We came to an agreement and she made me a packed lunch. She boxed it up in Tupperware and sat it next to Malcy's fare, identical in all respects, a cake, an apple and some crisps. I drank my tea and looked around. It had come to this. Going back to Bangor for two hundred and fifty quid. Thirty-five and finished and not allowed to drink. But I would be accompanied by my one consolation. Malcolm Tracey, formerly known as Mal Co-ordinated.

Malcy was the missing link between the perfume and the stink, between cheap Channel 5 stand-up filler, between a million sneering panel shows, between the alleged death of The Spirit Of The Fringe, between the stage of the Hackney Empire and the screen of the Empire Leicester Square, between squatted 1970s gigs in Stepney and the comedy colonisation of the provinces, between the transfiguration of the mainstream, between a new generation of prancing ponces, between all that and more, back to the first time anybody chalked upon a board the noble phrase, that presaged change, and turned the ripple to a wave, the secret signal to the brave, *Alternative Cabaret*.

No one knew how Malcy had begun, where he had sprung from and how he had grown, nor where he had gone to for most of the Nineties, when he appeared to disown his progeny and tied his talent in a sack and drowned it in the sea. The history, such as it was, was contradictory. Lisa Appignanesi's book on Cabaret included a photo of him in the final chapter. He was wild-haired in a leotard and snarling like a panther, at a venue called the Earth Exchange that the comedy circuit left to rot long before my first open spot. A pamphlet I bought at Leicester Art Gallery tied Malcy in to Seventies Arts Lab anarchy. Victoria Wood once mentioned him when asked who had inspired her to begin. A journalist called John Connor wrote a book on the Fringe in Edinburgh. But he had an ideological axe to grind, and Malcy's work got left behind. Someone told me it was Malcy who first coined the term *Alternative Cabaret*. Working in South Devon in 1972, he used it to advertise a Punch and Judy Show. From inside a stripy tent he increased the violence content, and threw in an act of anal sex between wooden puppets. In the beer garden of a plush hotel Malcy found he'd caused offence, and was compelled to grab his effigies and flee from the South West. Then there were the years of petty crime and drugs, the years spent dancing naked in Soho in gay clubs, and rumours of unsavoury acts and criminal convictions, and of time spent in prison for unspecified actions.

On release Malcy played folk clubs and festivals until the Alternative Comedy scene coalesced. He never had an act as such, it seemed, but still stormed the gigs with only a harmonica, a pack of cards, a dirty pair of Y-fronts and a bag of different wigs. Somehow he could usually hold a crowd. You could almost hear them thinking aloud, "Can this be it? It's fucking shit." They sat bewildered and entranced, waiting for Mal, as if by chance, to achieve something recognisable, something tangible and definable. But he never did. A harmonica solo, a poem, a song and then a joke. A magic trick, a puppet show, and then a puff of smoke. A purple wig, an inflatable pig, a visceral torrent of abuse, a spastic dance in a tight red suit. And then the climax, the coup de grace – Malcy turned round and dropped his pants.

I first saw him in '84, at a club in Birmingham supporting The Fall. The disgruntled fans showed their disdain for Malcy's refusal to entertain. Leaning drunk upon the mike stand with a beer bottle in each hand, he told the same joke again and again, until they tried to shift him with polystyrene cups and empty cans. Acknowledging defeat he said, "I'll only go if you throw glass," the immortal line that would one day be mine. But a shoe connected with his head and he died upon his arse. The performance was recorded and released as a seven-inch single. I knew every shout and jeer and each embarrassed giggle. But I did not know what I had seen. Had Malcy failed, or did he succeed? All I knew was that somewhere, beyond the suburbs where I went to school, it seemed there were heroic deeds, irrational acts and holy fools.

I next saw Malcy in Edinburgh in 1987, falling drunk down the Fringe Club stairs at a quarter past eleven, raising his glass and cursing heaven, dressed as Vladimir Lenin. And two years later at the Glastonbury Festival, he punched an inflatable woman in the face at the other end of the cabaret tent. My girlfriend called it a disgrace. She had a point, I must confess. Three months later, I moved to London. My fledgling career had begun. I won five hundred pounds in a new acts competition, got signed up to an agency with a handshake and no conditions. They took me to the top floor of a tiny West End office and pointed out across the land, beyond the upstairs rooms of pubs, at the uncharted territories of student union premises that they promised would collapse and fall into our waiting laps. And soon I was out on the road, only twenty-one years old, and support act to none other than Mal Co-ordinated. Or, as he was currently billed, *Malcolm Tracey, formerly Mal Co-ordinated*. Times had changed for the better in that respect at least.

Malcy didn't drive. So I chauffeured him hundreds of miles between bizarrely scheduled dates. Aberdeen to Derby in a day. Malcy was paid a thousand pounds a show, of which he gave me sixty. Some days he was convivial, other days withdrawn. Some days he was charming, other days a bore. Once in Leeds, or Bradford, he made me give him thirty pounds. I had run into an ex-girlfriend and slept at her house. Malcy had booked me a hotel room and felt I should pay. I couldn't tell if he was joking. But he kept my money anyway. Each night, I did my fifteen minutes then watched him work, knocking back the drinks rider, smoking in the dark. Nearly two decades since he first wrote *Alternative Cabaret*, Malcy's act, such as it was, had reached its apogee. After ten minutes' faff with harmonicas and cards and wigs and coats, Malcy held up a massive picture of four small brown stoats. Then he began an hour's speculation on their interconnected relationships, occasionally gesturing at individual stoats with a pointed wooden stick. Sometimes it worked, and the students were spellbound. But Malcy seemed to be seeing how he could confound expectations, amusing himself at the punters' expense, as if holding them in contempt. And in the closing ten minutes, when the space had thinned and the crowd was sparse, Malcy could always win them back by dropping his trousers and showing his arse. But even this traditional display, with which he had all but made his name, seemed to be dispatched in a perfunctory way. In short, Malcy's heart wasn't in it.

As we travelled the country, it became clear to me Malcy wasn't that concerned about his comedy career. It was of secondary importance to a social network he maintained, which indulged his other interests up and down the land. In Aberdeen a small fat man met Malcy after the show and they retired to practise card tricks in a hotel room, sharing junk food from the garage and a can of Irn Bru, lamenting Malcy's conflict with the Magic Circle crew. In Nottingham he was ensnared by the executive committee of The Robert Silverberg Appreciation Society, for whose annual newsletter Malcy had written an appraisal of the overrated 1960s science-fiction writer. In Sheffield, Malcy was the sometime beau of a seventeen-stone widow who had needs that only he could satisfy, apparently. In Bristol, fluff-faced comic book fans offered him a copy of *Superman* from the early Seventies which they knew Malcy, a famous collector, would not be able to resist. It included the first appearance of The Super Moby Dick of Space, a sentient, speaking whale in a short red cape, who patrolled the cosmos defending The American Way. I assumed Malcy's interest was an ironic pose, but he was hurt by the suggestion and didn't speak till we reached Preston. Malcy loved the Super Moby Dick of Space. He felt that its creator was touched by divine intervention, chosen to communicate something beyond his comprehension.

The route of our already strangely scheduled tour was further complicated by the side-trips Malcy insisted on making and the peculiar rituals he was determined to observe. After an average-to-bad show at Lancaster University, Malcy made me drive him twelve miles to the coast where he stood on the sea-front and took off his coat and urinated in the face of a statue of Eric Morecambe, who hailed from the area, or at least had done. He explained that he tried to do this at least once a year, and considered Ernie Wise a genius unsung. Malcy had sworn he would never play Glasgow, but on the way to Stirling he insisted we drive through the city centre while he, sporting a ginger wig and clutching a haggis, leaned out of the car window shouting, "Remember Culloden! That was tragic!" at small children and old women. Each day, Malcy would buy the dullest post-card of the town we were in, inscribe it with the same description of an imaginary Italian holiday and post it to an address in Ealing that he had chosen at random from the telephone directory. On an Irish leg, driving between Belfast, Dublin and Cork, Malcy insisted on eating only at tiny tea-rooms, where he would order a baked potato, with no butter, filling or salad, and then seek out the chef to compliment him on the meal. Whenever we were in Devon he always tried to have sex with men, but even in Exeter's only gay nightclub, the local queens could tell the difference between real lust and some Situationist conceit. Whenever we played a town with two 'b's in its name, Malcy would order me two full English breakfasts in bed and have them both delivered to my room at 5.45 a.m. The cost of the two meals would then be deducted from my fee. But I grew to love these idiosyncrasies, just as I grew to love Malcy, over and above his act, in spite of himself.

Malcy used to live in Peckham then, before he moved back to his mum's. At the end of our two-month trip I finally dropped him in his street. He did not invite me in for tea, say goodbye or thank me. Three months later in Edinburgh, Malcy performed his 'farewell' show, in a room above a shop. The signs had been there I suppose, but it still seemed hard to believe. What would Malcy do instead? He was dis-institutionalised. After midnight, Malcy stuck his face through a curtain and addressed us for a quarter of an hour in the persona of a head that had no body and was floating in the air. Then he laid his props upon the floor – the harmonica, the wigs, the pack of cards – and invited us to speculate upon the perfect order that these elements might integrate for the ultimate comic effect. Malcy lit an oil lamp and sealed his mouth with masking tape. He arranged his props in every possible way, like some Mondrian ballet, until at last, at half past one, with wigs scattered all around the room, he admitted it could not be done and that the totems of his trade were powerless to someone who no longer cared. Even against his will Malcy was still funny, but the friends that I took with me said it was a waste of money. Sold out for three weeks, then that was it, Malcy packed up and disappeared. The *Guardian* said the show was shit. The *Observer* disagreed. Five years later I saw Malcy on Oxford Street, hunched up, head down, staring at his feet. I waved at him, but I don't think he noticed me.

When the money well ran dry and I went back to my old promoters they laughed as if vindicated somehow and said they could find me something. Two weeks headlining on what remained of the student circuit that I'd help create. Of course I'd need a support. Had I heard Malcolm Tracey was back on the boards? No. He lives with his mum now in her council flat. No-one knows where he's been but he's blown all his cash. It'll be just like the old days. But if he really sucks, promise you call and we'll send someone up to replace him.

Malcy came in the kitchen where I sat with his mum. He looked older but content in an indefinable way, as if the black cloud that always used to surround him had risen away. "Malcy," I said, "It's Tim. Remember me?" "Ah Tim, yes. Did I see you on the TV? Good luck to you son, they'd never have me. I dare say I could have made it if I'd given it a try but sometimes these opportunities, well they just pass one by. Now. Bangor. In Wales. I assume that you'll drive.

Goodbye Mother, I am sure that we will meet again. But if I should die, think only this of me. The stash of porn under the bed goes to kids with cerebral palsy. Everyone needs a wank mother, don't you agree..." "Goodbye Malcy," she said, and passed him his packed lunch. Malcy kissed his mother on the cheek and handed me his props. "Sight gags dear boy. You can't have too many. You're still travelling light I assume? You think that a wig, no matter how funny, is not meant for the likes of you."

Malcy woke soon after Oswestry. So far I'd restrained myself from asking him where he'd been the past ten years. It seemed somehow impolite. Instead I said how much I had enjoyed his farewell show, in Edinburgh so long ago, when he had spent an hour trying to align his funny props for maximum effect. "Yes. Well, I got there in the end you know, while I've been away. I was five years gone before I realised anyone might have missed me." "What do you mean, Malcy?" I asked him. "The problem was I'd taped up my mouth. You remember, you were there. So I couldn't play the harmonica or recite even the simplest joke or sing a silly song. It was all very well moving wigs about but even to a foreign ear there's something in the rhythm of a perfect gag that can incite the involuntary act of laughter and, I believe, there are absurd images that transcend any cultural conditioning and whack us on our funny bones at a primeval level." My head was spinning. I'd never heard Malcy wax theoretical on comedy before. He'd always seen it as a chore. What did he mean? "A certain shape, a certain sound, a certain colour and a certain move, combined at a special moment and timed to perfection, will send a pulse of laughter out, so powerful the earth will crack, the lightning flash, the sky turn black, and everything will alter." I felt a little bit afraid hearing Malcolm Tracey talk this way, but kept my eyes upon the road and looked for signs to Bangor. "Everything I need to implement this comic day of judgement is in that bag on your back seat or here inside my skull.

And when I work my wonders everything I've fought against will wither, die and fall. Can we stop for a piss soon?"

We checked into the Regency Hotel, opposite the station. Outside the rain was chucking down and waves were crashing on the shore. I thought about the prophecy that Malcy had just made and wondered what exactly he'd been doing while away. If he really had the power that he seemed to think he did, then having him as my opening act might not be ideal. If Malcy had stumbled upon some comic formulae that unleashed the energies he had described then if I had to follow him I would surely die, and with it being Bangor I needed to do the time agreed, or with the petrol and the rooms I'd be in negative equity. I went into the hotel bar to get a drink and steady my nerves, and then I remembered I wasn't well enough. But as I sat there smoking I realised there were two options. Either Malcolm was a super-being or he'd just flipped and lost it. Tragically it seemed to me the second was most likely. I resolved to get through the gig tonight, then have a think in the cold hard light of day as to whether my childhood hero really was going to pay his way. If he looked like a liability I could just put him on the train, phone the promoters and have them find me someone new, who I could hook up with before the next show. I knocked at Malcy's door. "Showtime," I said. "Come in," he lay upon the bed, naked except for socks and an orange wig over his cock. "Get dressed, Malcolm," I said, "Bangor Uni will dock our fee if we're not there by six thirty for an ineffectual sound-check. This is no time for messing around." "On the contrary, dear boy," said Malcy, "There's never been a better time for it."

What can I say? Malcy did OK. His fifteen minutes came and went largely without incident. At first he faltered, as well he might, after ten years out of the light. But he cut such an eccentric figure with his tight red suit and revolving roster of wigs that the student pricks were initially too confused to go in for the kill, and before they knew it he had their good will. Twelve minutes in, Malcy put down his puppet rubber chicken and reached inside his jacket pocket and pulled out a piece of paper. I wondered if it contained some spell, some charm or incantation, with which he would make good his boast of earlier that day, to bring the mountains crashing down and make the doubters pay. But instead it was a poem he said he'd written that week, about his relationship with his estranged daughter. In all the time I'd spent with him, Malcy had never mentioned her. He read it sincerely in slow measured tones. It was funny, but not cute, and clearly heartfelt. The audience fell silent, with occasional laughs, but they came in the right places, and Malcy rode the pauses. At the end they applauded but I noticed from my corner that a girl by the toilets was crying. Then as if to acknowledge the hiatus he'd caused, Malcy bent over and pulled down his pants, showed his arse to the students and bowed.

I need not have worried. Malcy still had it, and more. After his set my own seemed a bore, if not to the crowd then to me. Once more I was learning from Malcolm Tracey. But hey, what the hell, we both did our time. The twat from the union paid us both fine and nobody had to go hungry. As we walked back to the Regency Hotel, Malcy stopped for a piss by the chip shop. "Though I say it myself," he said, to himself, "that went rather well. It might have been my best gig ever. Yes. I was on fire, so I think I'll retire. Things really can't get any better." Outside the hotel Malcy stood on the steps and looked at the sea and the sky. "A drink before bed," Malcy smiled. I said, "I'm sorry I need to get some kip in. I didn't tell you before but tomorrow I'm afraid we are both due in Glasgow." To my surprise, Malcy took it in his stride. "Good. Then we'd best be off early. If you don't mind there's a stop I should like to make somewhere West of Greenock." It had been a long time since I'd had to drive Malcy to his assignations. But I felt kind of proud to have him around and agreed, one last time, that I'd take him.

At Wemys Bay Malcy pointed the way across the sea by ferry. "We'll go to Bute, to a beach I know, and there we will put on a show to live in the halls of memory." Tired and perplexed, I acquiesced and drove the car on to the boat. Malcy hurried to the bar, already on his second jar, by the time I'd bought the tickets. I didn't think to question him, I'd seen it all before. He'd have a plan, to see a certain man or dally with a whore. But when we drove on to the land he took control and pointed out the way, to Skelpsie Bay, a little South West of Rothesay. I parked the car above the beach. In the distance I saw Arran, and in the rain I helped Malcy get all the props we could carry and take them to the shore. He handed me a pint glass that he'd brought with him from Bangor and told me to keep it safe as he would need it later. Across the sand he dragged his bags and set them up upon some rocks, that stretched some way into the sea, a small performance promontory. And as I watched him from the beach he got down on his knees and reached into his pocket and pulled out his old harmonica. The wind carried the notes away, but I assume he started to play, and as he did so little heads began to break above the waves. Malcy was surrounded on three sides by dolphins bobbing on the tide, clicking, waiting, watching him, wondering when he'd begin. "I'll test my theory," he cried, "on these far superior minds." And in between the wind and spray I think I heard Malcy say the first line of his tried and tested set. The story of a gherkin boy who lived inside a burger, the suicide note of mouse or something or other, a funny kind of lullaby sung to a sleepless child. I knew the pay-off, but before he spat it out Malcy called, "Throw the glass, throw it at me now." "What?" I answered him, appalled, as Malcy stuck an orange wig upon his sodden hair, and blew a last harmonica blast that cut the soggy air.

"I'll only go if you throw glass," he shouted. I threw it towards the waiting rocks. It shattered with a crash. The sea grew calm and duck pond still and then there was a splash. The dolphins dived beneath the waves. Skulls cracked smiles in ancient graves. A shadow fell across my face. The Super Moby Dick of Space! But no – a cloud had crossed the sun. I looked back. Malcy? He was gone. And lying there upon the rocks, his harmonica, alone, unloved.

I hung around the beach till dusk looking for Malcolm Tracey. If he had come back across the beach footprints would have betrayed him. If he'd swum underwater out to sea he'd have to have dived a mile from me without breaking the surface. I had to confront my fear. Malcolm Tracey had disappeared. I drove back to the ferry and phoned the promoters to tell them my support act had spontaneously combusted. But back in London they pre-empted me. There had been a complaint. Malcy's poem had made a student cry. This wasn't what comedy was for. Admittedly in any other form of art, tugging the strings of someone's heart would be considered worthy. But not in stand-up comedy. Malcy was sacked and there would be a new support waiting for me when I arrived in Glasgow.

There's nowhere to hide in the University of Strathclyde. The venue's on the top floor of a tower. You're crushed into a backstage room that doubles as an office and it was there that I met Malcolm Tracey's young replacement. A local lad, slotted in, new to the game, hungry, keen. He was playing Jongleurs gigs up and down the country and storming every one. He wasn't interested in doing Glastonbury – how was that gonna help his career? – but would do a couple of Edinburghs to snag a Perrier nomination and blag a TV deal. I felt old and irrelevant, like someone cutting peat, while dreaming of electric fires and cursing their wet feet. I offered him a cigarette, but he didn't smoke. I said the rider was no use to me, and he packed it away in his sports bag. A pretty young girl flounced in and said it was time. My support act stood and left the room and I went out into the hall and watched him walk on to the stage. The crowd applauded his entrance but his opening line, something about how he resembled an Australian soap star, hardly caught fire. It shrivelled in the spotlight and then curled up and died. He tried a condemnation of the students' refusal to laugh, and then flipped onto his belly, begging for their love. But the tricks of the trade were just tricks of the trade. The Emperor stood naked. The crowd were betrayed. The boy floundered, dry mouthed, then looked around, and bent his head, and bit his lip and bedded in for a battle. Something was different. Something had changed. I felt Malcy's harmonica in my pocket and put it to my mouth. It might have been seawater, or it might have been spittle, but as I ran my tongue along the openings I could feel that it was wet. I pursed my lips and filled my cheeks and blew the liquid out.

For Tony Allen, The Amazing Mr Smith, Andrew Bailey, Steve Bowditch, Arnold Brown, Ted Chippington, John Cooper Clarke, John Dowie, Greg Fleet, Stephen Frost, Boothby Graffoe, The Greatest Show On Legs, Malcolm Hardee, The Iceman, Kevin MacAleer, Oscar McLennan, Simon Munnery, Paul Ramone, Gerry Sadowitz, Andy Smart, Arthur Smith, Martin Soan.

Of London and Luton stock, Simon was raised in squalor near Watford. It was his own squalor: the result of ten years' stubborn refusal to tidy his room. Simon has performed at 17 Edinburghs, 3 Melbournes, 1 Adelaide, 1 Kilkenny, 1 Galway, 1 Halifax, 1 Aspen under various guises: The Security Guard, Alan Parker Urban Warrior, The League Against Tedium, Simon Munnery. In Edinburgh 2002 he won The Boothby Graffoe Award for his show Noble Thoughts of a Noble Mind. *He has appeared on TV and radio but denies this when asked.*

simon munnery

the true confessions of sherlock holmes

The first two cases were a fluke. After that, I coasted on my laurel. It began simply enough. I was at a party. It was one of those parties, common enough at the time, where someone gets murdered in an upstairs room and there's much rumpus and kerfuffle. Many parties in those days were organised at least partially for the purpose of doing someone in. I was banged up to the monkey nuts at the time of course and mashed on squinty puff as was my habit. On a whim I stuck out my arm and, pointing without looking, bellowed in melodious tones the phrase: "It was him what done it."

When I opened my eyes the man I'd been pointing at crumpled to the floor and began a long and blabbering confession at the end of which, naturally enough, the assembled company fell on him and took turns stoving his brain with a candlestick. It wasn't so much his guilt that excited the frenzy but rather the pitiful nature of his blabbering. It set your teeth on edge, it really did.

When a suitable lull occurred I was on the point of slipping quietly away – in order as it were to quit while I was ahead – when I was drawn back into the room by the sound of sustained and generous applause. The applause, nay ovation, lasted quite some time and while it continued I was given qua quas and merley drops and fondled rapturously by the crowd. Eventually a hush descended and a tremulous voice asked me how I'd done it. I was tempted of course to claim some kind of divine power or magical ability but, noting the change in fashion, plumped for science.

"I am a man of science," I said. "That is how I done it."

The crowd shrieked and giggled its approval. Science was new then and mention of it something of a novelty.

"A man of science," repeated one in hushed tones, savouring the phrase.

"Science man," said another.

"No. Not science man – man of science," I swiftly corrected. "I am of science; science is not, nor cannot be, of I. For science is science and I am I. Or am I?" I was on a roll now. The merley drops were kicking in. And I realised my best plan was to use the word science over and over again until I had convinced them. Fortunately this did not take long.

"Science!" I cried, raising a glass to my lips and slurping exuberantly.

"Science!" they replied, and drained theirs.

After repeating this procedure but a few times the word science began to take on a life of its own and I was no longer required to speak; which again was fortunate as by now I was hardly able. It seemed I had done enough when a sprightly maiden kindly muffled me with her chest.

"Science! Science!" The crowd began chanting unprovoked, the word ricocheting around the room like an aural musket ball. Gradually an informal yet beguiling round system developed, with a slow baritone *Sciiiience!* delicately counterpointed by several falsetto *Science!*es and, although the rhythm constantly changed, I was able to dance a passable lambada – at the end of which my legs felt suddenly stiff and almost infinitely long. Qua quas, I remembered and, laughing, curled my legs around my ankles and rolled into a corner.

There I clocked a portly fellow to my left wearing a steel fez. He winked at me in a most conspiratorial way and whipping out a quill began inking the word 'Science' on the thigh of any lady or gent willing to pay the fee and although it seemed exorbitant he was acquiring a considerable queue. He kept promising to cut me in but I saw none of it. More people were streaming in now, seemingly from every angle of the compass, the walls of the room being demolished to make way for a far larger banqueting hall, made partly of light and whose ceiling housed as fine a rendition of the night sky as one could hope to see in a painting and which would have been practically indistinguishable from the real thing had it not been made with two crucial errors: it was seen from above and there were too many clouds.

Soon I was unable to spook. Hours before, I had lost the power of speechifying, save to myself – who was not listening particularly – but now spooking was also beyond me and me – the other me who was now clamorously insisting on his existence. Before, I had not even noticed the power I had to haunt people, let alone my other self, but its sudden absence I felt keenly. Both of us did and he blamed me. Or was it she? I was begging forgiveness, therefore, from my other self when someone informed me that I had passed out and although we both vigorously denied this and dismissed the notion as absurd – if we were unconscious why bother speaking to us? – I could not deny the possibility that I might be capable of being more conscious. She/he didn't but, anyway, I accepted on our behalf a kind offer and began a course of head treatment which consisted of gentle-to-vigorous pummelling. Little more can I remember of that night. How I got home I have no idea.

I did not wake the next day, nor indeed the day after but, on the third day, I rose, Christ like, and began a careful self-examination for stigmata. I was still a little the worse for wear it transpired so I lay down and waited for the colours to go back to normal and my sense of messiahdom to fade. It was late in the evening by the time I surfaced again. Ambling to my door I found the letterbox stuffed full to overflowing with invitations, congratulations cards, offers of marriage and several small gifts – the petals of an orchid, various cigars and a fine pen-and-ink drawing of myself waving a banner marked *Science*. Clearly I was the talk of the town.

I felt flattered nay overwhelmed although this feeling was laced with a hefty tinge of doubt. Perhaps I had bitten off more than I could chew and would come to regret my party antics. I had just emitted a slight groan when the doorbell chimed but before I even had time to comport my visage the door swung open. And there stood the man in the steel fez.

Or at least it was *a* man in a steel fez. It may have been a different man, for all I knew. It may even have been a different fez.

"Ah Shylock! Good to see you, old fruit," he exclaimed and slapping me forcefully on the shoulder strode into the house as if it were his own, tossing his fez on to the hat-stand and gobbing copiously into my spittoon.

With the fez removed he was utterly unremarkable in appearance, this man that the world would in time come to know as Watson and who was only ever introduced to me as What's-his-name, but so utterly unremarkable as to be worth remarking. He had a face – certainly he had a face, its absence would have undoubtedly been noticed so he must have had one, but for the life of me and despite spending many years in his close proximity I cannot remember what it looked like; I cannot picture him in my mind.

"It's *Sherlock*," I corrected and added with my fullest indignatory face pulled: "…and this, sir, is my home!"

"Oh," he said, seemingly for a moment a trifle disappointed. "Never mind. What's in a letter? What's in two letters? Letters schmetters – Sherlock it is then; and this is your home – What a lovely home, Sherlock's home. Sherlock Homes why not even? –

that's what we shall call you; yes it has a good ring to it, already. Sherlock Homes. Does he? Just my little joke. Already..."

Whether or not he was Jewish I have no idea and I suspect neither did he. But certainly he pretended to be Jewish, or perhaps adopted Jewish mannerisms in times of stress. At other times he could seem Cockney or Italian. He looked me up and down, as a jockey might a racehorse, and began a cascade of fulsome praise:

"Yes, very nice. You have a fine accusatory nose you know. And what eyebrows! So decisive! Eyebrows I have seen, but yours! As fine a pair as ever graced a forehead. Expressive no doubt; expressive even by not being expressive – ah the subtlety of them! Very very detective."

Was I taken in by this? Not at first. But prolonged exposure to incessant flattery wears down even the most autosceptical ear.

"Don't you worry about these Sherl," he continued, nonchalantly sweeping the invitations into a bag: "I'll take care of details. Now, come on, let's get our glad rags on; it's time for work already."

He unfurled a fine green and black tweed cloak and proffered it towards me. I could only stare at him. He smiled back, slipping out an impressively large gold fob watch and began swaying it gently to and fro.

"Time is money and money time," he said patiently; and something in the way he twitched that watch led me to believe that it and much else besides would be mine if only I were to go along with him. No words or contracts were ever exchanged but that was the impression I was left with and he did nothing to correct it. I put on the cloak and we stepped out into the darkening night.

Why did I go with him? In the end it was a little thing. I had long been a hat wearer, almost to the point of obsession. Somehow, and without ever wordifying it as such to myself even, I regarded it as a kind of sin to be without a hat, to be *hatless*. Having lost my hat at the party the offer of a deerstalker I could not refuse.

We climbed aboard a large luxurious cab with a well-stocked *cabinet des drouges* and began slowly wending our way north.

"Where are we going?" I enquired

"To a murder," he replied calmly, "which you, the great scientific detective Sherlock Holmes, will solve."

He said my new name with relish and as often as possible, as if trying to drum it into me (and the world) by sheer weight of repetition. Even though I was aware to the point of irritation what he was doing, this did not diminish its effectiveness. It is with some sadness that I report that now, many years later, I can no longer remember my original surname. I think it began with a 'B'.

"I don't know if I can ..." I said, my voice fading with my confidence.

"I know you can. I have great faith in you. Scientific faith. I know you won't let us down. Perhaps we need a little marching powder?" He deposited a scoopful into my upper pocket and, snorting from it greedily, I sat back to enjoy the journey. I noticed we were moving rather slowly and that a man, perhaps several men, were running ahead of the cab – this was normally only required for motorised transport but our vehicle was horsedrawn. Later I discovered the purpose of these men: they were whisperers, sent ahead to drum up excitement at my approach. The manufacture of my reputation had begun.

Ah, Watson! A most unusual man, mysterious to the nth degree. A prism within a kaleidoscope within a maze could not be more mysterious. To watch him go about his business was mesmerising; like watching a clock with the face removed; an infinitely complex clock. To argue with him was a waste of time. He once lent me a book entitled *The Logic of Bold Assertion* which to my mind, far from espousing a form of logic, was in fact a manual of rhetorical technique. But rhetorical technique verging on poetry. Certainly Watson was a master of it; he may even have written the book. Where he had sprung from nobody could say with any certainty. There were many rumours – each of which was quite believable on its own but, in the context of the sheer number of other believable stories about his background, none could sensibly be held as true. Some said they were all true. To me that beggared belief.

For example, it was said that he had been a policeman himself at one time in Singapore and then Melbourne (in the Antipodes) where he had won the Maverick Cop's Maverick Cop award three years running. There he had gone about solving crimes – and more often committing them in order to solve crimes. His modus operandi was to do several spectacular burglaries, then waltz around bars flaunting the spoils, bragging of his deeds and luring any potential criminal in the vicinity into his next caper. On one occasion he arrested the entire town of Werribee.

Another story held that Watson had once worked as a humble clerk in the finance department of one of the Great Universities and, in the interim period between the leaving of one head of department and the arrival of the next, had taken advantage by making himself Professor of Professorology, the chair of a new branch of academe – academiology – the study of academics. This was basically the finance department in all but name, only with an inflated view of itself: rather than being there to serve the other departments its new purpose was to judge them and allocate funds accordingly. Holding the purse strings, he held great power and was able to end certain branches of study he did not agree with – Old Norse and Chemistry – and set up new ones – the Department of Crooning; Wholesale Studies; Canal Building. There was considerable opposition to these changes and the situation became violent. Bombs exploded and acid was thrown; and although nothing was ever proved it was the ex-Head of Chemistry who was arrested and later deported. Watson's position then seemed unassailable for a time but, in the end, he was forced to leave by intense and chronic nightmares in which Thor insisted on pounding his goolies with a furry mallet.

We did not go directly to the murder scene because, as Watson explained, it hadn't been committed yet and it would be unseemly to make accusations when there was no crime. Instead we stopped off at the house of someone he knew – he knew many people – an ex-detective known as Thinking Jack, whom he was anxious for me to meet. What I had to gain from this meeting I had no idea, but anything that postponed the gruesome business of detecting I welcomed.

I learned that I was one of several detectives that Watson had worked with, a veritable stable: Thinking Jack had retired now due to certain undisclosed afflictions of the mind, but before him there had been a string of others, some of whom still worked, each with his own distinct method.

Among others there was Maurice Chutney, the Musical Detective, who solved crimes by playing his flute; Desmond Cranbourne, the Psychic Detective, who solved crimes by contacting the dead; Virginia Lowry, the Female Detective, who solved crimes using her vagina; Albert, the Monkey Detective, a trained monkey, who would climb on to the head of each suspect and ascertain their guilt using phrenology; The Nobby Brothers, a pair of dissimilar twins who were possessed of remarkably astute noses – they literally sniffed out the guilty; and Stewart Wee, who used urine.

Over the years I met them all; some were high as kites, others mad as loons. I had a foot in both camps. Among them all Thinking Jack was perhaps the most interesting. His house, in a shy back street of Lower Clapton, had seen better days but felt warm and inviting. It smelled of books and rotting fruit.

Thinking Jack maintained as large a collection of wax discs as I have ever seen. These recordings, which numbered thousands and were arranged in a strict alphabetical order took up an entire room of his house and were a source of great delight to him. "Listen to this!" he'd often say, tenderly slipping a disc on to its playing device. "Now this! ... No, this! ... What about this? ... Do you like this? ...

Is this not good? ... Do you like this? ... Hear this!" and, before long, twenty or thirty discs would have been played. If you said you liked one he'd play it again; if you didn't he played another. There was no escape. The recordings were mainly of music, and mainly of the same piece of music, played in a huge variety of different ways, in different locations and by different musicians. The tune itself was hard to distinguish so low was the quality of reproduction.

Thinking Jack was most unusual in that he spoke in paragraphs. He hardly ever stopped talking and when he did he exhibited a fearsome glare as though he expected someone to throw money or at least clap. He kept pacing, not as a gentleman might pace, but with a low looping gait as if dodging an imaginary sniper. He was speaking even as we entered the room, his raven hair flapping like a glove as he emitted his characteristic rasping whine:

"... the present age with its sudden enthusiasms followed by apathy and indolence is very near the comic; but those who understand the comic see quite clearly that the comic is not where the present age imagines," he said, striding the room and waggling his finger. He was impossible to ignore, but I helped myself to a bottle of Rioja in order to try.

"Now satire, if it is to do a little good and not cause immeasurable harm," he continued, "must be firmly based upon a consistent ethical view of life, a natural distinction which renounces the success of the moment; otherwise the cure will be infinitely worse than the disease. The really comic thing is that an age such as this should try to be witty and humorous; for that is most certainly the last and most acrobatic way out of the impasse. What, indeed, is there for an age of reflection and thought to defy with humour?" The question hung in the air for a moment, but there was no time to answer it because he immediately continued:

"For, being without passion, it has lost all feeling for erotic values or for enthusiasm and sincerity in politics and religion or for piety, admiration and domesticity in everyday life. But, even if the vulgar laugh, life only mocks at the wit which has no values. To be witty without possessing the riches of inwardness is like squandering money upon luxuries and dispensing with necessities, or, as the proverb says, like selling one's breeches to buy a wig. But an age without passion has no values, and everything is transformed into representational ideas." Here, his face contorted into a venomous sneer, as if representational ideas were as loathsome to him as piss in the eye would be to another. He carried on, his strides across the room becoming larger, almost like leaps, and his finger-waggling like the wings of a humming bird in flight.

"Thus there are certain remarks and expressions current which – though true and reasonable up to a point – are *lifeless*. On the other hand no hero, no lover, no thinker, no knight of the faith, no proud man, no man in despair would claim to have experienced them completely and personally. And just as one longs for the clink of real money after the crackle of bank-notes, one longs nowadays for a little originality. Yet what is more original than wit? It is more original, at least more surprising, even than the first bud of spring and the first tender shoots of grain. Why, even if spring came according to agreement it would still be spring, but wit upon agreement would be disgusting!"

At that instant he fell to the floor in a seeming fit and whimpered, "No, not Preston. Please, not Preston." Watson was quickly at his side administering a calmative. I think this is where the title 'Dr Watson' first flitted into my mind. Whether he was a doctor or not I cannot say and – if he were a doctor – then of what? "A doctor of doctoring," some wag once quipped.

The calmative seemed to work. Within a minute of its application Thinking Jack had leapt to his feet and resumed his discourse: I cracked open another Rioja and rolled myself a doobrie.

"But, now, supposing that as a relief from the feverishness of a sudden enthusiasm things went so far that wit, that divine accident – an additional favour which comes as a sign from the gods, from the mysterious source of the inexplicable, so that not even the wittiest of men dares to say: tomorrow, but adoringly says: when it pleases the gods – but supposing that wit were to be transformed into its shabbiest contrary, a trivial necessity, so that it became a profitable branch of trade to manufacture and make up and remake and buy up old and new witticisms – what an epigram on a witty age!" Again he fell to the floor, this time frothing from the mouth. Another measure of calmative allowed him to finish his tirade:

"So that, finally, money will be the one thing people will desire, and it is moreover only representative, an abstraction. Nowadays even a young man hardly envies anyone his gifts, his art, the love of a beautiful girl, or his fame; he only envies him his money. Give me money, he will say, and I am helped. And the young man will not run riot, he will not deserve what repentance repays. He would die with nothing to reproach himself with and under the impression that if only he had had the money he might really have lived and might even have achieved something great."

There was a lull.

"On that note …" piped Watson and ushered me back into the London night. It is strange perhaps that I can remember such a long speech from so long ago; but over the years I heard it many times, always from Jack's mouth and always word-for-word the same. He had other speeches, many others, on many subjects and the merest mention of certain key words would set him off on one. I don't think he could help it. It was fascinating to watch, but one couldn't help but imagine how agonising it must have been to do, to be. It seemed as if poor Jack could not but make speeches and, far from being a blessing, his incessant thinking was an affliction. I don't know why Watson took me there. I suspect it may have been as a kind of warning.

We arrived at the murder scene in good time, the victim still warm and a large crowd gathered. It was somewhere near Highbury; the street name escapes me. News of our arrival spread like wildfire. "It's Sherlock Holmes – the *scientific* detective." I doused my nerves with Absinthe. With minimal ceremony we were led from our carriage to the scene of the crime though, en route, I found time to take a toot from my top pocket and when we arrived at the upper conservatory I felt confident enough to begin my investigating.

"Who he?" I commanded, indicating the corpse.

He, I was informed, was Sir Edwin Strood, the famous Mancunian entrepreneur, who had built a huge meat-processing factory near Bradford, become very rich on the proceeds and then fallen into disgrace when he was caught treating the pieces of meat like women. Any number of people would have reason to kill him: chefs, gourmets, business rivals, his wife, women generally. The scandal had meant his exclusion from society but had not diminished his wealth. If anything, meat sales had increased.

I looked around the scene of the crime slowly, carefully – or at least pretending to be careful – magnifying glass in hand and a keen scowl across my face. The crowd looked on enraptured. There was unfortunately a superabundance of clues. They littered the floor – one could hardly step anywhere without disturbing some suspicious object. There was the victim's diary with the pages from certain specific dates torn out; a pile of half-burned threatening letters; a portrait of a sheep, winking; the seeming murder weapon itself – a steel replica of a bull's member; and, in the dust near his arm, it looked as though the dying man had scribbled in his own blood: "Albert Fornby killed me." Apparently he had even made a last speech; but his voice had been quite feeble and no one had been able to hear it above the Bavarian Oompah band that even now continued to play in the adjacent room. The noise was doing my head in.

As a famous detective, it is well nigh impossible to arrive at an undisturbed murder scene: someone needs to have discovered the body for you to have been called and the process of discovery inevitably causes some disturbance. And then the excitement generated by your approach causes more: it is not unusual to find extremely large numbers of clues – some deliberately left by the perpetrator to throw you off the true scent but many others left by well-wishers, who have no malicious intent, indeed are only trying to help – reasoning to themselves that a detective needs clues as surely as a dog needs a bone and so, out of the goodness of their hearts, providing you with vast numbers of pointless and misleading clues. Yet usually one cannot simply ignore these clues without the risk of causing considerable offence. People have spent time and effort creating them, after all, and naturally expect their creations to be treated with due care and respect. Over the years I have learned not to panic in such situations and take my time, examining each clue in turn and making squiggle marks in my notebook but, then, I was far less experienced. It was, after all, only my second case.

On a whim and with a single confident wave of my hand, I dismissed all the clues before me as being "Far far too obvious," turned on my heel and proceeded to the drawing room where – to my relief – I found the house guests assembled. Here, surely, were the suspects! There were six of them – a convenient and human number. I smiled an inward smile. Perhaps I was on the home stretch.

Watson appeared, seemingly from nowhere, as was his wont – I once saw him swim and noted he did not leave a wake, hardly even a ripple. He handed me an impressive dossier. I smiled knowingly and opened it. The pages were blank, of course, but I skilfully prevented anyone observing this by slamming it shut and throwing it on to the fire. I stared at the suspects one by one as Watson whispered their names in my ear.

There was Lady Strood, wife of the victim and though of advancing years still a woman of bovine splendour; her brother Ned – tall and neatly dressed; Lord Applethwaite the notorious lily gilder; Calvin Roberts the formidable Welshman, his wild hair trailing to his knees; Albert Fornby, a rival meat trader; and Nelly Grant a vibrant and highly respected whore. What a party, I thought.

Now, it seemed to me, it was just a question of choosing one, as I had before, and then justifying my choice by repeated use of the word science.

Something told me, though, that it wouldn't be as easy this time and a grim terror gripped my heart. What if I made the wrong choice? An innocent man might suffer; my reputation might be ruined. It did not bear thinking about. To cover my nerves I laughed a little – a quiet chuckle to myself – as though thinking about some wry detail of the case. All six looked suddenly nervous. Intrigued, I laughed again, this time slightly more loudly. The room felt noticeably more tense; shoulders stiffened, breaths were held: They thought I knew and was about to spill my bean! I laughed again, this time my longest, loudest, most raucous laugh, like a navvy on payday, loud and mocking; it echoed in the rafters and around the room like cannon fire:

"Ha ha ha ha ha ha ha," I cried. "Ha! Ha! Ha Ha!"

On and on I laughed – I didn't know how long I could keep it up or where I was heading and had indeed begun to feel the dread fingers of doubt begin to work their way up my spine – what could I do next? – when, behind me, I heard a muffled crump. Had the Oompah band changed the beat? Surely not! I swivelled like a viper and seeing that one of the six had collapsed in a heap pointed at him and casually remarked, "'Twas him what done it. Clearly, and for scientific reasons."

The balm of warm applause filled my ear.

Now the difference between a guilty man and an innocent one is

not as might be supposed that the guilty one knows he's guilty:
Everyone knows they are guilty – they just don't know what of yet.
Hence the need for the police, detectives and the judicial system:
Not to create justice, but its illusion. There never can be real justice:
We are all guilty. And we all know that. But if all the world's a stage
then it is our duty in this world – to act.

The crumpled man was shaken back to consciousness and his
confession eagerly awaited. As none was forthcoming and, seeing
that he looked confused and alarmed but not particularly guilty, I
took the precaution of twatting him with a handy vase. Watson
swiftly finished the fellow off with a revolver.

"But how did you know it was Calvin?" asked one of the house
guests when the applause had subsided.

"Calvin!" I said, "That was not his real name. That was not even
his real face!" Taking a scalpel from my pocket, I cut the skin around
the murderer's neck and yanked the face off. There were gasps of
horror from the crowd.

"This is his real face," I continued, indicating the red morass.

"It's hideous!" cried a lady's voice.

"Yes, madam," I replied. "That is why he wore a mask."

"But how did you know he did it?" my questioner continued.
Now I had to be careful.

"He did it," I retorted, turning to face my questioner, "because
you did not. Look at you. Anyone can see. You have the heart of ten
men, the inquisitiveness of twenty perhaps, but the strength of less
than one. You would not hurt a fly, nor are you capable of so doing."

Her reddening face proved the validity of my point and sensing
victory I grasped for some grand phrase to encapsulate the moment,
and end the evening.

"In the case of the Mysterious Death of Sir Edwin Strood, I say
this. When one has eliminated the impossible ..." I began, pausing
dramatically, but a fraction too long:

"He wasn't impossible!" cried Lady Strood, climbing on to a stool, "and, even if he was, that's no reason to eliminate him! How can you speak of the recently departed in such a way? He may have been hard to live with. He had strange habits …"

"Strange habits? Why the fellow stuck his pinky into pork!" a voice in the crowd interjected.

"Yes! Yes! – and beef and mutton and sometimes even sea-food …" continued Lady Strood, "but he wasn't *impossible*. You can't say that …"

"Now, Maud, calm down; there's no need to be fennyweedling – I think Mr Holmes was referring to the murderer," said her brother and helped her from the stool, constraining her flailing arms with some netting.

Eventually I was able to finish my sentence and bring the evening to a close. I breathed a huge sigh of relief. As the saying goes: the first time it's impossible – from then on it just gets harder. Life: you get used to it then you die. Detecting: people die and you get used to it. Watson took me to an after-hours club frequented solely by detectives. There's nothing like a few bevvies when you've cracked a case – and the brotherhood of a shared profession. The Detective Club it was called. It used to have a more continental sounding name: 'Club Detective', but some people had taken that a bit too literally. There we drank till dawn, singing detective shanties, getting quinted on ferozene and puffing on a hookah, leaving no turn unstoned.

Born in Birmingham in 1950, poet, former stand-up, musician, direc-
tor and author John Dowie made his debut in 1969 at the Midlands
Art Centre alongside Black Sabbath. He released various musical proj-
ects on Virgin and Factory Records. His TV debut was on Revolver
hosted by Peter Cook. He has collaborated with, among others, Albert y
Los Trios Paranoias, Barry Cryer, Ronnie Golden, Neil Innes, Heathcote
Williams, Max Wall and Rory Bremner. His shows include Why I
Stopped Being a Stand-Up Comedian, The Joseph Story *and the*
Perrier-nominated Hangover Show *(which he co-wrote and directed).*
Published works include Hard to Swallow *and* Dogman!

john dowie

help me make it through the night

How many years? How many years in the same fucking shit-hole dressing room with the same fucking piss-green walls and the same fucking sink to piss in? How many years of sitting in the same fucking chair waiting for the same fucking face to peer round the same fucking door with the same fucking "all right Big Man?" and no, it's not all right, it's shite, it's fucking horrible is what it is – and "would you like a drink Big Man?" and yes I'd like a fucking cold magnum of fucking champagne and some fucking proper food but no, no fucking chance; it's the same fucking crate of German fucking lager and a bag of fucking chips, if you're fucking lucky, because there's no chip shops round here these days, it's fucking Chinese takeaways and fucking Indian restaurants and fucking pizzas and what the fuck has happened to this fucking country? It's fucking fallen apart. It's fallen into shit. It's fucking fucked.

But I'll get through it. I'll put on the fucking bowtie and the frilly shirt and the fucking cufflinks and the trousers she'll have ironed for me – Mam, the Princess – because she loves me and I love her, always have, always will, and I swore, I fucking swore from day one that I'd see her all right – because she's the reason I'm here. Her. The Princess. Not the fucking punters with their fucking wives and their fucking girlfriends and their fucking mates – all drinking

German fucking lager and cracking their own fucking jokes, waiting for me to come on and give them the same shite I give all the other fuckers night after fucking night. Her. She's the reason I do it, get through it, get the money – cash, son, cash – trouser it, get back home, and she'll be there – waiting – never mind what time of the day or night – six o'clock in the morning sometimes – she'll be there, with my breakfast ready, eggs, beans, bacon, mushroom, black-pudding, tomatoes, chips, brown-sauce, bread – fucking lovely, made with love, pal, made with love, because she loves me and I love her, always have, always will, she's the only thing in my whole fucking life that's ever meant anything, ever, and any minute now it's a knock on the door and then it's one last squirt in the sink, one last dribble of piss, and then it's on to the stage and I'll make those fuckers laugh, don't you worry about that, and not just laughs either, but *whooshes*, pal, that's what I get, *whooshes,* when the fucking beer runs down their fucking noses and when I leave the stage they're fucking cheering – on their fucking feet – and then they're off back home with their fucking wives and their fucking girlfriends and shagging each other fucking senseless and that's the job, pal, that's the fucking job, and I'm good at it. Fucking good. The best. Because I tell jokes, pal. Jokes.

I see there aren't so many Pakis on the street now the Chinese have found out they taste like chicken.

How can you tell when a woman reaches orgasm? Who gives a fuck?

Did you hear about the lion in the jungle? Ate a blackie. Then had to lick another lion's arse to get the taste out of his mouth.

How old are you, love? Nineteen? If you were my daughter I'd still be bathing you.

Good gags. Great gags. And why are they laughing? Because I'm telling the truth. Because they wouldn't fucking laugh if I wasn't. They wouldn't laugh if I wasn't saying what every other fucker thinks but hasn't got the guts to say. And that is why I'll have those fuckers in the palm of my hand tonight – like every other night – because I'm telling the truth. And that's power, that is. That is fucking power.

You'll never amount to nowt.

Well have a look now, you twat. Have a look at the fuckers cheering when I leave the fucking stage. And then have a look at the Roller outside and then have a look at the house – the house I bought for her – cash. Go on, have a good fucking look and then look me in the face and say it again you bastard – go on, I fucking dare you, say it again.

You'll never amount to nowt.

You shit-arsed little fuck. You fucking tossing bastard.

Never had that from her. Not once. Nothing like it. Ever. And why? Because she loves me. Always has. Always will. But not you. No, not you. Nothing. That's all I ever got from you. Fucking nothing.

I should have killed him when I had the chance. I should have smashed his face in with a fucking hammer when I was fucking fourteen. When I got the booking. First booking I ever had. Nelson & Colne. British Legion. Saturday night. Four quid. And I told him. And what did he do? He did nowt. Nowt. Just cleared his throat, spat, and didn't even look at me – didn't even look at his own fucking son – just spat and said it: *You'll never amount to nowt* and I saw the hammer sitting there and all I had to do was pick it up and smash his fucking head in, but I didn't. I couldn't. Because she loved him. She fucking loved him and I don't know why she loved him – but she did. She fucking did.

Thank fuck for cancer. Best month of my life, watching him go. Watching him being eaten up from the inside out, watching his face shrivel and the pipes draining the piss and the shit out of him and when he went into the ground I could have pissed myself laughing. I could have danced on his fucking grave fucking singing …

You'll never amount to nowt.

You'll never amount to nowt.

But I couldn't. Not with her on my arm. I had to be there for her. Be with her, hold her up, look as if I cared. But I *didn't* care. I didn't give a flying fuck. I was pleased as fucking punch, me. Glad. Just me and her now. Fucking good.

A knock on the door.

"Five minutes, Big Man."

Fuck.

* * *

Sixty minutes. Sixty minutes of solid gold. Hecklers sorted. Punters picked on and pissed on. Joke after joke. Pakis, nignogs, Jews. The organist behind him, sweat running down his face – because if he gets one note wrong ... But he doesn't. He doesn't get it wrong. He plays the notes and the Big Man sings *take the ribbon from your hair* ... and his body and his breath and the lights in his face and the punters looking up at him – that's all gone. There's only his voice, filling the air, filling the room – and it means more to him than anyone could possibly imagine. Because the Princess loves his singing. Always has, always will. For as long as he could remember, from his first days at school – *You've got a lovely voice, son.* And then he's off and it's over and he's wiping the sweat from his dripping pits and he's collaring the cash and he's into the car and it's "fuck off you carpark twats with your fucking 'sign this' and your 'shake this hand' and his 'all right son'" and then it's his foot on the pedal and Barbra Streisand on the stereo and he's back home in 20 minutes max.

And when he got back she was dead.

Slumped in the chair, telly still on, a sliver of blood running from her nose to her chin, the local rag on the floor, a pool of piss beneath her feet.

Mam, he had thought and "Fuck," he had said, the word wrenched from him (he never swore in front of the Princess) and then he was on his knees beside her, feeling for a pulse, finding it, faint, slow, but there, and then the sweat is bursting from him, bathing his body in cold wet fear, his heart hammering inside him, adrenaline driving through him, scrambling for the phone thinking *ambulance* and *fuck that, no, the Roller* then picking her up and *fuck* she weighed nothing – she was a bird – then out of the house and into the car – banging her sweet head against the door – unwanted tears suddenly blinding his sight, *no time for that, no time for crying now you fucking ponce, get her to the hospital you useless twat, get her to the hospital now and don't die Princess, don't die, because if you do, I'm dead, I'm finished, I've fucking had it.*

The doctor was a Paki. Of course. Always was. Always would be. Out of medical school for how long, son? A month? Been shaving for how long, son? A month? Ever had a fuck, son? Eh? Ever lay in bed with a woman and felt her warm body wrapped around you? Ever known love? True love? Ever woken up with her warm breath on the back of your neck and her warm body waiting – waiting for you to kiss her and hold her and enter her ...?

No. Me neither. But he hadn't said owt. He said nowt. He just sat there and listened to the shite he'd been expecting from the moment he'd found her.

At her age ... coronary ...
life support ...
may not make it through the night ...
nothing you can do ...
come back in the morning ...

Come back in the morning? Come back for what? A corpse? The Princess a corpse? And then the grief, the never-ending grief, the grief that goes with you all the way to the grave, a grief you can't even share, because there's no one to share it with. No one at all. Just you – alone – with your endless fucking grief. And no one to iron your trousers.

He couldn't believe he'd thought that. He couldn't believe that thought had entered his mind as he sat there, as the kindly-faced Paki spelt out his options of grief, of despair. He couldn't believe he'd thought of his trousers, of his fucking trousers with the fucking piping down the fucking sides, but he had, he fucking had.

He didn't want to cry in front of the Paki – he didn't want to cry in front of anyone – he didn't want to cry full stop – but the tears burst from him. Hot wet salty tears running down his face, a face that only she had ever loved. He found a rag in his pocket and wiped his eyes and blew his streaming nose but they wouldn't stop, the tears would not stop, and he knew that it was not the moment he was in that was making him weep but, rather, it was all the moments – it was every single moment of his whole fucking life – and if she hadn't been alone in her love for him – if there had been any others – one even – who had loved him – then it wouldn't hurt so much, do you know what I mean, pal, Paki pal, do you know what I'm saying? I'm saying that I loved her – always have, always will – and she loved me – and what hurts is this – no other fucker ever did. Ever. So what did that mean to her? How did that make her feel? That nobody loved her son? It must have broken her fucking heart.

He pulls himself up, blinded, and reaches for the fat cigar but there's no smoking in a hospital, no matter how much you need it, not even on the cancer ward and if you can't smoke in the cancer ward where the fuck can you smoke? Outside, obviously. Outside. In the cold.

A bench outside and the butts on the pavement and the wind blowing all about him and what do you do now? You have a smoke, pal, that's what you do. You light up and you drag the nicotine deep down inside you and it finds the pain and it sorts it out – for a minute. Only a minute but that's better than no minute at all and you can focus for a minute – for a minute you can get your head clear – and you can feel the tears welling up inside you, again, lining up, one by one, waiting to come streaming down your face, again, but you don't want tears, tears are no good, no good at all. What you want now is a clear head, so pull yourself together you twat because the Princess needs you, she needs you to get yourself sorted out, she needs you to be strong, so be strong you fucking stupid snivelling little ...

You'll never amount to nowt.

Shut him up. Don't listen. Smoke. Lean back. Look up at the sky. Look up at the sky and all those stars, those stars that go on forever. Stars. Stars in your eyes. A million stars.

And a newspaper blowing at his feet. He looks down. The local rag. The one she'd been reading, lying at her feet when he'd found her. Maybe the last thing she'll ever have seen. Not the stars. Nor him. Nor the casual tossing of another wedge – another grand – in cash – onto the sideboard as he came in. Nor his voice. "All right, Princess, my love?" "Something to eat, son?" No. Not that. Just this fucking rag with its fucking local news and its articles and its fucking adverts...

The wind whips the pages open. A headline takes hold of his eyes and drags them from his face. A familiar face looks up at him. His guts lurch.

Comedy festival ...
City's finest ...
Freedom of the City ...
Awarded to ...

Speccy twat.

He wanted to puke.

Speccy twat. The twat who killed Benny. Not that he'd liked Benny. Another sad unfunny twat. What kind of a twat runs around a field in his underwear pretending to be chased by women? Only a twat like Benny. But he made the fuckers laugh. And he'd done his time. The war years. The Windmill. The fucking grind. But speccy twat – what had he ever done? He killed Benny. He tried to kill me. And now he's here. In my fucking town. Getting what? Freedom of the city? For what? For fucking lying. For fucking coming on as a streetwise twat, an anarchist twat, a revolutionary twat, and the next thing you know he's entertaining royalty and fucking coining it hand-over-fist like all those other twats, the educated twats, the university twats, the twats who've had it made from day fucking one. While twats like me are sitting outside a fucking hospital waiting for their fucking mothers to fucking die. And the last thing she reads – the very last thing she'll have seen – is some other twat getting it all, as always, getting the fucking pat on the back and the fucking knighthood and the fucking awards.

Never mind the charity. Never mind the millions he'd raised for charity, for the nurses, for the firemen, for the hospitals, for the kids. Never mind the charity golf and the charity lunches and the fucking charity banquets when he'd gone out there night after fucking night and made those bastards laugh. And for what? For fucking fuck all.

And how would the Princess have felt? Eh? How would she have felt if they'd said, "Freedom of the City will go to..."

Her son.

She'd have felt proud.

But they couldn't do that, could they? No. And why? Because it's always the other fucker, never me. And now she's lying up there in the fucking hospital as some fucking doctor stands by her bed with his fucking clipboard and his fucking pen and then he turns off the fucking machine and takes her away from me for ever and ever and that's it. You bastards. You fucking heartless uncaring bastards.

Come back in the morning?

I'll come back in the morning, all right. Don't you worry about that. I'll come back in the morning for my Princess ... to be there. To wait for her to die. To gather her up in my helpless hands. But for some bastards there won't be any more mornings. Some bastards will never have a morning ever again.

* * *

It was in the attic. He feels his breath labour in his throat and his heart kick inside him as he climbs the ladder and pushes the trapdoor open. The joke comes into his mind, as jokes always did. *The wife asked me to clean out the attic ... dirty ... covered in cobwebs ... still she's good with the kids.* The light of his handheld torch flickers around the grimy space and there it is ... the little black box.

He'd been booked for a show and the grey-haired promoter had fucked up the advertising and part of him wanted to believe him and another part of him said, "They know you're here, Big Man, but they don't want to see you, you're finished." But that wasn't his problem. His problem was he was owed a grand and the grey-haired bastard said "I can't pay you, Big Man, but how about this? Compensation. You never know. Might come in handy." And it might. Explosives. "You run a club, Big Man, you know what it's like," and yes, pal, he knew what it was like. He knew about the gangsters and the drugs and the kickbacks to the cops. He knew about the guns and the knives, knew about what passes for currency in this town. And you never know when a few explosives might come in handy, so he'd taken the shit, the little black box, he'd taken it home and he'd stowed it away ...

And it was a piece of piss to work with. Had to be. Built by Micks for Micks. That was the beauty of it. Any twat could work it. A fucking chimpanzee could fucking work it. You wire the blue wire to the positive and the red wire to the negative and you take the detonator to wherever you want within five hundred yards and you press the green button and then the sky's the fucking limit. Literally.

Ten-minute drive to the hotel. Spotty-faced kid behind the desk. "Here for the awards, Big Man?" And he walks straight past him, the box under his arm, saying "That's right, son. Surprise appearance."

Freedom of the city? I'll give him freedom of the city. A bit at a time.

Lift. 8th floor. Banqueting suite. Podium. This is where the twat will stand. One hour from now. Here's where I place the shit. Right beneath his fucking feet. And when it's over – when I've blown those fuckers to Kingdom Come – then I'll go back to the Princess and wait for her to die and I'll hold her in my arms and feel the weight of her lovely body and maybe that will be enough for me – maybe then I can let go and I won't give a fuck what happens after that – because the best thing in my life will have been taken from me, forever. And the rest of you fuckers – you can sit around with your fucking wives and your fucking girlfriends and your fucking awards – and maybe, just maybe, one of you self-satisfied bastards will have the fucking decency to say, "the Big Man – he was all right. He made people laugh. Do you know what I mean? He made people laugh. And when they laughed – their troubles were gone. Do you see what I'm saying? Gone. And get this – try this on for size – when he sang he did something brilliant, something wonderful. He stopped them laughing and he gave them beauty ... absolute fucking beauty."

* * *

She is home. The Princess is home. She hadn't known she had such a home. She hadn't known anything until this moment when the universe fills her and she fills it and she is bathing in light, in total light. It is all around her and inside her and it is bliss, it is joy. And it will come to him, too, she thinks. To her son. It will come to all of them, to every soul, this bliss, this joy. It will fill them too, or they will fill it, and she wants to cry, she wants to weep, but she has no eyes to weep with, she has nothing at all, because she is everything. She is everything.

A presence comes to her, is inside her, outside her, surrounding her, bathing her in light and in love, glowing, luminescent, filling her with words, with liquid words.

"I did you wrong."

"No. Because there is no wrong. Only this light."

Then the presence becomes form and she becomes form and she is beside him in a railway café. On the wall, a faded metal plaque advertises a bracing seaside town. Between them, a table. On the table, twin mugs, an ashtray. He sips sweet tea and rolls a cigarette, not looking at her, his face unlined now, the same but not the same, and she too is the same but not the same, young but not young, human but not human, not human at all. She says his name.

"Reg."

"No, love. Reg is dead."

The Reg-that-used-to-be picks tobacco from his tongue and turns away, not speaking, not speaking as he always not-spoke. Typical, she thinks. But there is no need of words. She knows what he has to say. That he should have loved her son. But could not. Because the child was not his.

Poor Reg, she thinks. Poor sad lonely bitter betrayed Reg.

She had done him wrong, so he had done her wrong. Not by hurting her but by hurting her son. *What do you get when you raise a child with hate?* she thought. You get a hateful child. And now Reg is telling her, without words, or the light is telling her, without words, what her son is about to do – but she knows, she already knows. She had known from the moment she read the headline FREEDOM OF THE CITY and thought, *It'll kill him.* She had known from the moment she'd stood, too quickly, as something hard and heavy kicked inside her, as the pages of the newspaper slipped from her fingers, as she fell into swirling darkness. She had known then. Mothers know. Mothers know best. A woman's work is never done. A mother's work goes on forever.

It makes her feel so tired, so very tired as she slips away and back into the old dull body with the old dull skin and the aching joints, the tired muscles, the withered hair, the failing sight, the hospital gown, open, exposing her sad old skin, her veins, the hair of her sex. She pulls the drips from her arm, from her nose, from her mouth.

She wraps the gown around her and walks away, through corridors filled with light – light that is not light because she has seen light, she has been light, and light is not harsh, light does not hurt, but it leads her on, it leads her outside, the wind whipping the gown around her, as she climbs into the ambulance, turns the key and the sound of the siren fills her and she is driving away from the hospital and she is singing now, the Princess is singing, she is singing…

Yesterday is dead and gone …

* * *

Half past ten. Detonator on his lap, no bigger than a mobile phone, one red light, one green button. In his hand, the miniature TV – fucking Japanese, of course. He has the headphones on and a voice is in his ears, local news: "… and now we go live to the city centre where …"

Where it's all over, pal, where it's all fucking over. He sits back on the toilet seat, the plastic lid numbing his flesh, his eyes devouring the picture before him, of the smug-faced presenter four floors above. "Come on, my son, come on …"

* * *

The Princess stands in the doorway, hesitant. The dining has ceased, the drinking continues, the chatter from the tables is high-pitched, frenzied, laughter filling the room, but there is no pleasure in this laughter, no pleasure at all. There are only these egos, these bubbles of light, awash with alcohol and envy. Then she walks through the room, past all the tables, ignored, because this is their night, this night belongs only to them and they only have eyes for each other, and, besides, nobody is that drunk. Nobody is so drunk that they could possibly have seen an old woman in a hospital gown walking towards the podium, walking towards the presenter …

"And now, let's look at some of the many achievements …"

The presenter turns as the screen behind him shows the images – the stand-up, the sitcoms, the books, the plays, the musicals, the films, the lifetime's work achieved in a handful of years. An old woman in a hospital gown brushes past him, bends, picks up a little black box, and walks away. The presenter watches her go and a remark comes into his mind but he leaves it unsaid, because he couldn't have seen her. He couldn't possibly have seen her. He checks his nostrils. Turns to camera.

Outside, she stares at the carpeted floor. Where to go? A figure appears at the corridor's end. Uniform. Cap. She turns and walks away. "Excuse me love" coming from behind her, but then she is pushing the fire door open and running down the stairs, one floor, two, three, her heart beating too fast, too loud, and she needs to find somewhere safe, somewhere unsuspected and the fourth-floor gents is the obvious place.

He adjusts the volume on the Jap TV and does not hear the door open and close as she enters the cubicle next to his and sits, her breath laboured. *Now what?* she thinks. No idea. She hadn't thought this far ahead. She has no instructions with regard to this. Only obeying orders. Her eyes look down to the little black box on her lap. Boys and their toys, she thinks. Boys and their toys. Blowing things up out of all proportion.

The Big Man cradles the detonator in his hand, a happiness he has never known almost within his grasp, almost attainable, as speccy twat takes the stage, shakes the presenter's hand, takes the key – the big shiny glittering golden key – holds it aloft and the whole room stands, the whole room cheers, and *Fucking good* thinks the Big Man. His thumb presses down.

The explosion tears the Princess apart, shattering the partition between them. Her blood, her brains and her bones become ribbons, red ribbons that splatter into him, into his body, into his hair. There is no pain. There is only a ringing in his ears, a sense of bewilderment, and one word only leaving his lips.

"Fuck."

His body falls to the floor, falls into piss guts blood and shit, as the rest of him – the best of him – rushes towards a starry heaven where love, overwhelming love, embraces him, gathers him up and fills him completely.

Far below, he has become nowt.

Fucking nowt.

A former teacher and road sweeper, Arthur was a founder member of the National Revue Company and Fiasco Job Job. On TV, he hosted First Exposure *and* Paramount City *and his series include* Arthur and Phil Go Off. *On radio, he has presented* Sentimental Journeys *and he is a regular contributor to* Loose Ends *and* Excess Baggage. *His West End stage plays include* Live Bed Show *and* An Evening With Gary Lineker; *Fringe plays include* Arthur Smith Sings Andy Williams *and* Arthur Smith's Hamlet. *His books include* Pointless Hoax. *Nominations for his work include the Perrier Awards, Olivier Awards and Independent Theatre Awards. He lives in Balham.*

arthur smith

the man with two penises

I think Tony was more than surprised when, at the end of the evening at Ios Nicholais, I cut my little finger off. When I said to Tony, "Will you give me fifty quid if I cut my finger off?" he naturally agreed. He didn't expect that within thirty seconds I would produce an electric carving knife and slice straight through halfway down the finger. He got a bit hysterical, actually, and once I'd attended to the blood, I had to slap him with my right hand. I explained that I was going to get £3,000 from the insurance company and I had planned it all along, but he still seemed shaken and left soon after. I never saw him again but, to be fair, he did send me the fifty quid.

Now, that story is by way of explaining how it is that I come to have two penises. I am the sort of man who would do anything rather than work. You see, I met a rich man in a pub three years ago and he asked me about my missing finger. It turned out he was a plastic surgeon. The best plastic surgeon in London, he reckoned. He claimed that if he was paid enough he could transform Ronnie Corbett into David Beckham and he was really excited about some of the new ideas coming out of America. You can kind of guess the rest I suppose. Fifty thousand pounds he paid me. I didn't take it lightly. I made sure there was no real danger. The worst that could happen, he told me, was that my original penis might reject the new one. But in that event the new one would just wither away and he could cut it off painlessly. If it worked, then I would be the most extraordinary man in the world.

When I came round, my testicles really ached. They felt as though they had been whacked with a tennis racket solidly for several hours. My eyes were sore too because, as a cover for Dr Mike, I had also agreed to have a facelift and a nose job. It was some time before all the bandages were off and I was finally able to pull the blanket up and have a good look at my new prick. It was rather unimpressive – skinny and red with stitches all round the stump. I felt a bit sorry for it, poor thing – it had had an eventful month. One moment it was nestling happily in a pair of trousers on the M25, the next, it was being grafted onto an entirely new body. I had to stop this sort of thought. I didn't want to think about my new penis' previous history. It was important, as Dr Mike said, that I treat it as one of the family. He also suggested that I should not talk about 'the old one' and 'the new one'. So I decided to give them names. After some thought, I hit upon Ant and Dec, as I always thought they were a pair of penises. Besides the new one bore a passing resemblance to Ant. I hoped too that when Ant began to feel at home, he and Dec might begin to work as a double act, if you see what I mean.

Not long after I came out of the clinic, I was able to piss through Ant and not long after that I woke to find him winking happily at me and sporting an erection. I jumped out of bed to look at it in the mirror and was alarmed at its unusual shape: the first half stuck straight out, the second took a sharp turn upwards, such that it was parallel to my body. I had an L-shape erection. In profile, in conjunction with the limp Dec, I seemed to have the number '4' protruding from my abdomen. That night, Dr Mike gave me an injection. Next day, I woke up with aching balls and two erections. The effect was like some art house comment on Winston Churchill. I tentatively embarked on a double wank. It was terribly hard to co-ordinate my hands and I was still wary of the stitches. I tried to wrist Ant slower than Dec. Eventually I found a decent rhythm and Dec responded in the old-fashioned way and took a nosedive. Turning my attention to Ant, I suddenly felt delirious and ecstatic as my fingers ran the banana curve of his outline. When he fired his creamy message, I was so exhausted that I forgot to smear the contents of the sheets on to the slide Dr Mike had given me. I fell into a deep sleep, woke up and went to Kents.

I used to go to Kents to pick up girls. I'm quite good at it actually. I look a little bit like Jamie Theakston with a bent nose and I'm quite funny. Oddly enough, they really liked the half-a-little finger. One girl asked me to put it up her and wiggle it about. Matt, the barman, didn't recognise me at first and, when he heard my voice, he looked startled.

"What the fuck happened to your face?"

"I had a face-lift and a nose job."

He looked bemused.

"And I've had a second penis grafted on."

At this, he burst out laughing. To his further amazement, I ordered champagne. I sat down to wait for some girls to arrive and considered my plan of attack. Surely, I reasoned to myself, having two penises would be attractive to many women – just like my little finger. But, then again, I had an absence of finger but a double helping of penis. To lose a part of your body does occur; to acquire an extra bit might seem a bit abnormal. To have one eye and five noses is certainly unattractive. I never heard of Cyclops getting off with anyone. But two pricks – there's a thought.

Two blondes walked into the bar, I guessed Danish au pairs. A lot of Scandinavian au pairs go to Kents. I bided my time as they ordered two beers and I tried to imagine how wide my two dicks could spread. Eventually, I sent a bottle of champagne over to them with a note saying, "Are you Finnish air hostesses?"

They looked surprised when it arrived. You've probably noticed I'm good at surprising people. But they accepted, nodded and smiled at me. I walked over and said, "Well, are you?"

The one in jeans smiled and put out her hand. "We are students from Norway. I am Oola and this is Hannah."

Hannah was wearing a black skirt. She had long legs, small tits under a white vest and, on her feet, an ugly pair of trainers. She was unimaginably gorgeous. I thought immediately I would have to target Oola, but to my delight I was wrong and two weeks later it was Hannah sitting on my settee at midnight sipping brandy. I hadn't thus far managed to tell her about my unusual attribute. It's not something that slots easily into conversation. Perhaps my only opportunity had come when she remarked that I always wore baggy trousers.

"We shall go to bed, yes?" she said, leaping several pages in the script. Within minutes, she was beneath my duvet, looking eager. I was quite eager too, though I hadn't worked out exactly how I'd deploy my new selves. I was looking forward to trying because I not only fancied Hannah – I rather liked her as well. As I stripped and got into bed, I executed an elegant pirouette that expertly obscured Ant and Dec. Hannah bent over and kissed me on the lips six times. I could taste her lipstick and on the seventh, I kissed her back a little longer and a little harder. She gave a little gasp. Then she gave a very big gasp. Then she was standing by the bed, pinning the duvet to her chest with her hand and staring at me naked on the bed. Her eyes went from my two saluting penises to my two eyes and back again. On her face was more surprise than I've ever seen before. I realised in a flash I was going to have to get used to that expression.

Fair enough, be a bit surprised. But to vomit – I presume from shock – and flee the room naked, screaming "Monster!" was, I have to say, rude and a little hurtful. What was I? Some sort of freak? I sat back down on the bed, feeling quite unattractive. I lit up a fag and tried to think. In all my years of pulling women, I had never before caused physical revulsion on sight of genitalia. And I had really liked Hannah. My eyes burned with tears; I pictured my future self, in bed with a Bearded Lady or a Smallest Woman On The Planet, humping off the savage rejection of Everyone Else. Ant and Dec had by now retreated in misery. Flaccid and shy, they looked like some sort of newly discovered sea-creature – a hairy relative of the octopus.

"Hello Rick. Are you there?" It was Phil from downstairs on the intercom. I let him in, waiting to see how he would phrase things. He went for the direct approach.

"There's a bird downstairs, Rick, saying you've got two cocks." He paused, "She's starkers. Quite fit though." I asked Phil to bring Hannah back so she could get her clothes.

A minute later, trembling, she followed Phil back into the flat and put her arms around me. "I am sorry Rick. You are ill yes? I get awful shock." I could see her, doing what women do, meeting what she thought was a deformity, a handicap, with kindness and understanding. I reckoned I could easily get her back into bed. Cheered by this, I decided to let her and Phil in on the scam.

"I'm not handicapped," I said. Hannah cooed comfort, "No. You are just phallically challenged."

"I tell you what love," sniggered Phil, "not as challenged as you would have been if he'd whopped them both up you."

Tutting at Phil's lack of finesse, I continued, "I had a second penis grafted on for a laugh and to make a bit of money."

To my astonishment this seemed to really upset Hannah because she stood up and slapped me hard on the face. Then, she did it again and yelled, "You ugly pig. You disgusting pig. I am totally out of here man. You are making me sick." She stormed off in tears, leaving Phil and me agog.

After a brief discussion on the unfathomability of women, we shared a couple of pints and went through my earning potential. It was enough to make me forget all my worries of earlier, and Hannah along with them.

* * *

That was the real beginning, I suppose. I became a headline in the *Sunday Sport*: I Have TWO Dicks! a star guest on *Jerry Springer*. Guess What? I Have Two Penises and posed with the real Ant and Dec for the *News of the World*: Rick – A Man With Two Pricks! I became very rich. I did a buy-one-get-one-free campaign for Durex, an international lecture tour with Dr Mike and said I slept with Anna Nicole Smith. I sold my flat in London and moved to Las Vegas where my grotesque celebrity guaranteed a healthy income. I was no longer Rick, but 'Two Dick Rick: The Man with Two Penises'. My most popular venture was at a late-night stripclub. I would dress up as Elvis and wank Dec whilst Ant nestled in a bread roll, posing as a hot dog.

Women were everywhere. My fame, money and the perverse thrill I suppose two penises can offer to the insatiable female, meant that I pulled by the thousand. Beautiful, sexy, charming women who looked like walking advertisements for a dream would happily go to bed with me, in twos and threes, whenever I wished. And in bed I was having a very interesting time. My initial hope of having an orgasm at double strength and intensity never came off, so to speak. Instead, each prick would come alone and independently of the other. Also, instead of getting stronger with age, Ant never really achieved the heights of Dec's natural sensations, but withered slightly and was sometimes quite difficult to coax into action. That's why he always had to be the hot dog.

Nevertheless, there were a number of manoeuvres I particularly remember. One young lady, a former dancer called Shannon, manipulated me with her womanhood and her mouth, both at the same time. Exquisite. Another, an out-of-work Spanish acrobat whose name I'll never know, welcomed me with her back and her front and yelled lines from *Don Quixote* throughout. An Irish redhead called Bridget got them both to do a jig. Little things like that made it all worthwhile. Much to my chagrin, I could never get both Ant and Dec into a single cunt at the same time. The pain I felt was too great because – how shall I put it – the lads rubbed each other up the wrong way.

Thus I wended my wealthy way for the next eighteen months, until one day when it all started going wrong. I began that day like most others, brunching at Pete's Bar across the street with eggs, coffee and the local paper. A familiar face grinned out at the bottom of page seven. It was Dr Mike. He was now internationally renowned and, after his success with me, was looking for other men to 'help'. I read on – four other men, younger than me, had been through the same operation. A fifth was going to try for the triple. Refined techniques and lessons learnt from my body meant these men had none of my problems. And they had every intention of raining on my dicks' parade.

Sure enough, in the next few months two more Men with Two Penises arrived on my circuit. I had to change my name to 'The Original and Best Man with Two Penises'. But I wasn't the best. One of the newcomers could wank his two simultaneously. He could also sing and developed a popular act where he would pretend to be impotent and croon, *I've Lost That Lovin' Feeling*. As the song climaxed he would whip out his two big erections and come all over the stage, at which point he would change the lyrics to *I've Found That Lovin' Feeling*. It was stiff competition.

Things went from bad to worse. Younger guys with two, three, four penises apiece became as familiar as slot machines, at least in Vegas. One, a former music student, called his four 'The Members of the Orchestra' and used them to play Beethoven's Late Quartets. He was even in demand as an art house exhibit. There were rumours of a supermarket worker in Sacramento who was going for a quintet and whose wife was arranging to get six vaginas. I was outclassed, washed-up, finished. The work petered out and, I guessed, pretty soon the money would too. I took to sitting in a bar on the wrong side of the street from Pete's, spending my days and my money on Wild Turkey.

One afternoon, about four o'clock, I heard a little voice addressing the barman, "Hey Loser, serve me up a fuckin' double now or I'll trash the fuckin' joint." I looked down to see an old woman who barely reached my knee. "Who are you?" I said. "Who d'ya freakin' think?" she said. "I'm the Smallest Woman On The Fuckin' Planet. Ya lookin' for company?"

I spent a considerable chunk of my money getting it removed. Then I moved back to London and bought myself a flat. I met up with Phil again. He had moved on to be floor manager at Homebase and was now happily married, and still living in my old building. I expected that to be the end of all my best adventures. It nearly was, but not quite.

One evening in Kents I saw a beautiful, blonde woman rowing with what looked to be her husband. They argued, he left and she burst into tears. Sticking to a time-honoured winning formula, I sent over a bottle of champagne with a note saying, "Are You A Finnish Air Hostess?" She stopped crying and looked over at me with surprise and then recognition. And all at once I knew that this second chance was going to be better than any second penis.

arthur smith

dishonourable discharge

Roland's croissant was plump and apricot jammy. It looked, he thought, like a big, poignant, toasted wasp. He was eating it outside a Parisian café and to complete the cliché, it was a warm spring morning. He had a packet of Gitanes, a café crème and sitting next to him was his beautiful young lover. The bread, the coffee and life itself were, however briefly, sweet. Paris swarmed entertainingly before them. They say that to be happy is to inhabit a moment, a good moment, with perfect unselfconsciousness. Well then, for the first time since all that, he felt happiness. He, Roland Hooper, a forty-two-year-old computer-programmer, was conscious only that his risible misfortune had passed. He was sitting comfortably. He could begin – afresh. His eyes lazily scanned the scene, not really registering much until – bang! "Jesus, fuck, that's him isn't it? It is, fucking hell, that's Bernie." His body shuddered and his mind went online.

Bernie had been the undisputed king of the hospital Smoking Room, welcoming his new subjects, dispensing advice, medical, political and sexual. It was never clear exactly what was wrong with him; 'everything' was his own diagnosis. He had already been in hospital for six months when Roland first paid court to that brightly lit, windowless, toxic palace. During the next four weeks, it would be the only place he could get some air.

To clarify: Roland Hooper had been unlucky. October had been very warm that year and, when searching for an old computer disc in the attic of his Clapham home, he had disturbed a not-yet-hibernating wasps' nest. He was savagely attacked. A dangerous reaction to histamine had both nearly choked him and caused him to ricochet down the attic stairs and break his pelvis. If it had been a motorbike accident he could have reeked with the fumes of reckless allure; but he, Roland, had to fake the beetroot laugh of shame with every visitor, desperately insisting that it could have happened to anyone, and all the while aghast that it had happened to him.

There are lots of smells in hospitals but shit, piss and disinfectant are the ones competing for supremacy. So when, following medical advice, Roland began to walk the corridors, a sinful prick of tobacco was so surprising and so new that his nostrils got an erection. For the first time in three weeks he was alight. Also, he was desperate for a fag. He levered himself at such speed towards the thrill, even his fool's crutches seemed to exalt. Thus, they delivered him unto glorious temptation. There it was -- the Smoking Room.

No bigger than a prison cell, it contained six chairs, all of which should have been consigned to a skip years before. Three of them oozed dirty yellow foam rubber, while the others were covered in a network of gaffer tape. There was a small low rectangular table covered in paper cups, many of them holed in the side by the death gasp of a burning fag. Curiously, there was no ashtray, only a bin stuffed with papers, sweet-wrappers and butts. In one corner, an old cheese sandwich lay on the floor, like a raggy grey bandage sodden with pus.

"Fuck mine, it's the Archbishop of Canterbury." The speaker grinned to reveal three brown teeth. He was referring to the large hook which curved up, shepherd-like, from Roland's right crutch and held his drip. It did indeed look like a holy staff.

"Come in mate. Take a seat, not that one, a bloke pissed on it two nights ago, it's still a bit wet." Roland tried to explain that sitting with a shattered pelvis was painful and besides, he had no cigarettes, but he hadn't bargained on kindness.

"I'm Bernie. Have one of mine." And handing him two Embassy Regal, the three teeth grinned again.

Gingerly, Roland took a seat that may once have been blue. Then he lit up, inhaled and shut his eyes. He was outside an airport, at the end of a long flight.

"First fag for a while?" – Bernie's sludgy eyes nearly shone. "...Fantastic feeling. Better than pethadrone."

"Drin, Pethadrine," came a voice from behind the door. It opened to admit a short fat man wearing beige pyjamas designed for a tall thin man. The result, when he sat down, was a belly that hung over the edge of his chair like a sack of wet porridge.

"Actually my learned friends, it's petha*dine*." A South African voice silenced them, bulletlike from the corridor. "But when it comes to lung cancer, you're better off with morphine." Roland opened his eyes to see a bulging red face grinning down at them from a white coat. It disappeared and the door slammed shut.

"Drin. Drone. Fucking doctors. They're all cunts anyway," continued Bernie imperiously. "Can I get you a drink, Archbishop? Gin and tonic? Pint of Guinness? I'm getting a triple vodka myself. Belly here's having a rum and coke. Belly, meet the Archbishop of fucking Canterbury."

"Hello there," said Roland, eschewing all nicknames on this first visit.

"I'll have a white wine," rasped the other occupant of the room, a leathery woman in a velour tracksuit. "Fuck it, make it champagne, Bernie."

"You celebrating, Queenie?" Bernie smiled broadly. "Why don't you put a sexy frock on, we'll go dancing up the West End."

Everyone laughed, and then a silence came as all four attended to their cigarettes and roll-ups.

Queenie began an alarming story whose plot Roland couldn't quite follow. A man she knew from bingo had developed cancer as a direct result of twisting his ankle.

"He done his ankle in the March," she said darkly, "and come December he was dead."

Her message was clear. Another doctor had fucked up.

"I don't call them doctors," said Bernie, "I call them Shipmans. Shipmans and cunts."

Roland was to learn over the next few weeks that the Smoking Room policy on health was formulated by Bernie. Its main thrust was that all doctors were useless, or even worse, part of a conspiracy to keep him ill and out of the pub. His followers would bring daily bulletins detailing the incompetence and cruelty of the Shipmans. Bernie advocated confrontation with the medical ruling classes; always question everything, dispute every diagnosis, look for the hidden agenda and ignore all advice unless it suits you. His was the Jeremy Paxman approach – "Why is this lying bastard lying to me?"

Having taken this stance he was lucky that his own Consultant was the genuinely dislikeable Dr Pik Simmons, a man with the accent and views of a traditional Afrikaner. Feared for his sardonic humour, it was his lung-cancer gag that had poisoned Roland's first hospital cigarette. Much of his venom was reserved for Bernie, whom he addressed mockingly as, "Mr O'Hanlon". Then he would squash him underfoot, like the old butt-end of the joke he was.

Unsurprisingly Bernie stationed himself almost permanently in the Smoking Room, returning to his ward only for meals. He provided fags for the fagless and succour to the depressed. Roland could soon attest to that. A depressing problem for him had been his huge, swollen bottom, over which no underwear would fit. His hospital gown gaped so obscenely at the back, even his mother found it repulsive.

"Cover yourself up please, Roland," she had said, adding delicately, "It's not very ... nice ... for the other people." Miserable and humiliated, he limped along for a smoke and was met by Bernie, who snorted in agreement.

"We don't want no poor ladies getting a big flash of your arse, Archbishop." He then disappeared, returning with a piece of string to tie strategically round Roland and solve the problem.

Queenie was the principal lady in Bernie's kingdom, flirting and bickering with him, generally playing out the role her nickname decreed. Roland loved her unexpected stories and her medical expertise. This particular day, a day Roland remembered for other reasons, the day of the idea, an obese woman had heaved into one of the chairs.

"You in for fat?" asked Queenie, knowledgeably. The woman, breathing heavily, nodded.

"I only have to eat a piece of toast and I put on two stone."

"Yes," said Queenie, "and you've eaten the whole loaf, haven't you?"

"You're off the wall you are, Queenie," said Bernie after the fat lady had left.

"I'll tell you off the wall, Bernie. My mate, Dave, every time he gets pissed, he buys potatoes and puts them in the fridge."

"What? What are you talking about, you batty cow?"

"It's true. Every time he's pissed he buys potatoes and puts them in the fridge."

"Leave it out, Queenie. That's stupid. What do you reckon, Archie?"

The 'Archbishop' had been shortened; Roland belonged. His part was largely that of a willing audience for Bernie, but also to be something of an intellectual because he'd once been spotted reading a book on the ward.

Before he could reply Bernie embarked on a long, epic coughing fit. As he approached the end he suddenly produced a jar, unscrewed it and hawked vigorously into it.

"The Shipmans have asked me to keep my flob," he explained. "Look, that's just from today." He triumphantly displayed the aggregate of phlegm to Queenie and Roland, who suddenly knew he would never eat oysters again. It occurred to him that a room he often passed, the Patients' Discharge Lounge, might be a wholly different thing from what he had imagined.

The pissed potato man and daily mucus forgotten, Bernie was moved on to one of his favourite topics. France. He had recently heard of a survey that proclaimed the French Health Service the best in the world. This, allied with a vague story about a beloved woman who lived there, made him a confirmed Francophile even though he had never been to the country, or any country outside of England. Roland smoked and snatches of the conversation blurred around him.

"I'll bet the food you get in French hospitals is better than the rubbish you get served up here. Shit warmed up. They get it out the toilet."

"You'll get a nice bit of steak there," added Belly, who had arrived, his gut as big as ever, although the frame that held it seemed to be thinning, giving an impression of a balloon tied halfway down a stick.

"Steak," said Queenie, "with snails and frogs. No thanks."

"Steaks and frogs would be better than stewed rat which is what you get here."

"Lucky to get them stewed," added Belly, as ever seeking Bernie's approval, as they all did.

"I'm going to go to France," said Bernie, "if I ever get out of this fucking place."

A gloom descended. Inhale. Exhale. Cough. If I ever get out of this fucking place. Each of them was alone with their thoughts and their tobacco. Self-pity was frowned upon, but for a few minutes they all seemed to feel it, caught up in the endless succession of scans, operations, injections, sleepless nights, all the pain, boredom and indignities they had suffered and had still to suffer. There were no seasons in the Smoking Room but suddenly Roland was aware that it was winter.

Bernie spoke again.

"Queenie, come to the pub tomorrow?"

"What's wrong with tonight?"

"Tomorrow. I'm serious. Not a made-up pub. A real pub. There's one right by the hospital."

This was a radical idea.

"We'll all go," said Bernie, his eyes now dancing. "We can all just about make it, I reckon."

Woozily awake in the night, Roland considered the outrageous notion of stepping outside the bounds of the hospital into that other world where he used to live. It was forbidden, strange and fantastically exciting. And a pub. It had only been two months, but it seemed so long since he had been in a pub it was something he could only think of as a picture, a virtual image on the screen of his mind. A mind that was ill with boredom.

Next morning they gathered. Hobbling past the lift, Roland reflected that he had a kind of purpose to the day for once; if it had been physically possible there would have been a bounce in his step.

The others were already in position.

"Right," said Bernie briskly, "Here's the plan—"

"Bernie, I can't go," a small voice interrupted him.

"Why not?"

"I'm—"

"Scared?"

"I don't think I could make it physically, I've been getting worse. It's all I can manage to get here."

"And you're scared."

"A bit."

"Do you think you'll ever go in a pub again?"

There was a silence. Roland concentrated on putting his cigarette out and noticed again the tiny flies that hung around the overflowing bin. Bernie smiled.

"Don't worry, Belly, we'll bring you back a bag of crisps."

Belly's thin frame relaxed into his chair and his famous stomach, smaller by the day, gave a little wobble of relief. The planning continued.

Fifteen minutes after lights out, Roland stuffed two pillows and a book under the blankets to mimic his sleeping form. Ten anxious minutes after that, he discretely slipped out of the ward, straining to tiptoe on crutches. He stopped in the toilet by the exit and carefully put a large overcoat on top of his gown. He made his way to the Smoking Room, James Bond despite the swollen pelvis. Belly was standing outside it looking flustered. "It's locked, they've closed it!" he gasped.

There was a sign on the door. 'The Smoking Room is now closed. If you wish to smoke, please use the area provided outside Howell Wing.' Underneath, written in thick felt-tip letters, was SMOKING KILLS.

"The fuckers." Looking around, Roland was shocked to see Queenie wearing a dress and in full make-up. She was wearing slippers but carried a provocative pair of stilettos in her manicured hand.

"You look fabulous," he gasped. How old was she? Forty-five? Fifty? Just a few years up on him really.

Then Bernie came round the corner in pyjamas pushing a drip tree.

"You're on a drip, Bernie."

"Fucking Shipmans. What's this?"

"The Smoking Room is shut. For good."

"*Fuck*ing Shipmans." He shut his eyes a moment and groaned.

"So, is the pub trip off? You can't go with a drip."

"Bollocks to them. Of course we're going. It's all sorted. Vinny's arranged a lock-in. I was going to ring and put it off, but if that's the Shipman attitude, fuck them, I need a fag. And a drink. Come on."

They all followed Bernie down some empty corridors, new territory to Roland, and arrived at a battered-looking service lift.

"I'll say goodbye here," wheezed Belly. "I was just coming to give you a send-off. Have one for me." He waved and smiled weakly as the lift door shut. They never saw him again.

From the lift, it was a short journey to the side door. Once outside that door, far from the Smoking Room, an instant change occurred that was something like a loss. The reality of what he was doing had made Roland jittery and he started at every sound, some of which he unfortunately imagined. This irritated Bernie, a born aggressor, to such a pitch that Queenie had to combat him with her stiletto. Roland despised himself for the middle-class coward he knew he was at heart, but obedience had been his lifetime's creed and was at his very core.

"Gosh I hope we haven't been spotted ... I wonder what'll happen if we're seen ... Do you think we're breaking the law?" helplessly on and on he went, unable to obey Bernie's orders and just shut the fuck up.

Mercifully, out of the shadows it appeared, dark and shut, the pub.

"Let us in. I'm freezing my bollocks off," said Queenie. A tap on a door, a light flickering, a soft click and they were in. Into this warm room with its overpowering smell of beer, its sinful joy, its dangerous ordinariness. They fell into cushy seats while Vinny and his wife Justine attended to them. The bad humour of the walk evaporated and Queenie put on her high heels.

"Get me a pint of Guinness and a large vodka please, Vinny." Bernie was breathing heavily.

"Oi, your cousin said you're not supposed to drink."

"I'm not supposed to smoke or be here either. Come on you bastard."

Queenie ordered a gin and tonic and Roland resolutely ordered an orange juice and bitter lemon.

"Come on Archie, not having a drink?"

"The doctor said I can't drink on my antibiotics."

"Oh yes, that old shit. Another vodka, Vinny, for my friend the Archbishop."

"Don't have a drink Archie," said Queenie whom Roland noticed was wearing perfume. Her thighs were pressed against his. He realised he had not felt the warmth of a human body next to him for a long time. He drank the vodka down in one.

Bernie, who had seemed on the point of expiring when they'd pushed through the door, seemed more relaxed and happy than Roland had ever seen him. After gossiping with Justine he started playing pool, like a puppet manipulated through the thin plastic tube of his drip.

"It seems odd to be here. With you two." He smiled at her and clasped his second vodka.

"Yeah. You and Bernie keep me going. And the Smoking Room."

"What will we do without it? It's too far to keep going to Howell. Too cold."

"I won't be smoking for a while. I've got the operation tomorrow."

"Good luck with it, Queenie."

"If it goes all right I'll be home in three weeks."

"I'm sure it will."

"Didn't last time."

"You'll be home for ..." He tried to think of some milestone in the forlorn wilderness of the future. "...Valentine's Day."

Queenie snorted. "My husband's gone off with my daughter."

At the pool table Bernie cackled at a pot.

"My daughter by my first marriage."

"I'm so sorry. You never said." Another of her unlikely stories, but this one had remained untold.

"Well, we don't talk about that stuff. I don't know if you're married or whatever. I don't even know your real name. And you don't know mine."

"Bernie's Bernie though, isn't he?"

"Bernie's Bernie, poor sod."

"Why poor sod?"

"At least I've got my caravan by the sea. They'll have to find somewhere for Bernie."

"Where was he living?"

"Before here he was in prison and before that he was on the streets."

"Why was he in prison?"

"He burnt his ex-wife's house down."

"Why did he do that?"

"I'll tell you why," Bernie had returned from the pool and he and his drip installed themselves at the table.

"I was a butcher. Had me own shop and everything. Wife, two kids. I come home early from the pub one night and I saw her in the car, a bloke feeling her tits up. A fucking *doctor* as he turned out to be. I told her, you can keep the house, I packed my bags and I left. I haven't seen her since that day. Bring the vodka over, Vinny, and I'll have a pickled egg if you've got one. Cunts. Fucking doctors. Fucking Shipmans."

"We'd never heard of Harold Shipman back then though, Bernie," said Queenie unhelpfully.

Roland looked at her and imagined her after the operation, alone in her caravan without a womb, its only fruit off screwing its stepfather. He thought *Talk about irony* and sniggered hysterically.

Shocked at his own cruelty, he pulled himself back and could only conclude the vodka had sent him funny.

"I'm going to go to France one day. Go to my daughter's wedding, Queenie; she's getting married in France. I've never seen them since that day." Bernie was drunk and his tone was aggressive; he was not hospital Bernie, he was Saloon Bar Bernie, bitter and punchy.

"Come on, Archie, have another drink for fuck's sake."

"Leave him alone, Bernie."

"What's the point of sneaking out to the pub if you don't have a fucking drink?"

"Bernie, I don't want to. I don't want to stay in hospital one minute more than I have to."

"You've disappointed me, Archie. I thought you had bollocks. What are you – a fucking poof?"

Roland's head swam. He lit a fag, then noticed he already had one on the go. "I'm going to head back, Queenie."

"Wait a minute and I'll come. We'd better think about moving Bernie. They'll notice we've gone soon."

"You two go if you like," Bernie said contemptuously, "I'm staying. I'm having a couple more drinks and then I'm going to France."

"Don't be silly, Bernie …"

"Fuck you, that's where I'm going. No one's going to stop me. Je go in France, you make me sick, you two."

Queenie and Roland didn't speak as they battled their way back. He could smell the brandy on her breath as they waited for the lift.

"I'm probably being discharged next week so I won't see you after your operation, Queenie."

"Maybe no one will."

The lift arrived. As it cranked its weary bones upwards again Queenie suddenly shoved her hand up Roland's gown, instantly conjuring his first erection for two months. For some reason he laughed and then gasped as she roughly, quickly made him come. In the corridor Queenie kissed him once and then turned and walked away.

Next morning Roland Hooper was discharged early in disgrace which suited him fine. He could walk pretty much without pain and would only need the crutches for a further week or so. He took a last look at the Smoking Room on the way out. It was still locked and the notice was still pinned firmly to the door. Looking through the glass panel he could see it had been swept, hoovered and scrubbed, the chairs and table removed. It was bare and clean although the final traces of tobacco smell still lingered delicately. When he got home he sent a postcard to Queenie but never got a reply. The grim memory of that period of his life when he seemed to have nothing but life itself and a packet of fags, receded slowly.

Until now, because here on a grand Parisian boulevard, the image of Bernie presented itself again. It was not Bernie in the flesh, the taut sallow flesh of the long-term sick, it was a photo of Bernie grinning toothily from the English newspaper his girlfriend was reading. He grabbed it from her and read, filleting the article for the story. Bernie had been in a confrontation with a Dr Simmons, originally from Johannesburg. Simmons had been remonstrating with Bernie (Bernard O'Hanlon) about Bernie's visits to a pub, outside the hospital grounds. To try and emphasise his point the doctor had opened the window of the eighth floor hospital ward they were in. Instead of sneaking out, drinking and smoking, Dr Simmons suggested, why not just jump out of the window and save everyone, especially Bernie himself, a lot of pain and misery?

It was a bold and vivid gesture on the part of the doctor, but one that went badly wrong, because Bernie had called his bluff and before Simmons could stop him, had accepted the invitation and launched himself out of the window, falling to an instant death. He'd got his posthumous revenge on the medical profession, because Dr Simmons was now charged with manslaughter.

Roland sat silently for a while. The sun went in and came out again. Poor doctor. And poor Bernie, whose life had been transformed in one jealous moment and ended in one mad one. He never made it to France, but his picture had. He lit a Gitane and smoked it for Bernie.

Jenny Hargreaves became a punk performance poet in the 1980s and, according to legend, acquired the name Éclair while pretending to be French in a Blackpool nightclub. She was the first female to win the Perrier Award at the Edinburgh Fringe in 1995. These days, apart from stand up, Éclair dabbles in radio, telly, a bit of West End and writing. Her first novel Camberwell Beauty *was published in 2000; she hopes to finish her second before the publisher gets really pissed off.*

jenny éclair

metamorphosis – blue stocking blues

It wasn't a good day: my pre-packed 'healthy option' tuna pasta salad had proved disappointing and that put me in a bad mood. Friday afternoons can be very trying. I'd kept Emily Gibb in detention.

"This is as frustrating for me as it is for you Emily," I said.

She sneered her reply. "Yeah right, so you're going to Matt Partington's party tonight are you, Miss?"

I could have smacked her spotty face, but of course you're not allowed; hair pulling's out as well. To be honest, if I could have just opened her desk, positioned her head – guillotine style – and slammed the lid down as hard as I could on her cranium, we could both have simply forgotten about it and gone home.

I spend quite a lot of my time imagining how I would like to hurt the children in my care. When you teach chemistry you have a wide choice of torture to hand. Ammonia in the eye, nitric acid, sodium chloride, a ginger pigtail set alight by a Bunsen burner. *(Yes, Amanda Craig, I'm thinking of you, you Neanderthal slag.)* Sometimes I have to sit on my hands to stop myself from lashing out.

Ridiculous situation; no wonder these kids are out of control; how can you maintain discipline when you're not even allowed to throw the occasional blackboard rubber at their pig-ignorant skulls? Due to the fact that physical punishment is verboten, I find myself resorting – on a daily basis – to verbal sadism. However, I have been warned (officially) that comments about physical appearances such as "Hey you fat smelly girl" are out of order. This, I feel, is a shame. After all I know what they say about me; I have very acute hearing; I am yours truly – that 'fucking lesbo bitch'.

I made Emily Gibb write three sides of A4 on the displacement reactions of metals and confiscated her Nokia; she looked at me as if I'd amputated her leg! Emily Gibb is fifteen years old; she has a tide of fading yellow love-bites around her grubby little neck; by Monday no doubt there will be a fresh crop of little purple bite marks. I couldn't care less about Emily 'big tits' Gibb. I'd be gobsmacked if she stuck it out through her GCSEs; shop work or hairdressing beckons that one, though no doubt she will choose the tougher option of teenage motherhood and a bit of on-the-side dope dealing – that's how moronic she is.

I watched Emily Gibb squeeze blackheads out of her nose and chin and wipe them on the paper I'd provided for her. This, I presume, was to get back at me for returning her exercise book complete with a sliver of raw liver squashed between the centre pages. Petty? Maybe but we teachers don't get paid much: you've got to have some perks.

I had to let her go at 4.45pm (another typically soppy New Labour rule – any longer than an hour and we have to have parental consent). She approached my desk and handed over her work; halfway down the first page the words *You are a cunt* had been crossed out, but not rigorously enough.

"Thank you Emily," I said, in a really sarcastic way.

"Have a nice weekend, Miss," she replied, in an equally sarcastic manner; she was rather good, she managed to load the word 'Miss' with connotations of dried up vaginas. I was impressed.

At that moment we both bent down to pick up our bags. Hers was a bulging Top Shop plastic affair (the satchel is all but extinct in this dump) and our heads collided with a sickening thud. *I bet I've got nits* was my first thought. Emily Gibb is a scratcher – most of them are; sometimes I look out and I think I might as well be teaching gibbons.

I wasn't in any particular hurry to get home, my flat smells and I've no idea why. I have a horrible feeling there might be a dead rat rotting under the floorboards. I use a particular type of poison which, once ingested, causes internal haemorrhaging and your vermin's vital functioning organs turn to mush; it's a good job I don't have access to the school kitchens! Ha!

My car was the only one left in the car park; I got in and turned on the ignition. I stalled three times driving out of the gates; some workmen saw me and laughed. I wound down the window and called them "Fuck pig arse-wipes". I very rarely resort to the language of the gutter: good job all the other teachers had gone home eh?

The fuel gauge was hovering on empty so I drove to the garage; that's when it started – in the Esso station. I pulled up by the pump and I couldn't remember how to put the petrol in.

I sat there listening to Radio 4, some quiz. "Who wrote *I Claudius*?" – "Robert Graves," I replied smugly, a sentiment echoed a second later by a Mr Anthony Borovitz of Lincoln. But then there was a simple question about the chemical compound that makes up argon and I sat there stumped; for some reason all that I could hear in my head were the lyrics of a Westlife single, *bop, bop baby*. "I'll have to hurry you – the chemical compound of argon?"

I knew the answer: I'm a chemistry teacher for heaven's sake. The solution was lodged somewhere at the back of my brain like a nappy stuck in a clogged up drain. I attempted to punch myself in the head to dislodge the answer; it didn't work but all of a sudden I remembered how to get the petrol in the car. I had to press the little button which releases the fuel cap. Simple. I got out of the car; it's a whatsitsname – a silver one, a Golf – that's right.

My hand felt feeble round the nozzle, but I managed not to spill too much and crossed the forecourt to pay. The next thing I recall is driving away with a copy of *Heat* magazine on the passenger seat, a Yorkie bar and ten Silk Cut. Which was odd. I'm fervently anti-smoking. In fact, it was I who cast the deciding vote opposing a proposed smoking area for nicotine addicted teachers. It is thanks to me that certain members of staff are frequently seen hiding behind the trees on the playing fields puffing away like fifth formers. Unfortunately, this hopeless little band includes the headmistress; hence I am not a very popular woman. Cigarettes, *Heat* magazine and chocolate? I closed my eyes to think à la Hercule Poirot and almost went right up the backside of a Renault Mégane, a posh female voice yelled, "Cretin!" at me.

"Go fuck yourself!" I replied, which was odd as I'd meant to say, "Sorry."

I don't eat chocolate. I'm not that kind of woman! I have a savoury tooth; give me a jar of dill pickles over a box of Milk Tray anytime; and I certainly don't read daft magazines stuffed with nonsense about D-list celebrities, none of whom I recognise because I don't watch television. Well, occasionally I'll catch the news and the odd documentary on the History Channel. (Let's face it, I can watch that footage of Kennedy having the top of his head blown off till the cows come home.) But I've never watched a single episode of *EastEnders*.

The television is a legacy left over from my last partner, a man whom I went off rapidly after he bought me an apron with a pair of breasts on the front. He said it was ironic, a metaphor for witless. My ex is called Nigel Pothecary, a man who thought Evelyn Waugh was a woman. Idiot! A man who thought Pythagoras was the name of a Greek restaurant in Islington. Imbecile! A man who truly cooked his goose when he bought tickets for *Fame* rather than tickets for the Proust at the National which I'd been hinting at for a fortnight. "But it's *my* birthday," he whimpered – King Arsehole!

I was relieved when he left; we'd been like an experiment that went wrong in the lab. On paper the two of us looked like a winning formula: he had the letters after his name, the beard, the glasses, the corduroy trousers, all the outward signs of academia including dreadful halitosis, but he didn't have the brain. In the end we were like vinegar and sodium bicarbonate fizzing furiously against each other in this little test tube of a flat.

Since then I've been alone, which is good because I've managed to teach myself conversational Italian and the rudiments of French polishing. I truly believe that if you put your mind to most things they are achievable, from breadmaking to salsa. The brain is like a very big sponge. This is what I tell my students. They don't listen of course, they text each other stupid messages and fall asleep dribbling on their desks.

I am a self-sufficient woman. I cannot bear incompetence: there's just no reason for it; most things come with a manual; just stop bleating and get on with it. I have single-handedly rewired this flat, tiled and grouted my bathroom and cemented down great shards of broken-up bottles along my back wall so the little bastards from the estate can't get into my yard without losing a few pints of haemoglobin. I have also hand-reared a fig tree.

Most people make me despair, my pupils depress me, dull-eyed and bovine. We seem to be in the grip of some kind of epidemic of crass stupidity. A nation of fat imbeciles smoking and eating chips.

I had a lot of marking to do, but for some reason I sat on my self-re-upholstered sofa and read about Liz Hurley and teeth bleaching. I even attempted a quiz about Winona Ryder. It was rather hard: I only got four out of ten. Out of habit, I scrawled *v poor see me* at the bottom of the page in red biro. My horoscope (I'm a Taurus, not that I believe in any of that guff) said *expect changes this weekend*. By the time I'd finished the magazine, the Yorkie wrapper lay discarded on the floor.

I had a bath; that's when I got the next surprise of the day. I saw my toes: they were painted coral pink. I mean the toenails of course not the fleshy bits. Now I don't paint my toenails. I don't wear peep-toe shoes, apart from Birkenstocks in the summer, so there's no need. In fact I don't wear make-up period. Now and again I might pluck a few stubborn hairs that sprout from my chin, but that's as far as it goes. But there they were, all ten of them, all shiny. It looked a bit peculiar, considering that I don't shave my legs; they looked like they'd been grafted on by accident, Poodle feet on Alsatian legs. Very odd.

Before I knew it I was mowing my shins with a razor, the blade was rather blunt; my legs bled profusely.

I wanted to listen to a concert on Radio 3, but the radio refused to tune in properly and the only decent reception I could get was on Radio 1. "*Bop bop baby* ..." I sang along and, just for a moment, it almost made me cry. It was somehow incredibly moving, all that passion. It knocked spots off Elgar.

I found my hands soaping my body with Imperial Leather. I don't go in for floral scents. I find most perfumes sickly and cloying, like burnt-out sweet shops. Once, when I was in Peter Jones, a shop assistant grabbed my arm and squirted some foul-smelling liquid all over it; I felt like I'd been pissed on by a cat.

I don't tend to pay much attention to my physical state; as long as my legs can carry me the rest can do what it likes. What surprised me, then, were my breasts, I don't have breasts, I have always thought large breasts rather common. I mean fine if they were of any use, if they contained spare brain cells or a reserve set of organs, livers, kidneys etc. – but they don't. Breasts at the end of the day are two bags of fat. I was glad that mine have never been prominent, that I have never had any trouble with them. A fellow teacher at my school had very large breasts; once they were involved in an incident concerning a sash window. Very badly bruised apparently; she retired soon after; went to live in Wales.

I ran my hands over my breasts again and looked down. Truly I didn't recognise them; they appeared on my rib cage like two perfect orbs, nipples the size of mini courgettes pointed at the ceiling. My withered little English Cox's pippins had become Gala melons. I thought maybe I would try and bandage them up, suppress the swelling. But I didn't have enough bandage – I only had an elasticated sock bandage which I'd bought after the chain came off my bicycle and I'd taken a nasty fall last autumn.

There was no way the elasticated sock bandage was going to be of any use, ankles and breasts being so different in contour. I put some Savlon on the pair of them, swallowed a couple of Piriton (a handy antidote to most allergic reactions) and wandered into my bedroom. I held a breast in each hand, hushing them, encouraging them to settle, to stop jiggling. It was like trying to get twin babies to go to sleep. Eventually I wrapped my thick towelling robe around them, reckoning if I didn't look or touch, if I just ignored them they'd go away.

I decided that if they hadn't gone down by the morning I could (a) look up breast conditions on the Internet, (b) go to casualty or (c) attempt to prick them with a sterilised pin.

A stack of red exercise books sat on my kitchen table, 8A's homework; it could wait, I had all weekend, I watched *Top of the Pops*, ate a Pot Noodle and masturbated on the sofa – three things which I haven't done for a very long time. It was at this point I realised I must be ill, so I went to bed with a Bacardi Breezer I'd won at a school tombola three years ago and a packet of Munchies I'd confiscated from a Year 7. I didn't even bother to clean my teeth and that's not like me.

My new breasts woke me at sevenish; for a moment I thought I had a couple of labrador puppies under each arm. I scooped them up and tried to catch them in a bra. It was ridiculous. Even though I altered the straps and fastened it on the very last hook, flesh rolled out of the sides, over the top. I decided to take my mind off them with some marking, I brought the books into bed with me but my breasts kept popping out of the bra and getting in the way, everything got smudged and they ended up covered in red ink. I didn't want to have another bath because I was convinced that once they came in contact with water they would grow even bigger, so I pulled the duvet up to under my chin and had a good cry.

I was right about the water theory. As my tears soaked through the duvet the breasts increased their volume. I now had two giant pink pumpkins to deal with. I thought, *If only I could lop them off with my garden shears and make some soup.*

On a Saturday, I will often take a trip to the Tate Modern, have a walk along the river, stroll up to the Festival Hall, treat myself to a new book, sit in the café and have a Latte.

None of this was possible till I got my breasts sorted out. I needed to buy a bra. I felt a bit better once I'd formulated a plan. All I needed to do now was get dressed. I found an old rugby shirt at the bottom of my laundry basket that Nigel my intellectually-inadequate boyfriend had left behind. It was maroon with white stripes and a number 7 on the back. Fortunately, what with Nigel being a campaigner for real ale, the shirt was an xxx large, I managed to squeeze into it; the horizontal stripes accentuated the problem; I looked like Kenny Everett. Hysteria rose in my throat like an air bubble. I opened my mouth and I let out this noise.

I recognised the noise because I teach teenage girls. The noise could only be described as a giggle. A really high-pitched giggle, a cross between Katie Birtle's giggle and Ashling Morgan's titter. It was the sound of utter vacuity. My hand flew to my mouth and I bit down hard. This was the worst thing I could have done: I was now helpless, giggling fit to burst with snot and tears and the whole works *Hee heeheehee.*

This is not how I laugh. When I laugh – which is seldom – it sounds like a cross between a cough and a sneeze. Grown women do not giggle, unless they're drunks of course.

I tried to eat some breakfast but I dropped half a croissant down my cleavage and somehow, despite rummaging down there for a good five minutes, I just couldn't find it. I threw on a large mackintosh – even though it didn't look like rain – and some old trousers. Maybe the cold air would help, maybe the breasts were just dramatic heat lumps, whatever, they were affecting my balance and I had to lean backwards so as not to fall on my face.

A short bus ride from my house lies East Street market, I knew there was a stall – the one on the corner – that sold outsize ladies underwear. I'd seen it often enough – Union Jack-sized knickers, bras as big as Easter bonnets – so I wobbled off with my arms folded under my massively swollen glands to the bus stop.

I didn't have to wait long, a number 12 rumbled up and I hauled myself aboard. I fished my purse out from my pocket, being careful not to drop my breasts, and counted out some change for the driver. I got confused adding up: it was the five pences and two pences that got me.

I said, "There you go, that's a pound."

He said, "No it ain't, you daft cow, it's 94p."

No one in my life has ever called me a 'daft cow'. *Over-educated frigid miserable bitch* – yes – *emotional cripple* – certainly – *passionless control freak* – many times. But 'daft cow' – never.

My whole life seemed to flash in front of me – reading at the age of three, Grade Five flute at eight, National Junior Chess Champion at ten. All my old school reports that I keep chronologically filed scrolled across my memory. I could see the handwriting – spidery testimonies to my intellectual prowess. *A capable girl, well advanced for her age, academically gifted, a shining future.* I mentally checked the contents of my box of treasures: the O and A level certificates, the acceptance letters from both Oxford and Cambridge, the scroll heralding my double first, the photo of me looking justifiably triumphant in my cap and gown!

In seconds, all my golden memories of academic glory turned to dust. The red elephant of a London bus juddered beneath my feet and I was suddenly aware that I was on a number 12 being accused by a man with tattoos and no front teeth of not being able to add up!

I opened my mouth to spit my favourite little Latin put down but I couldn't remember it, my mouth hung open and I'm afraid I dribbled. All of a sudden he looked sorry for me, he changed his tone, he said, "Don't worry, love. Here, let Bobby do," and he put his hairy paw into my purse and extracted the requisite sixpence.

"Fanks," I spluttered, suddenly unable to form a 'th'. As I ricocheted down the bus, my breasts slapped a toddler's face. An old lady who had got on behind me said, "Poor love. Not all there, is she? I've a second cousin a bit simple."

I felt myself go hot and squeezed into a seat. My breasts sat on my lap like twin pigs on their way to market, my nipple snouts twitching.

I pressed my face against the window of the bus and amused myself by making goldfish faces against the glass, mouthing the words *Bop bop baby*. Suddenly the light on the bus changed and, as we lurched into a shadow, I saw my face reflected in the window – only it wasn't me. I am thirty-nine, I wear glasses, my nose is long and thin. Looking back at me was the face of Emily Gibb.

I decided to get off the bus; what I really needed was a fag.

Illiterate until he was in his early thirties, Ricky Grover is now a prolific, award-winning writer. He wrote and starred in two short films: the theatrically-released Punch *won him the prestigious Silver Bear Award at the Berlin Film Festival and his Channel 4 film* Hungry *won him Best Actor Award at the Brest Film Festival. Ricky has appeared in the feature films* Love, Honour and Obey *and* Bring Me The Head of Mavis Davis. *He was well-reviewed for his co-starring role in* 'Orrible *and other TV credits include* Red Dwarf, Friday Night Armistice *and* Black Books. *His character Bulla was not only regularly featured on Channel 4's* The 11 o'clock Show *but even interviewed chat show host Michael Parkinson for BBC TV.*

ricky grover

My first ever job was a jeweller's. At my school, you didn't choose which university or college you would go to; you chose which jeweller's you were gonna rob first and this one was only round the corner, so it was well-handy.

Dads usually advise sons on their chosen career. My stepfather was an armed robber, so he said, "Well, if you've set your mind on doing it, at least I'll get you a job with a good firm." And he did. It was like being in the London Docks in the old days. You had to know someone to get a bit of work but, once you was in, you was in.

I'll never forget Frank. He wore a big trilby hat and his coat collar was up. It was about 90 degrees. It was a very hot summer. I felt I was starting off a good career. I was gonna have a proper job with a proper firm and a proper uniform. I had a lady's stocking and a cosh. Frank wanted me on the firm because I was a boxer and I was in shape. I'm still in shape now, but it's the shape of an onion. We had a meeting in Bianchi's caff in Canning Town. Bianchi's used to be owned by a bloke called Horace who made the best jam roll in the world. People used to travel miles to have his jam roll and custard and meet in his caff and say, "Have you got a bit of work for us?" His rice and custard wasn't bad either, but you couldn't beat his jam roll. He had a big old alsatian dog who bit everyone, but no one minded.

So I walked in and I can remember the steam coming off the big urn thing – you used to press it to make these frothy coffees. I went up to the ramp and I saw Frank and the firm sitting in the corner. There was a bit of sniggering going on. I was only young. I didn't know whether they was taking the piss. So I ordered a coffee. A black one. Horace looked a bit surprised. He knew I didn't drink black coffee. I normally liked a glass of milk with my baked jam roll. So I got this black coffee. It must've been volcanic hot. I remember I could feel the heat through the handle of the mug. And I walked over and gave it to the geezer straight in the face. Scalding coffee. The geezer who'd been sniggering. That changed things. They'd thought I was a bit of a puppy but, at that point, they realised I was their guv'nor. Their arsehole fell completely out of bed. One of them took the fellah away. He had blisters all over his face. And that ended up his nickname – *Blisters*. He was the driver.

So I did my first job with Frank. He knew someone who worked at the jeweller's round the corner, which you need with any job that's worth doing. We had a look at it for a couple of weeks and, as our informant Shanie had told us, the owner used to take about £15,000 worth of jewellery out of the shop every Friday night and sell a bit of tom[1] on the side. This bloke always came out bang at the same time every Friday and kept his jewellery in a leather pouch which he carried quite openly, which people often do because it puts less emphasis on them.

On the Friday of the robbery, I wore a zip-up top and a hood and this bloke, as always, came out bang on time. My heart was pounding. It was my first job. I'd rehearsed what I was going to do in my bedroom mirror quite a few times. "Behave yourself, mate. Gimme the pouch!" We didn't want to hurt no one. The idea was just to secure the prize.

---

1. tom = tomfoolery = jewellery

I jogged up to him outside the shop in my zip-up jacket and hood and made eye contact with the geezer: "Behave yourself, mate. Gimme the pouch!" just as I'd done in the mirror. Sweet as a nut. Bang! The geezer gave me the pouch! Within no time at all I was back in the car. Bob Marley was blaring out on the car radio. Blisters was laughing hysterically; Frank was buzzing. They were both puffing gear. I didn't even smoke, but I was stoned out of my head.

We got back to Frank's house and his mum treated us like we were the Kray Twins. "Tea, boys?" She knew we were up to a bit of skulduggery, but she loved it. "Fairy cakes, boys? Anything you need?" Can you imagine my first ever job going as sweet as that?

Frank slammed the big leather pouch on the table and we all just stared in awe and anticipation at it for a few seconds. I remember cold drips of sweat rolling down my face and my heart pounding. I remember how proud I felt and, in the background, seeing Frank's mum smiling at me. She had a gold tooth: must've cost bundles. She hardly knew me, but even she was proud of me. Now she knew I was proper.

Then Frank started unzipping the pouch and it felt like the sound of the zipping went on forever. Zzzzzziippppppppppppppp May I never move. Gospel truth. The contents of the pouch fell onto the table ... It was four ham sandwiches.

Then it hit home. The geezer had been robbed before. That's why he was walking about with the pouch on show. He had the tom hidden somewhere else on him. Anyone who fancies nicking the tom is going to end up with his packed lunch.

My mate Frank, though, was experienced. He didn't bat an eyelid. Just picked 'em up and went, "One for me ... One for you ... One for you ..." There was only three of us, so I got two sandwiches. They was lovely. French mustard on them. It was like being abroad.

ricky grover

Nowadays it seems like everyone wants to be someone they're not. You've got all the posh people moving to Docklands and trying to speak Cockney and all the Cockneys, as soon as they get hold of a few quid, moving up the road and trying to speak posh. So no one really knows who's who.

Years ago, I tried to shrug off the rough-and-ready. I was trying to be somebody I wasn't. I was saying things in a posh accent like, "That's absolutely totally amayzing!" which sounded all right from a distance.

One night, I met this bird in a wine bar. I figured she must be posh or else she wouldn't have been in a wine bar in the first place. She seemed to quite like me. She thought I was a catch. It was a dark wine bar.

I saw her for a few weeks and I kept up the act. It got to the stage where she wanted me to meet her parents. The invite was for Christmas Eve – dinner at their house. When I say 'house' it was more like a mansion – in Manor Road, Chigwell – lions' heads, tongue-and-groove, flock wallpaper. I remember they even had a big glass ashtray. Real nice.

I turned up looking ridiculous, wearing a moody[1] suit that didn't fit. I even had a leather pouch to make myself look posh. I can't remember where I got that from. I looked like an insurance man gone wrong.

Everyone was there – all her aunts, uncles, her deaf nan, everyone – but they were the genuine Chigwellites – not the jekyll[2] ones. They'd lived there all their life and been to private schools and everything. You could tell there were no car dealers there, although the nan looked a bit iffy.

We all sat round this big glass table for dinner. They'd put on a good spread although I thought they was a bit shy with the stuffing and the turkey was on the small side. I had this big healthy appetite – and that was what caused me problems later on that night. But what I'm saying is it was blinding. There was a pineapple on the table and everything. It really was like being abroad.

After dinner, everyone stood round a baby grand in the back room and sang carols. I wasn't gonna fit in there. So I managed to slip off and flop on one of the big leather Chesterfields in their front room. Then in waddled their little family dog, a chihuahua about 15 or 16 years old. It had a dodgy leg and its belly was hanging on the floor. It was on its way out and I knew how it felt.

I picked little Chai up and began to stroke him. I knew his name was Chai by the tag round his neck. While I was stroking him, the deaf nan walked in and said, "Anyone for Christmas pudding?" I looked round. I was the only person in the room. But I put my hand up. Well, you've gotta make sure, ain't ya? She nodded and turned round and left.

What I didn't know is that if you're stroking a little dog and you stop, sometimes they go for you. How was I supposed to know that? They didn't have chihuahuas where I grew up. As the deaf nan turned round, little Chai went for me. I couldn't help myself. I just

1. *pretentious*
2. *'jekyll' = Jekyll & Hyde = snide = false*

went CRAAASH and give it a backhander. I hit the dog so hard, its head spun round. Right round. It just lay there and it wasn't getting up. I wondered what the fuck I was going to do. But it was easy. I hid Chai underneath a silk pillow on the Chesterfield.

I went back in the dining room and we all sat down and ate the Christmas pudding. It had squirty cream and everything. When I finished, they were all looking at me and the girl asked: "Did you find the ten pence in the pudding?"

"No," I said. "What's all that about?"

They looked at me a bit odd. Then I realised I'd said it in my normal East End accent.

Everyone was looking embarrassed. "We used to put sixpences in the pudding for luck," said the mother not looking at me. "But now we use 10p pieces so you can see them – to stop you choking."

I'd seen nothing. I didn't know it was a treasure hunt. I had an appetite. I must've just whopped it down. To make it worse, I was now desperate to have a shit. Dodgy food or nerves or what – I dunno.

I didn't think this was the right time to ask, so I held it and held it while the family pretended nothing was wrong and we played charades. I didn't understand what was going on. I started having the sort of stomach pains that force you to make deals with God. *Get me out of this. I'll do anything.* The tortoise had reared its ugly head. I didn't know what to do with myself. I thought, *I just have to ask* but I couldn't think of a posh word for khasi and the pain was getting worse. Then it came to me.

"Would it be OK if I used your washroom?" I asked, which I thought sounded quite salubrious. I must've heard it on an airplane or something.

"Of course," the girl's mother said. "It's upstairs, second on the left."

I went up the stairs but, by this time, with every step, there was a really dodgy fart which I tried to cover by coughing. The pain was spiteful. It was telling me *The shit's going to hit the water before your bum hits the seat*. I didn't think I was going to make it. I'd only got seconds to go when I made it up the stairs and reached the second door on the left. I knew I only had another two steps left – that's the one step in, then the turn. I opened the door and, inside, there was ...... a washroom. Where you freshen up.

No khasi in sight. Just a sink and a mirror. It was a fucking washroom! I'd never seen one before. What is the point of having a room like that? It was no use to me but I had to go, didn't I? I dunno how I thought of it, but there *was* a way out.

Go in the sink. Lob the shit out the window. Call me old-fashioned.

No one's going to know. It's Chigwell on Christmas Eve. It's dark. And this house was set back a bit. No one would know.

So I raised myself on my toes, sat on the sink, reached over, locked the door, just finished going and then the sink came away from the wall. There was a loud crash of metal and masonry and I thought *Leave off! I can't believe it!*

Within seconds, the whole family was outside, banging on the locked door and calling out my name: "Ricardo! Are you all right? Ricardo!"

First things first, I thought.

Get it out the window.

But it wouldn't open. It was one of them windows that had been painted so many times it just wouldn't open.

I'm pulling at the window; they're banging on the door; and in my panic I'm thinking *I've got to do something!*

I don't know how I thought of it. I must be a fucking genius.

I just punched a hole in the window – well, I've done a bit of boxing in my time – then opened the washroom door and said to them in a posh, outraged voice: "What sort of neighbourhood is this?" I pointed to the large log still steaming on the floor. "I was standing there washing my hands," I told them, "And someone threw that through the window. It's absolutely disgusting!" I even made the quotation marks with my fingers.

Then I realised they were all looking down at the steaming log on the floor. *What's all this about?* I thought. I looked down and there was a bit of a shiny 10p piece sticking out of the shit.

We stood there for a few seconds, just looking at the coin, then there was a scream from downstairs. Nan had discovered the chihuahua. I waited nearly an hour for the bus home.

Jeff Innocent is an established and popular stand-up comedian on the British live comedy circuit and has appeared on national television many times. He is from East London and had a typical 'East End' upbringing. Born in a workhouse, his mother dying in childbirth, he joined a gang of child pickpockets who preyed upon London's rich. He was eventually saved by one of his very victims, a Professor Higgins, who sought unsuccessfully to reform Jeff's street urchin existence. Inevitably 'nabbed' by the Peelers and transported to Australia he escaped back to the 'East End' where he briefly played inside-right for West Ham United. He later joined The Small Faces and worked for the Kray Twins. In his spare time Jeff enjoys Greyhound racing, listening to the music of Lee Perry and reading Walter Benjamin.

jeff innocent

in darkest england – cockneys explained

The front-room window of my rather modest two-up, two-down, 19th-century terraced house offers a remarkable panoramic vista which is in stark contrast to its geographical location, Custom House, pronounced 'ouse, in East London. To Londoners its mere name conjures up an image of postwar urban cultural depravation. It is all the more surprising then when I tell you that from my window I can see a Shire horse gambolling in a field, a llama staring over a fence and children stroking a rabbit. It is a city farm; part of a 'bringing nature to deprived inner-city kids' type project popular with trendy hippie left-wing Labour councillors in the 1970s.

'The Farm', as it is known locally, is in fact a last-chance saloon for dysfunctional animals who have been rejected from mainstream zoos. Baboons who have masturbated once too often in front of visiting parties of Catholic schoolgirls and gorillas that have a penchant for toddlers' arms. It even holds several camels which are rumoured to be captives of Bin Laden's Taliban army. The Farm's cultural significance was further entrenched recently with the visit of Princess Anne. The horse loving, plain-speaking granddaughter of the late Queen Mother was assured a warm welcome; her grandmother being second only to Bobby Moore, RIP[1] as East London's most revered personage. The Queen Mum's bravery while visiting the Blitz-ravaged East End during World War Two is well documented but what is not so widely known was her remarkable ability to play the spoons.[2] Whilst performing somersaults and headstands, sometimes showing her bloomers in the process, she played the spoons with gay abandon. Fuelled with cheap gin the Queen Mum would briefly forget her formal duties and superior social position whilst melting the hearts of the most violent petty criminal or local toothless matriarch. Establishing her forever as 'one of your own'.[3] The 'respect' shown to this special relationship was exemplified when the Council scrubbed the word 'slag'[4] from a piece of local graffiti so that the Princess would not be offended as she was being chauffeured past on her way to the farm. Whether Danny Jenkins is now merely 'a grass',[5] having lost his slag status, remains unclear.

Traditional accounts of the area have highlighted its more depressing features, Defoe on the Black Death, Dickens (beardist and chronicler of the Cockney), on crime and child labour; and General Booth (another prominent beard wearer and inventor of the tramp) who, in his book *In Darkest England*, compared East London to the dark untamed jungles of Africa, and described its inhabitants as savages. The contemporary media have even revived a Victorian term, the 'East End'. Less a geographical entity it is now a catchy buzzword to be used mainly in news items about gangland murders or on documentaries concerned with inner-city decay. This

---

1. *Former captain of West Ham and England. Widely regarded as the best football player ever. He won the World Cup for England single-handedly in 1966. A true gentleman.*

2. *The spoons held back to back to form a percussive instrument.*

3. *One of the highest compliments in Cockney culture. It has a similar standing to, "To me, you're like family."*

4. *In this usage, an insult to mean 'Out of order'.*

5. *A police informer.*

term has more recently been borrowed by estate agents to describe the location of converted warehouse apartments. Thus giving their stock both an air of tradition and metropolitanism, a heady mix for any budding urbanite.

East London has always been a place of contradictions, where Dickensian values grapple with the onslaught of Modernity. Where now, at the dawning of the 21st century, scrap metal yards, pubs, betting shops, domestic violence and petty crime all hang on tenaciously to survive under the ever-looming shadow of Canary Wharf. This is how it has always been for the indigenous people of East London and it is these historical contradictions which have forged the unique culture of the Cockney.

The word Cockney originated some time in the 14th century to describe townspeople in general but as London expanded it was only those that lived in the centre who retained the Cockney epithet. An old saying claims that to be a true Cockney one had to be born within the sound of Bow Bells. The Bow Bells belonged to the church of Mary Le Bow which stood in East London and whose peel played a variety of local favourites, particularly the songs of Lionel Bart and Max Bygraves. This could be heard as far north as Hackney, to the south as far as Deptford, as west as St Paul's and eastwards, towards Southend if it wasn't for the 'ouses in between. Sadly this quaint old adage no longer applies as the Bow Bells were melted down during the 1970s due to a shortage of sovereign rings[6] in East London. This incident is referred to by local historians as 'The Great Tom Riots'. 'Tom Foolery' being Cockney rhyming slang[7] for jewellery. These uprisings stand as an example of a tradition of political activism in London's East End and show how People Power can bring about social change. For they ushered in legislation which

---

6. *To East Londoners, sovereign rings represent ethnic jewellery.*
7. *An underground language originally used mainly by criminals.*

made it law that every major shopping area in East London should contain an Argos superstore, providing cheap jewellery for the Cockney masses.

The importance of jewellery in East London exemplifies the contradiction within Cockney culture. For though it is a culture which has been born and bred in the face of adversity, the Blitz, West Ham United's inconsistent form, the ubiquitousness of television documentary teams and their geographical location has meant that Cockneys, like no other regional working-class culture before or since, have had relative access to the finer things in life. Located next to the Royal Docks and the City of London, for centuries the commercial centre of the Western world, and, being close to London's West End, for decades the Mecca for popular music and fashion, has meant that as colonial subjects Cockneys have been nearer the table and have therefore gotten the biggest crumbs. For whilst Northerners, for example, were still racing whippets, eating tripe, putting ferrets down their trousers and marching to London for the right to wear shoes, the inhabitants of East London were usually "aving it large"[8] in beer gardens, wearing Italian designer fashions and rattling their charm bracelets to the music of Frank Sinatra. This North/South cultural divide is presented in Britain's longest running television soap opera, *Coronation Street*. Here the character Mike Baldwin personifies the Cockney 'up North'. Entrepreneurial, owning a local factory, driving a Jag, drinking brandy at the local pub instead of beer and living in a flat rather than a two-up, two-down terraced house (where undoubtedly he would relax to the music of Frank Sinatra). Distrusted by the provincial Northerners because of his Southern ways, Baldwin epitomises a prevailing image of postwar, petit-bourgeois Cockney man.

---

8. *To have a good time with dignity.*

Perhaps the earliest image of Cockney man to become established in the popular imagination is somewhere near that of the character Bill Sykes in Dickens' *Oliver Twist*. A bullish, drunken Victorian, wearing a scar, hobnail boots and a thick buckled belt for beating orphans. By his side a Bull Terrier, which incidentally are indigenous animals to East London. Living wild along the River Thames since the Middle Ages, they would swim alongside boats in the river like dolphins, taking it in turns to be in the lead. Now largely bred in captivity these dogs can often be seen languishing in the comfort of tower-block balconies or guarding car breakers yards.

The Edwardian Cockney man was a more friendly chap. He knew his place and would doff his cap in the presence of his social superiors, often with the phrase, "Gawd bless you ma'am". The technological advancement of braces over the thick buckled belt meant that he could sing and dance his way through life, overcoming his difficult circumstances (and the knowledge that he was going to die in the Great War) through the power of his Cockney spirit and his knowledge of music-hall songs alone. The character of Bert in the movie *Mary Poppins* typifies such a man. The historical bridge between the Victorian and Edwardian Cockney man came in the shape of Stanley Holloway who possessed both of their characteristics. Although often thought of as purely an actor playing a fictional character in *My Fair Lady*, the film version of George Bernard Shaw's *Pygmalion*, Holloway was in fact a genuine father of a flower seller whom he had sold to 'some toff'. And in true Cockney style he was 'one for the ladies'. The Victorian Cockney woman was usually a gin-soaked, syphilitic mother of fourteen who walked the foggy streets of the East End selling her body to earn enough money to keep herself and her husband in drink. Cockney women in the Edwardian period were less visible because they were either 'in service', as scullery-maids or else in hospitals run by nuns, discreetly having the illegitimate child of the master of the house for whom they skivvied.

The contemporary image of the Cockney as a duckin' and divin'[9] lovable rogue, emerged during World War Two against the backdrop of ration-book austerity. The 'spiv', as he became known, wore a pencil-thin moustache in the style of movie idol Douglas Fairbanks and dressed sharply in a suit, Crombie overcoat, suede shoes and trilby hat, aping the style of an English gentleman. The spiv served an important function during these depressed times, organising a black-market economy which provided goods such as stockings, Ovaltine and jellied ells (a regional delicacy) to the impoverished community. Even the local police, usually referred to as 'coppers' or 'rozzers', turned a blind eye, for they were themselves often the recipients of the spiv's resourcefulness. This romantic stereotype of the Cockney 'wide boy' with a heart of gold prevails into the 21st century, perpetuated by such TV fictional characters as Arthur Daley in *Minder* and Del-boy Trotter in *Only Fools and Horses*. Both these programmes have attained popularity as far afield as the USA and Australia, making the Cockney internationally recognised. East London of course already has a long-standing relationship with Australia, its convicts being the first settlers. Indeed it is the connection of the Cockney with crime which is probably the most dominant within popular thinking.

The story of East London gangland began in the late 19th century with the emergence of criminal gangs largely made up of Eastern European refugees who had settled in areas such as Aldgate and Whitechapel. Wearing large furry hats and wielding curved sabres, they terrorised the East End with their bareback riding antics and impossible dance routines. Dickens had previously identified embryonic gang activity and had brought it to the public's attention through the pages of his serialised stories.

It was not until the 1960s however, with the rise of East London's most infamous gangsters, the Kray Twins, that the mythology of East

---

9. *Living off one's wits. Also Cockney rhyming slang for conniving.*

End's gangland really becomes cemented. Feted by the media and courted by showbusiness personalities and even royalty, their story and those of their colleagues and competitors alike have been told and retold. Particularly during the 1990s when a spate of autobiographies appeared like *We Only Hurt Our Own* and *No Swearing in Front of the Ladies*. For Cockney readers these books blurred the boundaries between local history and true crime and ironically have earned the authors more money than the very crimes they have written about: in fact they now represent a specific tradition of East End writing. Their popularity nationwide turned people like the Krays, the Richardsons and 'Mad' Frankie Fraser into national heritage figures who seemed to came from a cosy old black and white world where you could leave your front door open and let the kids play out anywhere.

More recently, at the turn of the century, a wave of British movies such as *Lock, Stock and Two Smoking Barrels* and *Snatch*, drew on the casual violence and sartorial elegance of these postwar Cockney villains to develop a kind of gangster chic. Although highly stylised comic fantasies, these films influenced a generation of young British men and were largely responsible for the cultural phenomenon of the 'Mockney'. This is a term which is used to describe young men, largely middle-class and with no geographical connection to East London, who imitate the speech and general demeanour of an imagined Cockney geezer[10] in order to achieve street credibility.

Nevertheless this Cockney cool has obscured a harsh reality; the average Cockney man. Over fifty, with no criminal connections, unemployed, living on the 20th floor of a tower block, he has a drinking and gambling problem, and his wife and kids have left him long ago, but he still goes down to the local and sings *I Did It My Way* on a Saturday night. This more mundane image of the Cockney is portrayed in *EastEnders*, Britain's much-watched soap opera. Here

---

10. *Another word for bloke.*

Cockneys are presented as dysfunctional, neurotic and aggressive, spending most of their lives arguing, fucking and fighting. Apart from the occasional knees-up (of which more later) there is little evidence of a specific East End culture on offer. It does however feature a towering Cockney icon in the shape of Frank Butcher. Wearing a trilby hat, golfing knitwear, slacks, sunglasses and in winter, the regulation sheepskin coat, Butcher epitomises every Cockney male stereotype that has ever existed. His profession, that of a shady secondhand car dealer is one that is widely associated with East London and Essex men. Unlike previous representations of East London however, *EastEnders* does include women as Cockneys in their own right. Usually serving the important functions as bar-maids, prostitutes and more importantly opening the door to the Old Bill with the well-worn phrase, "I don't know where he is and if I did I wouldn't tell you."

As is common with most communities in the poorer areas of Britain, when possible, the contemporary Cockney attempts to overcome contradictory circumstances by having a good time. The Cockney 'knees-up', which feeds off a rich tradition of musical songs and dances, is as much a national folk institution as the Morris dance. Usually performed at 'family dos' such as weddings, anniversaries and the welcoming home of released prisoners, communal songs like *The Hokey Cokey* and *Knees Up Mother Brown* serve to reinforce Cockney identity as well as family ties. Learning the dance moves represents a rite of passage experience for the 'nippers'[11] and gives middle-aged aunties an opportunity to show they've still got it. For the ageing matriarch it is a chance for her to lift up her skirt and dance in the style of the late Queen Mother, herself totally proficient at the Hokey Cokey. Surely there can be no

---

11. *Children. Also known as 'saucepans' as in saucepan lids, Cockney rhyming slang for kids.*

other regional working-class culture that can count a member of the royal family as one of their tribe.

These events also offer the opportunity for inter-family feuding in the form of physical violence. East London has always been a breeding ground for champion boxers and the family do is often where a fledging pugilist might learn his or her trade. Women are often involved in such brawls but usually their role on such occasions is that of peacemaker, pulling their spouses away from the conflict with the traditional shouted phrase, "Leave it, Tel, it just ain't fucking worth it!" Usually however these fights are stopped by a respected male elder of the family with a long prison record for crimes of violence who uses the phrase "Behave yourselves, it's a family do." Realising that they have been, in Cockney parlance 'out of order', the protagonists usually forget their differences, take a drink together, sing a Frank Sinatra song and everything is forgotten. Sweet as a nut!

Family dos are also where Cockney cuisine is at its most visible. Ham sandwiches cut into triangles, mini sausage rolls, cheese and pineapple on a cocktail stick and, in a rare acceptance of French food, *vol-au-vents*. The traditional mainstays of the Cockney diet however, fish and chips, pie and mash and jellied eels, are usually eaten out in restaurants. More recently their popularity has been challenged primarily by Indian food and also other foreign foods such as kebabs (with or without chilli sauce) and Chinese all available from a plethora of restaurants and takeaways which have sprung up since the early 1970s.

The vast culinary choice on offer to East Londoners is largely a result of immigration to the area. In the late 19th-century East London became home to the largest Jewish community outside of Eastern Europe. Jewish culture has been fundamental in the shaping of Cockney culture itself, in the form of food, language and a steady supply of gangsters, boxers and tailors. To a lesser extent

Irish immigrants have also left their mark particularly in the areas of building construction, pub singing and Catholicism. By the late twentieth century many Cockneys could count at least one Jewish or Irish ancestor in their family tree. In the 1930s the Royal Docks, situated in Custom House and Canning Town, was the largest and busiest docks in the world. Merchant seamen from almost every known country would descend on East London and frequent the many pubs, brothels and tattoo parlours which had grown up to facilitate their needs. In the post-World War Two era, colonial subjects from the Caribbean and Asia were recruited in order to help rebuild the country. Many men and women from Jamaica, St Lucia, India and Pakistan to name but a few, settled in East London where they and their descendants have since become as much a part of the landscape as Jewish and Irish settlers had before them.

Going into the 21st century East London has become host to political refugees from countries as distant and diverse as Sierra Leone, Bosnia and Kurdistan. In turn they too will learn to do the Hokey Kokey and acquire a taste for jellied eels. Whether someone from Kurdistan could ever totally appreciate the music of Frank Sinatra remains to be seen. Nevertheless the unique cultural symbiosis which has always been integral to the identity of East London continues unabated. It is beautifully illustrated by any typical Cockney ice-cream salesman. He himself might be from Pakistan, a country not famous for its ice cream, the slogan 'Tony's Italian Ice Cream' might be emblazoned on the side of the van and the tune *Greensleeves*, an English classic, chiming its arrival.

Not all Cockneys have totally embraced East London's increasingly multi-ethnic demographic and, in seeking to maintain a more traditional way of life, have moved out to the county of Essex. Legend has it that Essex was discovered by Frank Butcher who upon hearing the voice of Charles Dickens in a dream went to Bethnal Green 'nick' and demanded the 'rozzers' to "Let my people go!"

Upon which he led the chosen ones, Moses-like, into the wilderness of Dagenham marshes until they came to no other place but Romford. And it was good. Situated to the east of East London and connected to it by the all-important A13, formerly the Southend Arterial road, Essex is also a retirement home for well-heeled Cockneys who have got just a little too old for all that duckin' and divin'. For successful younger Cockneys such as builders, hairdressers, black cab drivers and footballers (preferably those that play for West Ham), Essex represents an upwardly mobile move and the chance to give their children the things they never had whilst growing up in the East End – like bouncy castles. If Kent is the garden of England then surely Essex must be its patio.

Since the 1980s many parts of East London which had become desolate, like the old docks and canals, have been regenerated by property developers. Coffee bars, restaurants and luxury apartments now occupy the same places where cranes and warehouses once stood. This has attracted a growing number of middle-class people to the area, a process which estate agents call gentrification. Cockneys of course are no strangers to toffs and are generally ambivalent about their presence. In some ways aspects of middle-class culture have always been warmly accepted by the indigenous people who are totally at ease with sushi bars, futons and even feng shui. For their part the trendy new inhabitants of East London, such as artists and IT executives, have embraced existing Cockney institutions like beer gardens and Saturday afternoons spent watching football at West Ham. They have even developed their own culturally specific chants to sing against opposing fans, "You're going home in a Bupa ambulance" being an example.

This amiable cultural exchange has found some resistance however, in the form of the 'Cockney Nationalist Movement'. Dressing in the style of characters from the stories of Charles Dickens and rumoured to be the carriers of the popular 19th-century diseases smallpox and cholera, these disgruntled traditionalists have waged a war on all things posh. Noodle bars and New Age holistic centres are regularly picketed and in a strategy borrowed from the Welsh Nationalist Movement, these neo-Dickensian terrorists regularly restore original Cockney pronunciations of placenames by painting out the letter H on local road signs, thus Hackney becomes Ackney.

The defacing of road signs may confuse the yuppies but it is an action welcomed by the growing number of tourists to the area who enthusiastically seek out Cockney tradition and heritage. East London is now firmly on the national heritage map and coachloads of tourists from places like Japan, Sweden and the USA pay regular visits. For Australians it is a trip which represents a chance to visit their roots and rediscover their convict past. In true Cockney spirit some locals have cashed in on this phenomenon by setting up tours which might include visits to the location of famous underworld activity such as building society robberies and gangland murders. The Krays tour is very popular, making available souvenir branded Kray merchandise like autographed baseball bats and for the nippers, knuckledusters. The distinct culture of East London has even attracted a small number of sex tourists to the area. Mainly from the north of England they have developed a penchant for Cockney love. The accent, sharp dress sense, ostentatious jewellery-wearing and social confidence all proving too much for the culturally impoverished and sexually frustrated Geordies and Scousers. And in a perfect example of the Cockney's ability to adapt and survive, it is now common to see men dressed as Frank Butcher walking the streets plying their trade.

The history of the Cockney then is like a case study in Darwinian evolution. Crawling out of the mucky depths of Victorian poverty, scraping their knuckles against the class injustices of the Edwardian period and finally standing upright against the Luftwaffe during the Second World War, the Cockney, part-myth, part-reality, just adapts and survives, ducks and dives. As I glance again from my front-room window, I could never believe that I live in 'Darkest England'.

One of Britain's most renowned stand-ups, Hattie is known worldwide for her role as Holly in the TV series Red Dwarf. She has appeared on everything from Have I Got News For You and Friday Night Live to drama series Jonathan Creek and US sci-fi series Lexx. She has scripted for Rory Bremner and Jasper Carrott as well as Spitting Image.

Linda is a British Comedy Award nominee for her stand-up work and Radio 4 listeners recently voted her the 'wittiest living person'. She was first woman team captain on radio's News Quiz, has guested on Just a Minute and I'm Sorry I Haven't a Clue and had her own series Linda Smith's A Brief History of Time Wasting. Her TV appearances include Have I Got News For You, They Think It's All Over, Call My Bluff and Question Time.

hattie hayridge and linda smith

a day in the life of an urban nobody

Wakey Wakey, rise and shine, up with the lark, start of a new day.
Can't waste it, best part of the day, the morning. Better get started,
can't mess about, got to get going. Get on the road, hit the road, hit
the road, Jack. Hit the road. Hit the Hut, Hut, Hut. Can't hang
around here all day, got to get going, get moving. I'm the sort of
person who likes to make the most of life. Start the day early, go to
work on an egg, that's the sort of person I am.

No I'm not. I hate mornings, I hate work. Count to five, then I'll
get up. Get up then. I'll start from five in my head. Five, four, three,
two, one, zero. If I don't get up now, I'll be late for work, then I'll
be annoyed and irritated all day. Get up, get a head start. Start in a
minute. Ten, nine, eight, seven, six, five, four and a half, four. For
fuck's sake get up!

Yes I like being my own boss. I like going out to work. Not *out*
to work, I don't go out. I go out-to-work. For the company. Get
out, get out of yourself. Get out. Yes, I like being my own boss. And
so I work from home. Homework, day work, night work, part of the
network. Trucking along on the information superhighway.
Homeward bound. Start of a new day. Boot in, boot up. I enjoy my

work. It's lucky I've got a job I enjoy. Very lucky. And it's an important job. Very important. Most important part of the whole process. Everything would grind to a halt if I didn't do my job.

Go back to bed.

I can't do that. It would cause total havoc! There'd be no quality control! No quality control, and then where would we be? If you didn't have quality control, you'd have substandard apple turnovers. Every one crossing the screen has to be checked. Can't have substandard apple turnovers. Certainly not. Every single one that crosses my screen has to be checked. Morning, noon and night. Can't have substandard apple turnovers unleashed on to an unsuspecting public. Dear me no. It's a very important job. Which luckily I enjoy. Used to go to the factory. Every day, all that travelling, going outside. Yes! all that travelling, and going outside! Don't do that any more. No need. Miss that. Get more work done working from your home. Not got anybody breathing down your neck. Not got anybody.

They don't take anybody! Had to be trained to do this job.

Join the professionals. It's a life of challenge, adventure, Discovery, Golden Delicious, Russets and Cox's orange pippins.

The training? It's tough.

The pastry? It's puff.

The wages? Just enough.

Your section? Should you choose to accept it, is Quality Control. By the time we reach you, the pure and perfect apples have been pulped and pumped into the pure and perfect pastry. Only the best survive. One bad apple don't spoil the whole bunch, girl. Now go back to your homes and prepare for apple turnovers.

If there's a job to be done, I'm the sort of person who likes to get that job done. Tick. Job done. Tock. Job done. Tick tock tick tock. You are feeling sleepy. Concentrate! Concentrate. Orange juice. Shaken not stirred. Keep my mind on the job. It's an odd job. Oddjob! The drinks! Yes, feeling sleepy, Mr Bond? Yes, the drink.

Every time you fool. Every time you fall for that same old trick, that same old drink. Mr Bond, Mr Brooke Bond. Tea time! Time for tea. I like a nice cup of tea in the morning, just to start the day, you see, and round about eleven, well, my idea of heaven is a nice cup of tea. No! Concentrate. If a job's worth doing, it's worth doing without tea. Do it for yourself, and the company. I do it for the Company.

What Company, that's the question. The Company is always changing. What's the Company today, Jim? 'Worldwide Conglomerated Farmhouse'! I wonder whatever happened to 'Mr Betcheman's Bootiful Bakeries'? Must be another takeover. The man from the Company, he say "Yes". I'm part of a Conglomeration. Achieving amalgamation. A mood of elation. Sweeping the nation. Hey Bossa Nova. Apple turnover. Hey Bossa Nova. Annual turnover. Hey Bossa Nova. Another major takeover. Hey Bossa Nova. I have a new boss. That's the rough translation, I suppose. Bossa Nova. Same as the old boss. Get back to work!

Back to work. Back to routine. Get a routine. Back to the old routine. The old routines are the best. I say, I say, I say, sometimes I think I must be going mad. I wouldn't say that. Say what? Say that. I didn't. You did. Did I? Yes. Sometimes I think I must be going mad.

Used to it now. Can't imagine doing anything else now. Can't imagine. Done it so long. How long? A long time. It must be. A good few years. A couple of years at least. Time flies when you're enjoying yourself. High time. Radio time.

Yes it's that time of day again, when 'Time Flies' with an hour, roughly an hour, of fun packed phone-ins, celebrity interviews, competitions and chaos theory. So let's start with a bang. Your chance to win points because 'points mean prizes'. No points, no prizes.

What is the point? Workers of the world unite you have nothing to lose but your chains. I've got to have a chain. A chain on the door. Got to have a chain on the door. Insurance won't touch you. Insurance won't touch you without a chain on the door. And a Chublock. Chain on the door and a Chublock. Insurance won't touch you without a chain on the door and a Chublock. Chublock, deadlock, chain on the door. And a mortice-lock. Got to have a mortice-lock. Insurance won't touch you without a mortice-lock. Chublock, deadlock, mortice-lock, chain on the door, five hundred Chinese terracotta soldiers. And the insurance still won't fucking touch you. Still it stops them getting in. No, it slows them down getting out.

What's the recipe for disaster today? Jim. Well, Trevor, the mood here is one of fear and trepidation. Moira. Thank you, Michael. Any update on the extent of the casualties? Fiona. Is it an accident waiting to happen, Kirsty? Well, Jeremy, it's a tidal wave of human misery. On a lighter note, Martin, cat up a tree. Too little, too late. And the Business News? Well, Valerie, there's been another major takeover by Grandma Frinton's Farm Fresh Pharmaceuticals.

"We are a Grandmother. Rejoice." I feel all warm and glowing. All misty-eyed.

I fancy listening to something emotional. Something to make me feel I'm alive. Click.

Thank you for listening to Emotional Classics. One in a series of psychological self-improvement workouts for the well-being of your psyche. In today's modern living, we need to keep our emotions in tip top condition for when they're needed.

Thank you for buying Emotional Classics and for recognising that your life is not fulfilled in any normal way.

You must feel pretty excited about the purchase of your Emotional Classics tape, huh? So let's exercise that excitement.

Let's say it is your birthday, and a friend has given you a cute little fluffy puppy dog. Using the emotion, 'excitement', repeat "It's a cute little fluffy puppy dog".

Good. You love your puppy dog very much. Now let's exercise the emotion 'love'. "Aaah" ... repeat, "Aaah".

Good, but your cute little fluffy puppy dog runs out into the main dual carriageway. You are shocked and alarmed. You have a feeling of panic. "Oh" ... repeat "Oh!"

Good, and he is hit by a 36 ton juggernaut. That is sad. Let's try and exercise as much sadness as we can. "Boo hoo" ... repeat, "My puppy has been run over. Boo hoo."

Let's try harder. You are overwhelmed by a wave of grief and bereavement ...

He was only 82. No age is it? He promised me those brass candlesticks. More tea vicar? Can't mourn for ever. Life goes on. It's a mad, mad, mad, mad, world.

I think they missed one 'mad' out when they said that. You don't have to be mad to work here. I like that one. You don't have to be here. You don't have to be.

There's one! There!! Across the screen. It's the unthinkable. A reject apple turnover! I'll handle this. Don't panic, Binty, this one's mine. I've got the blighter in my sights. Papers, papers, show me your papers. I will give you nothing but my Rank, Hovis and cereal number. Direct hit! Got the blighter. Jolly good. I'm losing it, I'm losing it. Back to base. I'm losing it.

That's what I like about this job, it's never boring. Bored?! No time to be bored. So much to do. The day's not long enough. Never two days the same. Different every day. Never know what's round the next corner. It's a roller-coaster.

Attention please. Company Welfare Announcement. Please stand by for an announcement from your employer. Return to your screen. Attention.

How may I help you?

We are pleased to announce that the Teddy Trouble Spots Mild Mustard Gas and Farmhouse Bakery Company has now achieved its optimum growth challenge. Your unit may now be released into the Serengetty plains of the wide open market. Run free little module, out into the sunshine of opportunity, happy in the knowledge that you leave your Mother Company right–sized.

Will there be anything else?

We are having to let you go. The Company is now right–sized without you. You are a person with employment needs. You are available for work. There is a skip outside; climb into it. Your future lies in Steptoe's backyard. Welcome to Dumpsville; population: you. Somehow we're going to have to make do without you, we're going to have to muddle through as best we can. Is that really the time? Won't your mother be wondering where you are? We're going to have our tea now, you'd better go home.

Will that be all?

To be absolutely frank. You're sacked. You're fired. You are redundant!

It's the unthinkable. Something's wrong with the screen. It's crashed, that's all. It's gone down, that's all. Something simple, that's all. Lucky I got talked into that extended warranty. Not such a bad idea. Not such a stupid bastard idea, that extended warranty. Here's the small print. So it's not to exceed … that's only parts and labour, an optimum time, now that's if it's a leap year … in the event of an expanding universe … Lucky I took out that extended warranty, because if you pay an extra supplement, over a period of so many years, then you're covered …. oh for parts only. So with the premiums on that, and I know it does seem a lot all at once, but once you've taken out an extended warranty, it takes the worry out of consumer durables. I've taken out an extended warranty for all my things. Everything. I think it's worth the extra. Not to have that worry. Because it doesn't work out that much. Because over the specified years when the interest payments are spread in a flexible repayment system, well it's only, well, not that much is it? But then there's a call-out charge, and I know it does seem a lot all at once, but once you've taken out an extended warranty, you'll know that disposable camera is insured for life. All my things have got extended warranty. But it's not the screen, it's me. The plug's been pulled on me.

Where's my extended warranty? Here's the large print. Jaws of Disaster old celebrity endorsed Life Insurance Health Death Pension Scheme. Getting on in life? You're never too young to think about a pension. Funeral expenses can be a worry, but at the Softly Softly crematorium, see the face you love light up, for less cost than you'd think. So, now that you're nearly dead, I'm sure you'll be thinking about your loved ones, and making sure they don't get their grubby little hands on your hard-earned cash. Those money-grabbing nieces and nephews never came to see you when you had that hip replacement operation. No, so you'll want to spend that money on golf, Caribbean cruises and ballroom dancing on the QE2. Hasta la vista grandchildren. Swivel on that! because I am off to Grey Leisure Heaven. To play golf! golf! a bit more golf! and the occasional game of bowls. Bowls! yes, and six months of the year in a flat on the Costa Del Sol. Because after all, no one wants to live out the twilight of their life in poverty and misery. Who wants to live like that? Living in a rat-infested slum, car alarms going off all hours of the night, driving you fucking mad, too frail to haul yourself off your feeble little bed with its urine-soaked threadbare blankets, and a dangerous electric fire, just near enough to fall on and burn, but not near enough to keep you warm, and costing you a bleeding fortune, with the bailiff's knock knock knocking at the door.

I didn't take the policy out. I'm beside myself. Beside the seaside. Beside myself with panic. Repeat. Panic. Time ticking away. Tick tock tick tock. Shock and alarm, repeat, shock and alarm, but mixed with, yes, sadness. Sadness, repeat sadness I know that one. Boo hoo. Excitement? no, frustration, grief and bereavement, impatience, disillusion, disappointment ... Help me Brucie! distressed, dis ... dis ... disembowelled, gutted, I'm gutted. Anger Anger. I'm so angry, I'm so bloody angry!

I feel like a joint of best British beef in a butchers in Dusseldorf. I feel like the last 1000 lire note in Euroland. Those scratchy competition things you scratch, what they called? Those scratchy little squares? You scratch them off with a coin and see if you've won, what are they called? I feel like I've got two wins and a no win; two cherries and a melon. I feel like my song's got nil points from the Belgian judge. I feel like I've gone to the 24-hour garage and it's shut. I feel like a section of the superhighway that's been coned off.

Tick Tock Tick Tock. Nothing to do. I don't go out to work, I'm out of work. Tick Tock Tick Tock. Tick, job done. Tock, job over. They think it's all over. It is now. Tense? Tense? Tense nervous headache? Lucky I got talked into buying that relaxation tape. Not such a stupid bastard idea, that relaxation tape. I like easy listening, it's so soothing, those waves, those wind chimes, those whales, I wish this music would last forever. What a world that would be!

Thank you, now sit up, pay attention, I said thank you for listening to Relaxation Classics. In today's modern living, we aren't always able to relax as much as we'd like, are we? I said, are we? If you wake up in the morning with your pyjamas soaked right through, you're suffering from stress. Now, I don't like stress, none of us do, I know that, now come on, keep up, right, you're lying on a beach. I don't know where, it doesn't matter for the minute, any bloody where. The sun's shining, for once, but right in your bloody eyes, so you've got a hat on, some kind of hat, doesn't bloody matter what. The sky's blue, the sand's sandy, it's getting between your toes, it's getting every bloody where, don't even think about having a picnic. You're eating a lolly, it's dripping all over the place. You've got some bloody bluebottle now buzzing round your sodding lolly, bugger off you little bastard. Now some kid's screaming it's bloody head off.

Now relax, come on relax. You've got to relax, you must relax. Are you taking this seriously or not? Come on relax. It's no good not relaxing, you've got to relax. You're feeling sleepy, you're feeling sleepy, you're drifting, you're drifting …

I'm on a lilo. I'm drifting out to sea. Far far, far out to sea. Drifting, drifting. Past the lifeguard. Look, he's waving. Past the little red flags. Look, they're waving. Past the lighthouse. Look, it's winking. Ooh the sea's a bit lively. Too lively. It's too lively. I'm feeling sick. I'm feeling seasick. Can't be sick on an empty stomach.

Sick on my stomach. Out on my ear. Dead on my feet. Sick on my ear. Sick on my feet.

Food, that's what I need. Have I got what I want? Do I want what I've got? I haven't got what I want, I'll have to have what I've got. Have I got anything in? Can I keep anything down? How hungry am I? Just have something little. Just have a small one. Don't have a small one. I've got regular and large. What is regular? Well, medium, really. How big's medium? Quite small. Just serves one. Serves One Right.

This 'Boil in the Bag' beef curry. I wonder if it's alright. It keeps. What's the 'sell-by' date? Hasn't got one. Must be alright then. Made stuff to last in those days.

I like to keep stuff in that keeps. I like to keep stuff in. I like to keep stuff in the fridge. I like to keep stuffing my stomach. Shelf life. Sheltered life. Life shelved. On the shelf. It's got a long shelf life. What's that in human years?

I remember 'Five Boys' chocolate. Yes, five little boys' faces. On the chocolate.

Shouldn't this chocolate be brown? There's white fluffy bits around their faces. It must be the Christmas Special. Christmas. Special. Snowballs. Babycham. Cherry B Cherry B Cherry B. Eat Me Dates.

Eat me dates, why don't you, you had those brass candlesticks quick enough. Wasn't cold in his grave. Cold gravy on that dried up old bird. Who are you calling a dried up old bird? You leave my mother out of this. It's your sister you want to worry about. Pudding Club again. Peak Freans Christmas pudding. Can you buy an even cheaper one? I doubt it. Your family. *Your* family. Your family, at least my family aren't ... Your family, at least my family aren't ... Aunt Beryl pissed again. At least my family aren't here. Christmas. Special.

Yes, I remember 'Five Boys' chocolate. Five little boys' faces on the chocolate.

Miserable, Suicidal, Manic, Psychotic. And one with no idea what the fuck is going on. Company though. When you're sitting all alone.

When you're sitting all alone, make new friends on the telephone. What's that chatline number? 0898 double eh? double eh? double eh? I suppose I could talk to Tony. I remember Tony. Every day he used to ring me. Wouldn't leave me alone. He was keen he was. Couldn't get him off that phone. Any time he used to ring. Any time of the day or night. The flimsiest excuse. I could easily talk to Tony. How well I remember Tony. Every day he loved to ring me. Wouldn't, just couldn't, leave me alone. He was keen. He certainly was. I couldn't get him off. That phone. Any time. He'd ring any time of the day or night. The flimsiest, flimsiest thing. I'm sure he'd love to ... No, he wouldn't talk to me now. After all, I never did buy the double glazing.

I've got his number somewhere. I've got a phone somewhere. Where did I put that number? Where did I leave that phone? I know where it is! Now what did I come in here for? I came up the stairs, turned round, opened the door. Now what did I come in here for? Stairs, turned, door, now what the fuck did I come in here for?

That ringing. What is it? Where is it? Who is it?

Hallo, is that the householder?

I don't need this, Tony. I need some space. You're just crowding me, Tony. You've got your life and I've got mine. Look for God's sake, we've had our laughs, we've had our good times. Now let's just leave it at that. It's over, Tony.

That droning. Who is it? Where is it? What is it?

Something's got in. I've got aluminium shutters on the doors and the windows and still things get in. It's taking up all the room, I can't move. It's taking up all the air, I can't breathe. It's a wasp, no, it's a bee. Bees don't come in. Or do they?

Wasps come in. Bees don't come in, bees are too busy making honey. Wasps come in. Wasps have got too much time on their hands. They don't want to work.

How embarrassing, what if I was having a dinner party? People round. People nosing around, looking at my things, seeing what I've got, eyeing up my goods, sizing up my stuff. It's none of their business what I've got. What business is it of theirs? They've got no business creeping around my place.

There's somebody else here! Someone creeping around my place. I'm not here on my own. No, I've got a dog. I've got a big dog. There's a big dog here with me. A great big dog. He'll have your leg off. He's lovely though. He's vicious. He loves me! He'll have you! I've got him on the leash now, but I can let him off. If he's off that leash, he'll have you. He's got a lovely shine. He's a pit rock. He's a pit rock terrier. He's a Pitlochry terrier. He's one of those mad dogs. He's a sumo. He's a Yamaha. He's lovely. But he's vicious. He loves me, he'll do anything to protect me. He loves me, but he'll have your leg off. Leave me alone! If you go away now, no one gets hurt. Go now, and we'll say no more about it!

That nasty intruder's gone away now. He won't be back in a hurry, that's for sure.

Good boy, seen him off, seen the last of him. You're a lovely little puppy dog. You're a lovely little fluffy puppy dog. You're a good boy, aren't you. Yes you are, you love your mummy. You can't be cooped up in here all day! Not right is it, cooped up in a little flat. You want to go walkies. No wonder dogs go mad and attack people. It's the owners, I blame. I was going mad cooped up here, all day. I hate to think of the effect it's had on you, Poopsy. You want to be in the park running about. What was I thinking of?

It'll get me out, the dog. Get me out of myself. I'll go out to walk. Not out to work, but out to walk. Your mummy would go mad cooped up in here all alone, I'd be your mad mummy. Walkies! He loves his walkies. Let's go for a walk beside the main dual carriageway.

I've got a door somewhere. Now where's that door? Go find, boy! Find!

John worked as a bus conductor and social security clerk until he went to Bradford University, eking out his grant by working as a nurse in a local mental hospital. His first notable media exposure was the John Peel Sessions *(Radio One) with his band the Popticians. He sang about spectacles and the misery of human existence. After publishing* Glad to Wear Glasses *in 1990, another six books followed filled with verse, prose, drawings, drama and photographs of potatoes – and the CD/cassette* Saint and Blurry. *In 2000, John received an honorary Arts Doctorate from Luton University and had his most notable live engagement at a women's prison in Medellin, Columbia.*

john hegley

easy on the butter

John and Tony were sat in the caff, their huge mugs of deep brown tea before them. John was awaiting a toasted teacake "with very little butter on, please – just a scraping".

Tony was talking about his father.

"... he was like a father to me. Someone else's father, but a father none the less."

The teacake arrived. It was drenched in butter. Drenched. It was wet outside, also.

"I'm going to go and see my Mum for Easter, John. Want to come?"

"I'm going to go to Greece," John responded. "Greeceter at Easter, Tone."

Tomorrow was Good Friday. Did the train run on Good Friday? Yes. John felt sure of it. He wished Tony well with his journey and received likewise sentiment.

Early the next afternoon, Tony was on the sunny side of the train to Chester with a costly chocolate egg which he'd opened, emptied and filled with small potatoes. His mum being something of a potato fanatic. From Chester, a bus deep into Welsh territory. The buses were running too. Tony was sat behind a couple of Morris dancers and eavesdropped, as he took in the passing green.

"Didn't you enjoy it today?" advanced one of the dancers.

"Tom took the skin off my thumb in the first dance," complained the other one.

"That was handkerchiefs that one, wasn't it?"

"I *think* so. I don't know how he managed taking the skin off my thumb with a hanky. It's ridiculous how rough he is."

Tony thought that English Morris dancers going home to Wales was strange but never said so, in case they thought he was talking out of turn, especially with the one so disgruntled.

"Did you put plaster on him?" asked the uninjured one.

"Him?" the other returned, confused.

"The wound, I mean."

Tony shared the wounded man's surprise and wanted to say that he'd never heard a cut personified either. In Bristol he'd heard people speak of their car as a 'he' or a tap, perhaps, as in "I think he needs a new washer", but a cut, no. Tony passed no comment for the same reason as earlier.

The injured one continued. "I *did* use a plaster," he said, proffering the hurt. "But I didn't have any big ones and had to cut a small plaster along the edge of the gauze and then join it to another one of the same size along the edge of *its* gauze, thus doubling the area available for dressing purposes."

"Let's have a look!" said Tony, containing his curiosity no longer.

Arriving at the cottage, Tony asked: "What's for tea, Mum?"

"Potato pie, love," came the reply.

Tony knew only too well what his mother meant: a bed of whole boiled potatoes with mashed boiled potato on top. The pie aspect was paltry, the potato part complete.

"You'll need the carbohydrate to give you energy for your work tomorrow."

"Potato digging would that be, Mum? ... Why *do* you have this potato fixation, if you don't mind me asking?"

"Because if I turn into a potato then I'll be happier being buried."

"But you won't be *alive* when you're buried."

"I will be if I'm a potato."

* * *

John went to Athens by plane and from there by bus to the ferry and by ferry to the island. Being Easter, the summer season was not yet underway and the decks of the ambling boat were overcrowded, as you might say and may imagine – slow on the water, in a romance of gathering darkness. Upon disembarking, people came up to him with photos of rooms they had available.

"I have my room in my bag," said John to one persistent woman clad like the night all in black. She was not enlightened by his words.

"I have a tent," he said uncryptically.

Still no understanding. John removed the tent from his rucksack and made a tent shape with his hands.

"*No bus* to the campsite. Not tonight," said a young man named Andros, whom John soon discovered to be the son of the black-clad woman, whose offer of accommodation he now accepted.

Back at their house, the Greek asked John what he wanted from their island.

"What's here?" John asked.

The Greek explained … "The cave where the revelation was gave to John … The Monastery …"

"Which John was that?" asked John.

"It is Saint John the Divine. God has spoken to him from a cleft in the rocks and John has dictated these words which form the Book of Revelations."

John imagined a little scene of dictating revelations from a speaking cleft and chuckled. "Is the monastery to do with this?"

"Yes, it is to celebrate the maracle of God's speaking."

John smiled further at the mispronounced 'maracle'. He was enjoying himself and had taken a shine to the lad who offered to be his unpaid guide and translator – for a small fee.

John accepted and that night slept well in the sheets of well-starched cotton, although he had not yet come to appreciate such things.

The next morning on the big Mercedes bus on the way to the big town with the campsite, John asked Andros if anything special happened at Easter on the island.

"You have missed the washing of feet."

"What feet are those?"

"On the Thursday of Easter in the square of the town the feet of the monks are washed with water of the potato."

"Why this potato water?"

"It is the tradition."

"What about today?"

"Today there will be Easter Epitaphs."

"Epitaphs?"

"I will let you see them, not spoil them by telling."

John was surprised to see, relaxing in the foregoing seats, a couple of guys in the guise of Morris dancers.

Andros explained that Morris dancing occurred throughout Europe and stemmed from the Moors – hence the Morris or Moorish dance.

"What, the Yorkshire Moors, you mean?"

"What are they?"

"They are a little joke."

"… that I do not understand."

Andros said there were many places to 'dance' in the big town.

When they reached the big town, John discovered that his tent had disappeared from the back of the bus.

"There is a hotel nearby," Andros told him.

"It's not the same though," said John gloomily.

"What do you mean?"

"A hotel; it's not the same as camping."

Andros agreed but saw little sense in this self-evident statement.

At the hotel desk, Andros asked about a room for the two of them. John also heard the word 'epitaph' mentioned in the conversation.

"We should get to the square. The epitaphs will arrive shortly," advised Andros.

"The epitaphs?" asked John. "Where are the epitaphs?"

"Soon you will see. First make sure your room is good," advised Andros.

In John's room was a big white marble-tiled floor and a mosquito.

Nothing else.

He came back downstairs and firmly complained: "I'm sorry, but the room is completely unfurnished."

"There will be no problem," said the owner.

John and Andros made their way to the centre of the town. Upon their arrival the crowd was expectant of the epitaphs, the large ornate boxes which the people chaired to the square, one from each of the nearby churches.

In the throng, John recognised the hotel owner and his bus driver, as voices started to raise to an excitement with the coming of the first of the epitaphs. It was like one of the coffins in Westminster Abbey that has a knight in armour lying atop, except that the figure in this instance was a Morris dancer.

The second epitaph was similarly dressed.

Others entered the square, no figures on them, just flowers and potatoes. Finally the offering from the monastery itself.

The excitement was a cacophony now.

"It's cacophony," said John.

"A Greek word," said Andros.

"Greek ... really?"

"Of course – from the Greek *caco* meaning bad and *phonos* – voice." Andros liked to draw attention to any etymology from his native tongue. 'Etymology' – that was another one.

John could see the mystery monastery box more clearly now.

Its shape was different from the others: wider, taller, but not quite as long, with a roof.

"It's a kennel," John gasped.

"What is it?" asked Andros.

"A kennel."

"What is a kennel?"

"Where a dog lives."

"We do not have this word in Greek. We say 'House of the Dog'."

The monks put down their epitaph and, as the crowd began cheering, John felt an inner motivation to movement …

"Come on, Andros," he said squeezing through the unenthusiastic hordes.

Andros edged up behind him.

"Where are we coming to?" questioned the native.

"My tent. I've got this funny feeling that my tent is in that House of Dog!" said John, on his knees now at the entrance.

John feels an onus to seek out his tent

he feels that the kennel's the place where it went

but it wasn't

That night at their table outside the café, they discussed Orpheus' entrance into the underworld to retrieve his beloved Euridice.

"Why do you think he looked back?" asked John. "Come on, Andros, you're a Greek…"

"John. It's crazy …"

John agreed: "He'd done it all; he'd got round the boatman and the naughty dog. All he had to do was keep looking straight ahead."

"I know … perhaps it is this which the gods tell you you cannot, which you must do," suggested the Greek.

On arriving back in his bedroom, John discovered all the epitaphs from earlier, stacked fillingly furnishing the space. Again, he went downstairs, to complain.

* * *

John and Tony are sat in the same caff as at the outset. Outside, it is dry but overcast.

The Morris dancers opposite are tucking into their full English breakfasts. Tony has described his spuddified weekend and explained that his mother has asked him to look after her naughty dog. John is in the midst of relating his own adventure.

"... and so, once again, I went downstairs to complain ..."

"But there wasn't anything suitable in the phrasebooks?" suggests Tony.

At this point, John's teacake arrives. He has asked for a toasted teacake with very little butter – "No, could I have the butter separately, on the side? I'll put it on myself, please."

The newly arrived teacake is dry, but with a huge pâté container dollop-full of butter.

John begins putting the butter on himself.

'Scampi, IN YOUR BASKET'

Boothby made his first US Network TV appearance in January 2003 on Late Night with Conan O'Brien *and followed it with live appearances in Melbourne, Bermuda, Paris, London and Edinburgh. He has won the Adelaide Fringe Award for Excellence, London's* Time Out Comedy Award *and been nominated for the Perrier Award in Edinburgh. His first stage play* Condition of the Virgin *premiered at Edinburgh in 2001 and his second* God & Adam *in 2002. His BBC radio series include* The Big Booth, Big Booth Too *and* Boothby Graffoe in No Particular Order.

boothby graffoe

are we there yet?

"Wake up," said the man. She was pretending to be asleep and ignored him. The man slapped his hand hard on her head and spoke again, "Wake up." He was loosening the tether now and taking the bracelet from her ankle, "We have to go." He spoke with panic but acted calmly, dragging aside the canvas to make an opening big enough for her to walk through. The cold wind jumped inside the tent and splashed her legs like water. She shivered involuntarily and made a big show of suddenly waking. She snorted and spluttered and flapped her ears. He stood in the new doorway and spoke as forcefully as he could in a whisper, "We have to leave. Come on." She waited and sniffed at the air. He produced the apple from his pocket and held it out for her. She stretched to reach for it and he walked backwards. She followed him.

The vibration and hum through her feet was exciting and there was a sliding partition to the front that allowed her to reach in and change gears. He didn't like her doing that and pushed her away and blew up her nose. She hated it when he did that and she hit him in the face, and pressed the horn, and turned off the lights and changed channels on the radio. She knocked the gearstick into neutral for good measure and then withdrew from the cab. The man put the engine back into the wrong gear and the van lurched, invisible, from one side of the road to the other. The man battered the dashboard like an arcade game and turned on the windscreen-wipers. He battered again and the de-mister breathed into life. He felt the weight behind him pull the van round, like the fat one on the end of a long line of roller-skaters. The radio was an angry insect. One of the windscreen-wipers fell off. The world went around then it all stopped suddenly in a cloud of crunchy white dust. It ended with them neatly parked on the hard-shoulder, facing the oncoming traffic. The man was in the passenger seat. He slid back across behind the wheel and swatted the radio, suffocated the de-mister and started the engine. She leant through the partition and flicked the switch that turned off the lonely wiper.

The news report had mentioned them, but only in passing, at the end, on a lighter note. No name was given, no description of him or the vehicle, and no supposition as to their direction or design. By the afternoon broadcast they were forgotten, bumped by a man in another country, who was so obsessed with the Enid Blyton character Noddy, he had taken to dressing in similar clothes and driving around the town where he lived in a little yellow car.

Behind him she shifted position. The van swayed. She pushed the left side of her face up to the partition so she could just about see him and said, "Are we there yet?"

He turned to look at her. "No."

"I'm bored," she moaned, "and I want to go."

"You should have gone before we left."

"I didn't want to go before we left. I didn't even know we were going anywhere. Where are we going?"

"I don't know."

"Are we there yet?"

"No."

"When will we be there?"

"Soon."

"But I want to go *now*."

* * *

It was the scenic route but it was way out of season. He parked up on the side of the road, near some trees at the foot of a hillside. It was cold. He slid up the concertina-door at back of the van and the elephant climbed out. He walked her round behind the trees and stood and waited with her. She sat down against the bank of the hill-side and sniffed at the air.

"What?" she said, eventually.

"I thought you wanted to go."

"I can't do it with you looking at me. I'm embarrassed."

He sighed and walked back around the trees to the driver's door of the van. He waited. "You can still hear," she said, "Get in and shut the door." He climbed inside and banged the door shut. "And turn the radio on," she shouted. "Turn it up loud."

The music was loud. The man was now deaf and blind. The elephant took one last sniff at the air and set off up the hill.

The music was very loud. The door, open wide, at the back of the van acted as an amplifier, blasting out sound far into the early evening. It was loud enough to be heard by the farmer who left his cottage-door open in his rush to investigate, thinking it might be one of them illegal rave-parties. The farmer wondered how they danced to Wagner? He took his shotgun, just in case.

The elephant mosied, as only elephants can, breathing in the end of the day and slowing down here and there to investigate interest-ing smells. She passed the farmer on the hilltop. He didn't see her. She was as big and as grey as the sky, and appeared only for a second in the corner of his eye as cloud moving low against the wind. A cloud that looked remarkably like an elephant. The farmer stopped. The music snapped into silence a second later. The elephant kept walking but now towards the farmer who dithered for a moment then, in turning to run, fell forwards, landed heavily on his shotgun, and mended it. The elephant rested one of her front feet on the farmer's back and sniffed around his body. She walked away, down the hill, towards the cottage.

When the man turned off the radio the silence took a little while to settle. He opened the door and listened for the elephant. The day was dying, they had survived the day. He saw no reason for them to look for him. He had taken nothing. He climbed out of the van and walked around the trees. The elephant, of course, was not there. At the top of the hill the man met the farmer. The farmer spoke first, surprised by the lack of surprise in the tone of his own voice. "I was attacked by an elephant."

"My car has broken down," said the man, looking at the shotgun. "Do you have a telephone?"

Inside the farmer's cottage the man picked up a half-empty bottle of brandy from the kitchen table and slipped it into his pocket. "I think it's broken my ribs," called the farmer from his bedroom. He was in front of the wardrobe mirror, lifting his shirt, looking for reflections of bruising. The man took a bread knife from the sink and quickly cut through the wire connecting the telephone to the wall.

The farmer entered the kitchen and the man folded his arms hiding the knife. The shotgun leant against the wall by the door. The farmer walked over to the door.

"It's been in here," he said. "It's had my apples."

"I've to go now," said the man, "I've to wait with my van. My car."

The farmer narrowed his eyes and the man walked forcefully towards him. The farmer's eyes widened and he moved aside. Outside the man stood by the farmer's little car. "Is this your little car?" he said. He put his hand on the roof. The farmer nodded. The man took his hand away and turned as if to go. "My car is like your car," he said, walking backwards. The farmer closed the door. The man walked forward, back to where he'd left, and, using the bread knife, slashed the front and back tyres of the farmer's little car on the blind side to the cottage. He set off up the hill.

"Are we there yet?" said the elephant. She had eaten all of the bag of apples she had stolen from just inside the cottage door. She was bored again, and had a tummy-ache.

"Yes," said the man. He had finished drinking the contents of the half-full bottle of brandy he had stolen from the table in the kitchen of the farmer. He slowed the van to a standstill and opened the driver's door. The smell of the sea washed over them both. "Let me out," said the elephant. They walked along the beach together leaving the van looking incongruous in the half-light of the early morning.

Later, on the clifftop the man released the elephant for the final time.

"On you go," he said, patting her side.

"On I go where?" she asked. The driver's door was left open, the engine still alive. The man climbed back in behind the wheel. He shut the driver's door and put the van into gear. He pushed his foot down on the accelerator, lifted the clutch and drove the van over the cliff edge.

The farmer picked up his shotgun from the wall by the door and set out to find the bastard that had nicked his brandy. As he stepped outside the first barrel of the shotgun went off and liquefied a large part of his right foot. He fell backwards, discharging the second barrel at the ceiling of the porch, which shattered and rained down on him, lumps of plaster and broken glass.

The elephant stood on the clifftop, watching the van sink.

The farmer sat weeping and bleeding to death, cradling the ruined telephone. He realised his only hope would be to try and drive himself to the hospital. He bandaged his foot with carrier bags and sticky-tape and took a walking stick to help him operate the pedals.

The day was starting now and the van was just bubbles. The elephant sniffed at the air. She turned away from the sea and walked inland.

boothby graffoe

quid pro quo

She was fumbling around with one hand on the table next to the bed. He was lying back, catching his breath and smiling. She was looking for cigarettes. She found an empty packet of Silk Cut on the floor and crumpled it into her fist.

"I'm going to the 24-hour garage," she said.

He pulled her back down on top of himself and kissed her. "I have cigarettes."

"I don't like your cigarettes," she said. "They're too strong. I'm going to the 24-hour garage. Do you want anything?"

"Wait," he said.

He was mooching around the room, pouring wine and putting on music. She was sitting on the bed, smoking his cigarettes. He stretched out naked next to her, deliberately uninhibited. He handed her a glass and drank from his own.

"Tell me," he said, as the music began. "What is your sexual fantasy?"

"I love this song ... I ... what?" she said. "What did you just say?"

He drank again, and took the cigarette from her fingers. "I said," he took a drag and lowered his voice, deepened it, playing with the emphasis, exhaling as he spoke. "What is your darkest sexual fantasy?" He'd added 'darkest', he'd never said 'darkest' before. He made a mental note to remember 'darkest' for next time.

She looked blankly at nothing and opened her mouth for a second. She closed it again and looked at him. She looked away, "I don't think you want to know that," she said.

"I do," he said quickly. "I do, tell me. Tell me about the pictures that find their way, uninvited into your head, that make—"

"What?" she interrupted.

He reined back, began again, "Tell me what you think about when you're on your own that you would never tell anyone else because you're scared what they might think. You know."

"When I'm on my own?" she said, uncertainly. "You mean when I'm...?"

"Yes." She looked at him and frowned, "I haven't got any cigarettes. I'll go get some."

"I've got cigarettes."

"I don't like your cigarettes." She blushed.

He knew in time she would tell him, and tell him in time she did, though walking around the room with her dressing gown on, rather than as he'd hoped, reclining seductively, in his arms. She began to speak and he relaxed with familiarity.

"I'm wearing, that dress, you know, that dress ..." He had given her specifics, a scaffold to get her started. What are you wearing? Where are you? It was taking too long. She seemed, almost, not to realise that the point of his question was not to hear her answer but to hear her question at the end. The same question he asked her, asked back. He knew what he was going to say. He was all prepared for this.

"I'm in this room," she said and he almost sighed but he turned it into a smile.

"It's a fantasy," he said. "You can be anywhere you like."

"Oh, yes, well, I suppose I could. It doesn't really matter where

I am." She laughed, he laughed with her, she was relaxing. "You're there," she said, moving towards him, sitting next to him on the bed and taking his hand. "You're with me."

She continued and he looked into her eyes, pretending to listen. In his head he was sorting out his reply, the reply to her question at the end. His question, asked back. The point of it all.

"You're in my mouth," she said and she suddenly opened her dressing gown, ran a hand down her breasts and slid her fingers in between her legs. He started to become interested despite himself. "I keep taking you out of my mouth and asking you if you're going to cum."

Her legs were open now, she was rubbing herself and breathing heavily. He was mildly bemused, it didn't seem like much of a fantasy so far, giving him a blow-job in her own bedsit.

"I make you tell me," she said, "I make you tell me, just before ..." Her voice was getting louder now. "Just before you cum, I make you tell me." She saw he was hard and immediately put his cock in her mouth taking him down to the back of her throat and slowly sliding him out. She'd never done it like that before. He was quickly becoming as excited as she was. "I make you tell me just before you cum," she said, repeating her actions. "I make you tell me."

"Then what?" he gasped, feeling the rise.

"Then you tell me," she said. "You say *Any second now*."

"Any second now," he said. "Any second now."

"Then ..."

"Yes?"

"Then ..."

"Yes?" "Then ... I grab the can of petrol from the bedside cabinet and pour it all over you and set fire to you as you cum! Then I wank myself whilst you run around the room burning and cumming!" She put her fingers deep inside herself and screamed the words, "Burning and cumming! Burning and cumming!"

She fell back on the bed with squeals of delight which became slowly, by degrees, a contented sigh. She was sweating and smiling. He was on the other side of the room, near the window.

"I haven't got any cigarettes," she said.

boothby graffoe

the worst serial killer in the world

Ordo Moonst stood outside the door that led to the lair of The
Floodgate Key. He carried a bag. He rang the bell. He waited a while
then took a small crowbar from the bag and jammed it in between
the door and the frame. He knew there was nobody home; he had
planned this very carefully. Ordo held the crowbar like an oar and
pulled hard; the wood of the doorframe splintered. His hands lost
their grip and he fell on his arse. The crowbar followed him down.
It landed across his shins. He screamed and jumped up, grasping the
doorframe for support, burying splinters into his fingers as he did so.
He screamed again. He danced from leg to leg and then suddenly
began bashing at the door with his shoulder. The door gave way just
as suddenly and he fell inside with his damaged hand underneath his
chest; he landed on it heavily and buried the splinters further in. He
cried out and rolled over and turned around and pushed his back
against the door to shut it. It was broken and wrong and he had to
force it into the frame. He hit it again and again with his back,
jamming it into place. It complained loudly but it closed; he leant
back on it and rested. His shins were dull and sore but his fingers
were alive with agony. He began to pick at the tiny slivers of wood
with his uninjured hand. Many were deep beneath the flesh. He
remembered he had a scalpel with him and a local anaesthetic. He

would anaesthetise his hand and gouge the splinters out painlessly with the scalpel. He looked for his bag which contained the things he needed. The bag was not there. It was outside the door, the door he had forced shut and would now require the crowbar to open, the crowbar that was outside in the corridor, with the bag.

Ordo Moonst entered the lair of The Floodgate Key, which was really just a living room in a flat like all the others in the block. A sofa and a TV and table lamp. And a gas fire on the wall with a painting above it. A painting of a horse which Ordo took down immediately, wincing as he held the frame with his porcupine fingers. The wall was now bare and waiting for The Message.

In the kitchen Ordo noticed a claw-hammer lying on the work-surface next to the cooker. That was what he needed: a claw-hammer. He began opening drawers and cupboards, emptying them out, searching for a claw-hammer, with their contents of cups and plates and cutlery smashing and jangling on the floor. Eventually he found one, a claw-hammer, out in the open, just lying there, on the work-surface next to the cooker. He smacked his hand against his forehead at his own stupidity for not seeing it earlier. His fingers! He grabbed his own wrist in pain, dropping the hammer, which landed on his foot. Nobody heard Ordo as he thrashed around in the mess on the floor, holding his hand and then his foot and then his hand again, screaming expletives and banging his head against the cooker, bang, bang, bang. Nobody was home in the flats either side. Ordo Moonst knew that, he had planned this very carefully.

Ordo limped back through the flat and, with his one good hand, used the hammer to claw the door out of its frame. His bag was still there, things were going well. He grabbed the bag and forced the door shut. It was more ruined now and took a great deal of pushing and kicking to persuade it back into place. When he was finally done he looked at the door. He was going to need the crowbar *and* the hammer to get it open next time. He peeked through the letterbox.

He could just see the crowbar, outside in the corridor, it was lying next to the claw-hammer that he'd dropped when he picked up the bag.

Ordo Moonst had been planning this for weeks, or months, or perhaps hours. He had very little understanding of time. Ordo lived in a country where, if you were seriously mentally ill but still able to shop, you were left pretty much to your own devices.

When he was much younger, or maybe just recently, Ordo had decided to kill the cat. He'd heard that the eyeballs of dead people retain a picture of the last thing they saw before dying. Ordo figured the same would apply to cats. He was going to strangle the cat so it could see him doing it and then cut out its eyeballs and have a look. It was the intention of Ordo Moonst to be the worst serial killer in the world.

Ordo approached the cat wearing a false beard. He didn't really believe the cat's eyeballs would retain an image of him murdering it but he didn't want to take any chances. He grabbed the cat by the throat and held it up to his face. The cat, who was *already* regarded by the surviving small furry wildlife in the area as the worst serial killer in the world, had little or no intention of becoming an Instamatic. It regarded its attacker for less than a second before it lashed out one sharp clawed paw and tore Ordo's left eyelid clean off. Ordo didn't realise at first what had happened. All he knew was that there was something pouring into his left eye and blink as he might it didn't seem to make any difference. And it hurt. It hurt a lot. He dropped the cat who calmly left the house through an open window. It may well have taken the eyelid, Ordo couldn't find it anywhere.

The doctor said that even if Ordo had brought his eyelid with him they still wouldn't have been able to sew it back on. Ordo had a disability which meant it wasn't possible for surgeons to re-attach severed parts of his body with needles and thread. Ordo was not unique in this. It affected a lot of the people who visited the hospitals in the country where Ordo lived. The medical term for this condition was 'uninsured'.

The cat had done a good job of amputating Ordo's eyelid. The wound healed quickly and Ordo found he saw a lot of things he used to miss before he blinked in mono.

Local children had spray-painted WINKER on the front door of Ordo's flat. He knew it was children because they spelt it wrong. He did not hate the children. They would honour him soon and act out his life in their games. Soon he would be remembered as the worst serial killer in the world. Badder than Berkowitz, more prolific than Pedro Alonso Lopez and making Bundy and the rest of the boys look like mere beginners. Ordo Moonst had found The Floodgate Key. He was going to use it to open the Floodgates.

Ordo wrote about this often on pieces of paper that he would immediately destroy by eating them. Ordo thought that if he ate a piece of paper he would be able to remember what was on there better than by just reading it. After a while he began to think that there was no real need for him even to read what was on the paper, just by eating it he should be able to assimilate and remember what was written. Ordo went on to eat many great works of literature.

The Floodgate Key was Ordo's name for the first person he was going to kill. Once the Floodgate Key was dead then The Floodgates would open and out of them would pour the many, many further victims of Ordo Moonst, the worst serial killer in the world. As, indeed, he would shortly predict with the blood-written message of the first.

The Floodgate Key was an essential part of Ordo's stratagem. The Floodgate Key could not be just anyone. There were a strict set of rules regarding the selection of the Floodgate Key which Ordo wrote down on a piece of paper and ate. Immediately afterwards Ordo chose The Floodgate Key at random from the many hundreds of single men who inhabited the block of flats opposite his own. He watched them leave every morning; he watched them come home again every night. Ordo knew that, sooner or later, the young man who lived in the flat would return home. Ordo would kill him and write a message on the wall in the young man's blood. The world would be aware that the Floodgates had opened.

Ordo knew that he had been in the young man's flat now for only a few minutes, or perhaps an hour, or maybe all day. There was no time to lose. He began with repairs to himself.

Ordo took the scalpel from his bag. He made a deep incision in the back of his hand and poured local anaesthetic into the open wound. He sighed as the pain disappeared from his splinter-filled fingers along with the feeling in the rest of his hand and his arm up as far as the shoulder. His anaesthetised arm was difficult to control and often slipped off his knee as he cut and sliced and tugged with his teeth at the tiny pins of wood. He began to delight in the utter lack of pain and experimented with deeper cuts. Before long Ordo had lacerated his fingers to such a degree that his hand looked like a paint brush. When he took it by the wrist and wiped it down the wall he found it worked like a paint brush too. Ordo realised he had no idea how long or how short a time would pass before the Floodgate Key came home. He realised too that the door to the flat looked tampered with at least, and might draw unwanted attention from returning neighbours while he Ordo Moonst was still inside, writing The Message in the victim's blood. With a flash of realisation that blinded him in the eye he couldn't close, Ordo saw that if he wrote the message in his *own* blood then all he would have to do was kill the Floodgate Key and scarper.

He only managed to paint one word on the wall before he had to cut into his fingers again for more blood. After three words he had no fingers, he had thinly sliced shiny red ribbons. He cut down between his knuckles and had only three letters of the final word to complete, requiring one more incision across the palm to the wrist providing enough blood to make him consider perhaps that he might even write The Message more than once. No. Once was enough. He was feeling cold and tired and there was pain beginning to invade parts of his hand that no longer existed. Ordo looked up at The Message and smiled. He was no longer holding his paint-brush-arm and it hung by his side pouring blood onto the floor. He glanced down into his open bag and wondered where he'd put his crowbar? He would need it to open the door. He crumpled into a heap and bled to death in front of the fireplace.

The young man who lived in the flat came home many hours later and found his front door battered and scarred. He pushed it gently. It fell off its hinges. Walking warily into his living room the young man found a stranger on the floor. The stranger, who had died with one eye open, had cut his left hand to slivers and apparently used his own blood to write a message on the wall above the fireplace in the young man's flat. The message read: *There Will Be Others*.

Prince Charles's favourite comedian, Jim has appeared on three Royal Command Performances together with his double bass. He made six short films called Jim Tavaré Pictures Presents *(BBC2) and his* Jim Tavaré Show *(Channel 5) received a Montreux Golden Rose nomination. He appears as Tom The Innkeeper in the forthcoming film* Harry Potter and the Prisoner of Azkaban. *With Dave Thompson, he wrote for ITV's BAFTA Award-winning* The Sketch Show.

Dave wrote ITV's BAFTA Award-winning The Sketch Show *with Jim Tavaré. Dave has also written for* Harry Hill's TV Burp *(ITV) and for many other comedians. His acting work includes the movie* Maybe Baby *and the sitcom* Time Gentlemen Please. *He has written for* Esquire, GQ *and* Time Out *and has worked as a stand-up in Britain, America and Europe. He is also the man inside the Tinky Winky costume in* Teletubbies.

jim tavaré and dave thompson

kissing in the wind

Arnold Watkins walked into the small interrogation chamber, removed a cigarette packet from his tweed jacket and put it on the battered old table. He took off his jacket and draped it over the back of the chair.

"Right 12C," he said gruffly, "you'd better start talking sense or you'll be in solitary confinement until you're seventy."

"I told you. I didn't steal that sausage."

Arnold's bald head shone beneath the naked light bulb as he sat down, all the time studying 12C's face intently. He knew he could crack her. The question was, could he force her confession and still have time to get to the pub before they stopped serving food?

12C flinched as Arnold slapped the table so hard his hand stung and the cigarette packet jumped close to the edge. The bang reverberated due to the tiled floor and walls.

"I know you stole that sausage, 12C. Like I know you were behind the escape of 1C and 2C."

"I'm familiar with your technique, Mr Watkins. This is the hard and soft interrogation method. You come in all aggressive and threatening. Then Matron will come and be nice to me. Offer me a cigarette. Use the gentle, understanding approach."

"Correct, 12C. Up to a point. We do employ the hard and soft interrogation technique here. But *I am* the soft interrogator. Nurse Vlad is doing his warm-up exercises as we speak. He doesn't want to pull a muscle during sudden movements."

"Please, sir. Not Nurse Vlad!"

Arnold slowly rolled up the sleeves of his Marks & Spencer country shirt, all the time staring into 12C's eyes.

"It's *your* choice."

When 12C blinked first, Arnold knew he'd get his confession and still have time for the pub. He might even be in time for the pub quiz.

"Have a smoke," said Arnold, smiling and pushing the packet towards 12C.

"I haven't smoked since I was twenty," replied 12C, proudly.

"I said *Have a smoke*," said Arnold, deliberately removing a gold-plated lighter from the pocket of his jacket as it hung on the chair back.

12C fumbled with the fliptop pack: "Please don't force me. Tobacco smoke makes me cough, even if the cigarette's on the other side of the room." Her fingers trembled as they removed a cigarette from the packet. "This is torture. You're not allowed to force me to smoke," protested 12C, as Arnold held the lighter towards her face and ignited it.

"Unfortunately for you, there isn't a telephone in solitary confinement," smiled Arnold, his clean teeth showing white in his well-kept mouth.

12C hadn't even touched the cigarette to the flame, when she fell into a fit of coughing.

"Alright, it was me," she blubbed. "I took the Zone Six keys whilst nobody was looking. I felt sorry for 1C and 2C and helped them escape. And I stole an extra sausage. I was hungry after being forced to knit jumpers all day."

"You're lucky it was only a council sausage," said Arnold, as he removed the cigarette from 12C's fingers and carefully replaced it in the packet. Satisfied with the confession, Arnold stood up and opened the door. "Alright, 12C, you can go back to the others."

"You mean I don't get solitary confinement?"

"Correct," answered Arnold, as he unrolled his sleeves and put his jacket back on. 12C's confusion arose from there being only one solitary confinement cell but eight people doing solitary confinement. They endured more crowded conditions than anyone else in the institution.

Arnold called to Nurse Vlad, his second in command: "Cancel the lock-down, nurse. 12C has confessed. I'm off to The Blue Anchor for a drink."

Nurse Vlad nodded at Arnold, took another look at the CCTV security monitors and pulled the microphone to his mouth. He spoke in a Serbian accent.

"Attention! Attention all residents! Mr Vatkins has seen fit to cancel the lock-down. Council Residents are free to vander at vill vithin Zones Vun and Two. Private Residents are free to vander at vill vithin Zones Vun, Two and Two A."

* * *

Arnold Watkins went through the hall of the Sunny Cliff Retirement Home wondering if he should wear his puce tanktop. He unlocked the front door and stepped outside. It was a clear evening over the Sussex coast and he didn't want to feel chilly later on. "I'll wear it anyway," he said aloud to himself. "That puce colour suits me and I want to look attractive." If the evening went according to plan, he would be warm in the arms of Susan Brown, Seahaven's Caring Lady Funeral Director.

Arnold bounded up the main stairs to his private quarters – or Zone Seven as he called them. Situated on the sunny, southern side of the house, the lounge afforded a nice view of the sea, blue as it was beneath the cloudless spring sky.

His Uncle Boris stared down at him from the portrait that hung above the original Victorian fireplace. Uncle Boris had died before

Arnold was born, but still dominated his life with a legacy of extreme success. The gilt-framed portrait depicted him in his naval officer's uniform, standing on the deck of the merchant ship on which he'd made his fortune. Some twenty years older than Arnold's father, Uncle Boris had bought Sunny Cliff with the money he'd made in the Far East, before dying of malaria and leaving the house to his younger brother, Arnold's father.

As a boy, Arnold's parents had told stories of Uncle Boris' talent for making money and Arnold had stared above the roaring log fires at the stern figure, pointing down to the sea across which he'd carried so many profitable cargoes.

The fact that he had never achieved anything like the success of Uncle Boris made Arnold feel inadequate. He looked up at that finger as it pointed downwards. If only Arnold could fathom the mystery of what his Uncle Boris was pointing at. He turned his back to the portrait and his lanky legs carried him swiftly down the stairs towards the oak front doors of the cliff top house Uncle Boris had endowed to the Watkins family.

His chauffeur saluted and stood to attention beside Arnold's green two-door Nissan Micra. "Thank you 14P," said Arnold, as he climbed into the back seat. As a trustee, 14P was allowed to leave the grounds of Sunny Cliff, as long as he was driving Arnold. He liked to wear the commissionaire's uniform he'd worn at the main entrance to Eastbourne's Grand Hotel until his enforced retirement at the age of 75. He was the only chauffeur in the country with gold braid hanging from his shoulder. A former soldier – and, before that, a stable boy in a Welsh country house – 14P lived to serve. As long as he could salute a man wearing tweed, his life had purpose.

As 14P coaxed the ten-year-old car along the unpaved, pothole-strewn track that led to the coast road, Arnold saw a couple strolling along the verge and ordered 14P to stop.

"Good evening, sir and madam. Are you, perchance, prospective clients of the Sunny Cliff Residential Home for the Elderly?"

"No, we're just on our way to enjoy the clifftop walk. We can reach it this way, can't we?"

"Get off my land, it's private!" barked Arnold Watkins to the male rambler.

"But this is a public right of way, according to the bye-laws. We're completely within our rights."

"I don't care what you're within, this is my land. No Gypsies. No ramblers. Off."

"I work for the Department of Highways. According to your letters, this track is public and therefore not your responsibility to maintain. You can't have it both ways. If you won't pay to fill in the potholes, I hardly see how you can claim ownership."

"You enjoy rambling, don't you?"

"Yes, but I can't see what it's got to do with—"

"Then take a hike! Hoppit."

"You haven't heard the last of this," said the rambler, as he began to retrace his steps back towards the coast road, his female companion following. Arnold commanded 14P to gun the 1.1 litre Micra forward and steer it purposely into one of the water-filled potholes. It was a risk, because some of those potholes were ten inches deep and could swallow a wheel. He was in luck, though, and succeeded in sploshing dirty brown water over the corduroy legs of both ramblers, without getting stuck.

"Good work, 14P. You can have sugar in your tea for tomorrow only."

"Thank you, sir."

If I'm not keeping them in, I'm keeping them out, Arnold complained to himself, as anger for the trespassers mixed with concern over the recent escape by 1C and 2C. When they reached the end of the track, 14P turned right on to the coast road and headed east towards Seahaven and Arnold's favourite pub, the Blue Anchor.

The coast road undulated as it followed the lush South Downs. Arnold recognised the hefty old Volvo coming in the opposite direction and, leaning forward from the back seat, flashed the headlights at its driver. Then his thoughts returned to 1C and 2C. They were his most troublesome residents for several reasons. Reasons he feared he could no longer face ...

* * *

Reginald Bowden, or Skipper as he was commonly known, didn't notice Arnold's flashing lights, because he'd just rounded a curve and the sinking sun was in his eyes, causing him to squint. He lowered the sun visor and tapped the indicator stalk, whereupon it snapped off and landed next to his foot.

As he turned off the coast road, the Volvo slowed to negotiate the unsurfaced short track leading to the Sunny Cliff Retirement Home. As he weaved around the puddles, his left indicator still blinking, Skipper felt glad that he'd avoided Arnold, who was seldom in a good mood.

Arnold had gone through a difficult time since opening Sunny Cliff. Several of his staff had objected to the conditions and deserted him. He was badly behind with maintenance payments to Deirdre, the mother of his seven-year-old daughter. Several years ago he had made a living as a bit-part actor but, as he approached his forties, the work dried up. They'd bought a terraced house in Seahaven, offering bed and breakfast. He'd hoped to cater for touring thespians, but an old actor friend had got too familiar with Deirdre. Or so Arnold thought. After he'd punched him in the face, most of the theatrical business was lost. Then they were featured on TV as runners-up in *Britain's Worst Bed and Breakfast* and that was the end of their career as hoteliers.

They decided to diversify and reopened as a hostel for asylum seekers. A boom period ensued, where the guesthouse was full of

Dover's overspill. Their good fortune continued when Arnold was engaged for three weeks' continuous work on *The Huge Dead Thing*, a horror film that was being shot in Brighton. It was a small part, in which he played a maggot. His face wasn't seen, which was just as well as he was replacing another actor who had been sacked for drunkenness. The costume reeked of his predecessor's stale sweat. But seven hundred quid a week was too good to refuse and one could make the role sound more impressive than it was.

Things were good. Then, the bombshell came. Whilst Arnold was busy in the maggot costume, Deirdre spent a lot of time in the company of Rashid, the Albanian refugee staying in room four.

The first Arnold knew about the affair, they had married in Lewes Registry Office and Rashid and his brothers had changed the locks to Arnold's house. A short period of emotional devastation ensued, fuelled by Arnold's discovery that Deirdre had legal right to their home. Then he'd inherited Uncle Boris' house and converted it into the Sunny Cliff Retirement Home.

* * *

Skipper parked his old Volvo in front of the weather-beaten façade of Sunny Cliff. His feet crunched in the gravel as he trudged round to the boot. He did not look up at the house, as he'd been a regular visitor here for over a year. He didn't need to see the cracked drain-pipes and the way the extension, built seventy years ago, didn't align properly with the original house. The conservatory seemed to have been tacked awkwardly on to the side of the building, offering residents 'breathtaking views of the South Downs' according to the Sunny Cliff brochure (which omitted to mention the pylons and electricity sub-station in between).

Skipper opened the boot, to reveal several boxes of cheap French sausages. He was called Skipper because he worked on the ferry that plied between Seahaven, four miles to the east of Sunny Cliff, and Dieppe. He subsidised his meagre earnings by procuring French produce from the Dieppe market and selling it to Arnold for a small profit. French food prices, combined with the strength of the pound against the Euro, meant that Arnold saved a considerable amount of money by using Skipper. Sunny Cliff's glossy brochure boasted *All our cuisine is sourced in France.*

As Skipper was about to take a box of sausages towards the kitchen door at the side of the house, Nurse Vlad emerged, looking very distraught.

"Skipper! Residents 1C and 2C are escaped last night."

"But 1C and 2C are Category A and kept in Zone Six."

"I am know this!"

"They definitely got away from the house?" asked Skipper, as he looked at Vlad's broad Slavic face.

"I must have forget to locking the Zone Six door. We find hole in the rear France."

"Do you mean Fence? France is where my ship brought you from."

"Yes, Frence."

Nurse Vlad was highly distressed about the escaped residents. He'd paid Skipper to smuggle him into Britain from Dieppe six months previously. He was glad of the live-in job as a nurse at Sunny Cliff, where he was slowly learning English. Arnold paid him a mere £12.36 a week but, until he knew more English, he had poor prospects outside Sunny Cliff. He had a personal interest in preventing escapes. A rogue resident could talk to Immigration.

"I'm sure they won't get far," Skipper assured the giant.

"Thank, Skipper. Would you like some hand with your job?" asked Vlad innocently.

"Yes, please."

As they unloaded the sausages, Skipper wondered if Nurse Vlad chose to wear that female nurse's uniform or if it was all Arnold would supply.

* * *

In the snug of the Blue Anchor, Arnold was finishing off a portion of sticky toffee chocolate pudding with pistachio ice cream. The Blue Anchor's jukebox pumped out a steady stream of Seventies hits. Susan Brown, Seahaven's Caring Lady Funeral Director, cradled a large Southern Comfort in her soft white hand, the nails of which were varnished black. She enviously watched Arnold put away calories in their hundreds, without increasing his weight. Susan was tall and thin, like Arnold, but lacked his fast metabolism. Her slim figure was the result of careful calorie control. She attributed Brown's Funeral Director's position as the premier undertaker in Seahaven to her glamorous looks and she wasn't entirely wrong. Arnold couldn't resist her sophisticated black dresses, which matched her shiny black hair and dark lipstick so perfectly. Not to mention those sexy, black-stockinged legs and four gleaming hearses. He'd already stated in his will that, should he die, Susan Brown should personally embalm him.

True, Susan had a professional interest in Arnold, as he was in a position to put several bodies a year through her chapel of rest. But there was more to it than that. His bald head, aristocratic thin face and lean body got her juices flowing in a way that the beery, bearded men of the town failed to do.

The last orders bell rang in the Blue Anchor. Susan was several Southern Comforts over the limit to drive her black Mercedes 500SL and readily accepted Arnold's offer of a lift. "Would the lady like to take her carriage?" slurred Arnold, who had a bottle of wine inside him and another clutched in his left hand. The temperature had plummeted since night fell and the cloudless sky twinkled with stars.

Arnold and Susan shivered as they walked across the car park. He bleeped his Nissan Micra, causing 14P to stir suddenly on the back seat. He got out of the car and stood to attention, saluting Arnold despite his arm being stiff with cold.

"Permission granted, 14P," said Arnold, anticipating that, having been locked in the car for several hours, his chauffeur would need to relieve himself round the back of the pub. A moment later 14P spent a penny as best he could with fingers numb from cold. Arnold chivalrously opened his passenger door.

"Are you sure he's not too old to drive?"

"He's fine."

"Come on, then. We'll go back to my place, but I want to stop at the Chinese takeaway. I fancy crispy duck."

Arnold had desired Susan Brown ever since first opening Sunny Cliff's doors to care for the elderly. Or, rather, ever since his first client had passed away, the day after Sunny Cliff opened for business. His heart had leaped as soon as he'd looked into Susan's soft brown eyes and savoured her figure-hugging black suit. When he'd seen her face, he'd quite forgotten his anxiety over the first resident fatality. Luckily, Dr Shipley had agreed to enter *natural causes* as the reason for death. This was technically true, as it was the wind that had caused that roof tile to fall on to the head of Resident 3P. And the wind is natural. Regardless of the fact Arnold was on the roof attempting a repair at the time. Or that a bottle of tax-free whisky fell naturally into Dr Shipley's hands every time he found the cause of death to be natural.

* * *

Arnold Watkins looked at the photos on the wall of Susan Brown's hallway.

"Hey aren't these all famous people?" asked Arnold, a little impressed.

"Yes. That's Daddy with Will Stewart, the Scottish comedian. That's Daddy with Johnny Brambles, Grand National winner 1952. That's Daddy with Dolores Monk the actress. Daddy was fascinated by celebrities."

"But, Susan, they're all in coffins!"

"He was an undertaker. I inherited the family business. Here he is with the racing driver, Colin Stokes."

"That doesn't look anything like Colin Stokes."

"He died at 180 mph."

"Oh."

"Would you like some duck?" asked Susan.

"I beg your pardon? Oh, duck. No thanks, I'll stick to my sweet and sour prawn balls."

"Is your chauffeur alright in the car? It's a very cold night."

"He's fine. The Welsh are a hardy species."

"He's welcome to come in the warm."

"Never mind 14P. He's guarding the car. Let's talk about me. I used to be an actor, you know, before I ran the old folks home. I starred in pantomime once. At the Palace Theatre."

"In the West End?"

"Cape Town, actually. A production of *Robinson Crusoe*."

"You played Robinson Crusoe?"

"No. Man Friday. It was during apartheid and blacks weren't allowed in the theatre. I had to buy my interval sandwiches before the show. Once I'd blacked up, they wouldn't let me in the artistes' bar."

They both chuckled, Susan Brown somewhat nervously. "Where's your corkscrew? I'll open this Chianti…"

Meanwhile, 14P passed away peacefully in his sleep on the back seat of Arnold's parked Micra.

When Arnold left Susan's house at two-thirty in the morning and found 14P's body, Susan obliged with her Chapel of Rest. Luckily Dr Shipley lived nearby and entered *natural causes* as reason for death. This was true enough, as in sub-zero temperatures it's quite natural to stop breathing.

The next morning, Nurse Vlad was pleasantly surprised at how well Arnold was taking 1C and 2C's escape. He'd been alarmed at first, but then they'd found the hole in the fence at the back of the property, near the sea cliffs. Arnold had stared into the distance and declared: "Best place for them. They'll probably be dashed against the rocks by now."

* * *

At breakfast time, Arnold stood behind the serving hatch and pulled the shutter up.

"Right, private residents first. Come and get it!"

Several elderly people made their way to the serving hatch and formed an orderly queue.

Arnold dolloped mashed potato and two private sausages on each plate. They all helped themselves to a slice of bread and margarine and returned to their tables. After the private residents had been served, the council residents were given the same except their sausages were council sausages, made of horse offal and rusk.

Whilst they were eating, Arnold made the day's announcements:

"Today is *Radiator Day*. We are switching the radiators on."

"Hooray!"

"And this morning we will be learning life skills. This will take the form of planting carrots. Private residents will be knitting jumpers. Later, platinum class residents will receive an educational lecture entitled *Timeshares in Normandy – why now is the time to buy*."

"Excuse me?" asked 9C. "What's the point of having the radiators on if we're out in the garden?"

"Don't be negative, 9C. And, by the way, I can see you wearing the hearing aid."

"Pardon?"

"You don't fool me, 9C. You are wearing the hearing aid and you know perfectly well it's 15P's turn between the hours of 5.36am and 11.17am. Give it to 15P."

9C didn't move. The other residents watched worriedly. Last time the hearing aid had been worn illegally, there had been a lock-down lasting three days.

"Alright, 15P, get the hearing aid from 9C."

15P looked up from his cup of nettle tea, brewed from home-grown nettles. "Quarter past four?"

The Sunny Cliff residents weren't served normal tea, for health reasons. The tannin was bad for them. Similarly, Arnold had banned milk on the grounds that it was bad for their cholesterol levels.

"I'll say it one last time. Give it to 15P."

"It's my hearing aid! You stole it off me, Watkins. I can provide a valid receipt."

"Right, 9C. For illegally wearing the hearing aid – and insolence – I sentence you to a half-hour session of aromatherapy."

The sound of knives and forks on brittle crockery, which was decorated in the ferry company's logo, suddenly stopped. Aroma-therapy was worse than solitary confinement. The dining room was silent, but for the whimpering of 9C.

"I'm sorry, sir. Please don't give me aromatherapy. I beg you!"

The residents watched in horror as Nurse Vlad and a trustee carried 9C screaming towards Zone 6 and the dreaded aromatherapy session.

"Let that be a warning to you all," said Arnold and he closed the serving hatch shutter with a bang.

Alone in the stainless-steel kitchen, Arnold leaned against the greasy wall and sank to the floor, his head in his hands. As he heard the sound of the residents booing him from the other side of the shutter, soft tears of self-loathing rolled down his finely chiselled cheeks. The screams of 9C receded across the hall, or Zone Two A, as it was now called. Had his life come to this?

He needed Nurse Vlad to keep discipline at Sunny Cliff, but the way he enjoyed administering the aromatherapy punishments! Arnold didn't want anybody hurt for the sake of it. If only he could get 1C and 2C off his mind! What if they got to the police? "I just wanted to be a successful actor," sobbed Arnold. "But I was never appreci-ated by my agent." His favourite puce sleeveless jumper, which had been knitted by 4P before he passed away from natural causes, felt damp on Arnold's back, such was the abundance of deep fat fryer grease on the bespattered tiles.

"I wanted to play in comedies in the West End. To star in funny sitcoms on ITV. To make this glorious nation rock with laughter. And look at me. I've become a ..."

"... a Gestapo torturer?" interrupted Susan Brown. She looked resplendent in her black velvet dress, her thirty-year-old neck a perfect background for the platinum necklace she won in a raffle at the British Board of Funeral Directors' Annual Summer Ball.

"Oh Susan," wept Arnold, "I can't go on!"

"They've found 1C and 2C," said Susan.

"What?" Arnold's head jerked up and banged against the sink. "Ow!"

As Susan's upper-class Sussex voice uttered these words, 1C and 2C appeared in the kitchen doorway.

"You came back!" exclaimed Arnold.

"Yes, son. We came back," said his father.

"But you're not allowed in Zone F—"

"Arnie ... It's alright, little soldier," said his mother. "We want to help you."

"Come on through to the lounge, Arnold," said his father.

"You mean Zone Seven," replied Arnold.

"No, Arnold. The lounge. *Our* lounge."

* * *

Bright April sunlight streamed through the lounge windows, affording a glorious vista of the English Channel. Arnold had kept the majority of the residents on the bleak northern side of the house, so he could charge a few platinum class residents extra for south-facing seaview rooms.

He'd told everyone his parents had died and that he'd inherited this house where he'd seen such happy childhood days. The truth was, after being deprived of the right to live in his own house (by Deirdre, Rashid and the ridiculous English marriage laws), Arnold had enslaved his parents in the family home. They had been made 1C and 2C. Secure residents confined to Zone 6 – or The Attic as it had been when he was a boy.

Arnold had converted Sunny Cliff into a residential home for the elderly with the intention of running it along humane lines. But the nursing home business is even tougher than the entertainment business and soon he had to economise to the extent that the residents were forced to do 'life skills' classes. These were thinly disguised slave labour, such as knitting jumpers for sale to Brighton's trendy shops.

This and more was explained to the horrified Susan Brown, who blushed when she heard of Arnold's crimes.

"I've developed an infatuation for you, Arnold. I came here this morning because I wanted to hear your voice and see your smile. The sea looked so blue, I went for a stroll in your back garden and bumped into your parents. They're very nice."

"We forgive you everything, son. If you'd only asked us, we'd have remortgaged Sunny Cliff to fund your business aspirations."

"I feel such a fool. I was so ashamed I never became a famous actor," said Arnold, as he poured everyone a second cup of the Twining's English Breakfast Tea that he kept exclusively for his own use. "I was too embarrassed to come to you begging for money."

Suddenly the threshold darkened, as Nurse Vlad appeared in the doorway.

"Vat is this? 1C and 2C in Zone Seven? This must not be!"

Nurse Vlad went for the handcuffs on his belt. Suddenly he froze and looked up. "Oh yes. I forgetting to say ze police are arresting Dr Shipley. A detective sergeant stands at your door, for speaking vith you."

"I'm finished!" Arnold's voice broke as he realised he was going to be swapping the keys of Sunny Cliff for the wrong side of a prison window.

"Oh Susan!" he wept.

"Oh Arnold," said his parents. "You're a very bad boy, but you're a Watkins; and a member of the Watkins family is giving you the chance to escape into exile."

"Who? Where?"

"Look at the portrait of your Uncle Boris. He's going to save you."

Arnold gazed up at the stern bachelor Uncle Boris. As always, he stood in his naval officer's uniform, pointing down to the sea from the deck of his ship.

"How is a portrait going to save me?" replied Arnold, running out of patience.

"Where's he pointing to, son?"

Arnold thought for a moment. Then it dawned on him: "The cellar? He's pointing to the cellar!" said Arnold, getting anxious as he heard the sound of voices coming up the stairs.

Before his parents had time to reply, Mrs Lawson, one of the platinum class residents, burst into the room.

"Sorry to be in a forbidden zone, but there's been a breach of security by the council residents. They've let the sergeant in through the front door, Mr Watkins."

"Go to the cellar, son, then look for the secret tunnel. It's how we escaped. That hole in the fence was just a ruse to fool you."

Arnold, Susan and Vlad all ran down the back stairs and down into the damp, cold cellar that Uncle Boris had hewn from the rock beneath Sunny Cliff's basement. A moment later, they'd discovered the trapdoor that Arnold's parents had used so recently and were trotting down the rough steps that had been cut into the limestone. Soon they saw natural light coming from the end of the shaft a long way below.

Shortly afterwards, their feet crunched on the wet shingle of a cave floor and they emerged on to a small beach at the foot of the cliff.

Suddenly a whistle pierced the crisp April air. "I recognise that whistle," thought Arnold. "It's Skipper's!" As if to confirm his pleasant suspicion, the whistle carried on the wind again and there was Skipper, at the helm of his thirty-foot-long motor cruiser. Its twin 1.6 litre turbo diesels throbbed in neutral.

"All aboard!" he called. "I want to get to France before dark. I've got a table booked in a little bistro where they have fresh lobster and a jazz quartet."

* * *

Susan and Arnold looked back at the receding cliffs and small tidal beach. By the time the police discovered the secret tunnel and looked out to sea, they'd be far away. Nurse Vlad emerged from the cabin, with a bottle of Beaujolais and four tumblers.

The red wine danced in their mouths and, as if in sympathy, the sun dyed the horizon red too. Susan gazed longingly into Arnold's eyes. As they kissed, the wind blew her long hair so it caressed the sides of Arnold's head. Arnold purred with contentment, unaware that from where Skipper and Nurse Vlad stood, Susan's lush black hair made it look like he wore a wig. After a long, delicious kiss, Susan smiled at Arnold and cooed: "Arnold, love, I want to sell my funeral director's business and spend the money travelling around with you. We've got the whole world to explore."

"That's fantastic, Susan. I think I'll call it Zone Eight."

Host of Channel 5 quiz show Whittle *and one of the members of ITV's BAFTA Award-winning* The Sketch Show, *Tim won the Perrier Best Newcomer Award at the Edinburgh Fringe in 1995 and has since hosted a vast number of TV series including Channel 4's* Fluke *which he devised and which was shortlisted for a Montreux Golden Globe Award. Tim is known as king of the one-liners.*

tim vine

the map of elorza

Hello. My name is Urgle Protap. And before you start mocking I know that my first name rhymes with gurgle and that my whole name sounds like the answer to a lazily thought out anagram question. I also know that it sounds like the name of a cream you put on severe eczema or an obscure variation of tap dancing for only the very skilled. And I'm aware it's the noise a dog makes when he drinks the last mouthful of water from a dish. And finally, yes you're right it does sound like the kind of name a writer uses in a story when he can't be bothered to make up something realistic. Satisfied? I've heard them all before. They've come at me thick and fast for the last 34 years and there are no original ones left. So don't think you're witty. You are not. I know I have a stupid name. Anyway like I say, hello. My name is Urgle Protap.

I live on my own. Yes, ha ha, "I'm not surprised with a name like that." Can we get on? The name of the village I live in is called Little Pitty. That's right Urgle Protap lives in Little Pitty. Try and get these scoffing thoughts out of your system. I agree it is a strange name for a village and I have heard visitors doing the *What a pity living in Little Pitty* line. And in case you're about to ask, no there is not a small coalmine in Little Pitty either. And here's another question I hear from a succession of smirking strangers: "Is Little Pitty pretty?"

Well yes I believe it is. But for those of us who live in Little Pitty we've long since got over finding our address amusing.

Incidentally when I say 'for those of us who live in Little Pitty,' I mean for me. I am the sole inhabitant. When I moved in twelve years ago there were 47 locals but now it's just me. Yes good point, "What does that tell you Urgle?" Well, actually they didn't choose to leave because of me. In fact there was no choosing about it. But I'll get to that in a moment. Suffice to say they were not driven away by the weirdness of my name or the fact that I keep African weasels.

Yes, you did read that correctly. I've got four of them and until recently they lived in a refrigerated hutch at the end of my triangular garden. Well why not triangular? Who was it who made the rule that all gardens should be oblong? Yes it does mean it's not easy to mow it. And you're absolutely right I can't get that nice neat strip effect that lawn mowers leave on a rectangular patch of grass. Can I be honest? I don't care. I've never been over-bothered by the aesthetics of a lawn. As long as I can see my feet I'm happy. Well, alright my ankles. OK my knees then! You've got it out of me. I don't mow my lawn and I never have mowed it. Happy?

I know the word you're thinking because I've been called it before. It's a three-letter word that begins with 'o' and ends in a double 'd'. If I'm odd what does that make you? That's right I don't know because I know nothing about you. But you know a bit about me, don't you? I'm Urgle Protap and I live in Little Pitty with my African weasels and a triangular lawn underneath which is a bunker the size of a football stadium where I spend most days working on the construction of a 300 metre hydraulic arm.

I'll explain. When I was just two years old my father gave me a hydraulics kit. From that moment on I was hooked. Hydraulics in simple terms is the science of water-power. By pumping water through a piston system one arrives at a machine which is capable of powering very large mechanical devices. What fascinated me from such an early age was the following question: Could I build a 300 metre hydraulic arm?

Over the last two years the answer had finally materialised in the affirmative. After more than 24,000 man hours, which included hiring hundreds of unemployed asylum seekers to work blindfolded so they wouldn't know what they were working on, I had a fully functioning 300 metre hydraulic arm underneath my house. It was too big to use but that wasn't the point. I made it and it was there.

The African weasel is possibly one of the most rare and endangered species in the animal kingdom. Its Latin name is *Gerictacus Balentum* but that's irrelevant; except that it's a better name than mine. (I know that's what you were thinking.)

I first took an interest in the plight of the African weasel when I was at college in Fiji studying the English house sparrow. It was my second year and I still hadn't seen a single sparrow so I began to spend my afternoons in the oncology section of the college library. It was some weeks before I realised my mistake and so I moved to the ornithology section. Yes I know Oncology is the study of cancer and Ornithology is the study of birds. I later discovered that Ornciology is the study of birds with cancer.

It was while reading a frankly dull book called *Ravens and Their Sleep Patterns* that I overheard an elderly librarian answering a query about the African weasel. He whispered in a frail voice, "We haven't got any books about the African weasel." I stood up immediately and made it my business to find a library that did. I soon found one and excitedly read all I could about this beautiful and exotic dung rat.

The reason the African weasel is endangered is because it can only survive in temperatures that are zero or below. (Hence the refrigerated hutch.) The problem arises when they are born in Africa. They die almost immediately. The only way to save them is to put them straight into an icebox. It's not much of a life in an icebox but the alternative is frying.

I purchased my African weasels at a sledge boot sale in Greenland. I bought a litter of five although sadly now I only have four. I named them after the Osmonds. I call them Osmond One, Osmond Two, Osmond Three and so on. They're not particularly demanding as I only have to feed them once an hour. They just eat frozen chicken because they have a very sensitive digestive system. (On the weekends I give them chocolate and beer as a treat.) And when I get home from work at the toothbrush factory I check their hutch temperature.

Yes that was *toothbrush factory*. Here we go again. It's my job. That's right, it is a little bit unusual. I sew the bristles on to the brushes. Well, perhaps it does sound ridiculous but it also happens to be quite dangerous. Inside every toothbrush bristle there is a tiny trace of plutonium. One toothbrush of bristles is not enough to be a risk to a human but a group of toothbrushes is a different thing. That is why most dental organisations suggest you dispose of your old toothbrushes. Let a cluster gather in your toothbrush mug over the years and you could be courting disaster. Thankfully this is not a problem for me because I have never been one of life's hoarders. Not including my collection of Ordnance Survey maps of course.

That's right. Urgle Protap collects Ordnance Survey maps. What a laughing stock. Well, I'll have you know I take it very seriously. I have been accumulating them all my life and have a map for every inch of the entire planet except one small town in Venezuela called Elorza. It should be arriving in the post any day now. The map of Elorza will complete the set.

Taunt me if you wish but this is my life. I am used to being taunted. My name, my address, my pets, my job, my hobbies, my family. They're all easy targets. Now I've said it, haven't I? You want me to tell you about my family. Well, I'm not going to. If I do, you'll point the mocking finger. It'll be just like when I was wrongly accused of burgling the Little Pitty Torch Museum.

I remember the date because it was the day after my 34th birthday. March 2nd. The night before I'd been out celebrating with my friend, Louisa. Yes I have got a friend. Yes her name is more sensible than mine. Yes, she is more of an associate than a friend. OK, I don't even know her surname. She's a vet and when Osmond Three was at death's door with salmonella it was Louisa's expertise that saved his life. Can we stay on track please?

Louisa and I had gone for a meal at the Italian burger bar on Walsh Street. Well, actually it was more of a takeaway than a sit-down meal. And Louisa didn't eat much. Anyway after I'd eaten my burger it was getting a bit late for Louisa and she said she was feeling tired. Apparently she always goes to bed early on a Thursday and although it was only eight o'clock she made her excuses and returned home. I was a little disappointed she couldn't stay out with me for longer because I was enjoying her company. But she did appear to be yawning almost constantly so she was probably right to call it a day. Before you ask, no it's not a romantic thing. No I do not secretly love her and I certainly don't spend long hours in my attic painting watercolour representations of her smile just trying to capture it so that I can have her smiling at me whenever I please. Anyway the only reason for mentioning my birthday was so I remembered the date of the Little Pitty Torch Museum injustice.

This is what happened. On the morning of March 2nd I was in a very upbeat frame of mind. I think it was because I was still buzzing from having such a wonderful four-minute birthday meal with my platonic friend Louisa (the vet with the memorable smile).

So with an extra bounce in my slippers I made myself breakfast. It was my favourite: two boiled eggs on toast and a decaffeinated orange juice. I'm aware that no one has ever found caffeine in orange juice. But why take the risk? I put on my string dungarees and set off up the high street giving the Osmonds their morning walk.

It was then that I noticed it. The whole town was silent. Every street, every alleyway, every shop was empty. The people of Little Pitty had completely vanished ... I'll pause there for effect while you imagine a *Day of the Triffids* scenario or an *alien abducts whole village* situation. Well, actually they hadn't disappeared at all.

As I wandered with the Osmonds up the narrow, cobbled pavement I heard the sound of voices coming from the town hall. Forty-seven voices to be precise. The whole village, except me, was having a meeting.

I began to approach the building slowly. This was partly because I didn't want to be heard and partly because Osmond Two has a habit of circling my left leg when I walk so every five steps I have to unwind his lead from my foot.

The voices became more distinguishable as I reached the Gothic wall of the town hall and crouched wide-eyed beneath a half open window. Even the Osmonds seemed to stop their sniffing and grunting. The five of us pointed our favoured ear upwards and listened.

Mr Brown was speaking. Another normal name I know but I'm not going to dress up the truth. His name is Mr Brown not Mr Apple-twister and that's that. Mr Brown is the owner and manager of the toothbrush factory where I work. The company is called Brown Toothbrushes. As he spoke it was obvious he was very angry.

"The man is a disrupting influence!" he yelled. The whole village erupted in agreement.

"He is an idiot who embarrasses himself and everyone around him!" Another eruption. This one louder and more in unison than the first.

"Little Pitty is better off without him!" A third roar of red hot hatred. Whoever Mr Brown was referring to was certainly disliked with a volcanic unanimity. My heart went out to the poor fellow.

Just then Mr Brown appeared lost for words because I could hear nothing from my shadowy hiding place. Then there was a smattering of polite applause like the bubbling of lava. "Ah he's stepped down," I thought. "Maybe it's someone else's turn to address the crowd." I was right. The next voice was higher and a bit squeaky. I recognised it as Stephen Worthington, my next-door neighbour.

"He is a weirdo and I don't like him."

The audience aggressively cheered again. This man everyone was talking about was the most despised man I'd ever heard of. Who was this horrible person they spoke of?

Well, my question was answered when the next speaker took the platform. And I only had to hear one sentence for a dark cloud of foreboding to drape itself over me like a heavy black groundsheet.

"I saw him last night at the Italian burger bar."

Louisa's voice chimed a frightening tune. Inside my head alarm bells began to tremble. I felt my stomach swell with an empty ache.

"I agree with you all," Louisa continued. "Little Pitty must get rid of this strangely named twit."

That was it. I knew then. The realisation swirled in me like an uncontrollable whirlwind. *Strangely named twit.* That's me. Urgle Protap. Somehow I've turned a whole village against me. And the person who broke these gruesome tidings was Louisa. A woman that I … liked with all my heart and soul. I should have known it. Nobody has ever respected me. Why would it be any different here in Little Pitty? As my mother once said to me, "Urgle you have a stupid name and you are an ignorant, embarrassing person who everyone will make fun of for your whole life." Actually she didn't *say* it to me. She wrote it on a birthday card. Every year she wrote the same thing. My dear sweet wonderful mother had turned out to be right. I was stupid and I always would be. How I missed my mother. I thought about her death at the hands of Osmond Five and how sad I was having to have him put down because of his mad aggression that day at the lido.

So many terrible dreads that in the past flew around my head like arrows looking for a target. Well tonight, as I crouched with four

African weasels under an old window ledge, those arrows had all hit the bull's-eye simultaneously. I imagined the ghost of my mother standing by the target dressed as Robin Hood. Smiling from ear to ear and glamorously chewing a stick of rhubarb as she did so often in her later years. I remembered too my father's words to me. They were a constant source of discouragement. "Don't listen to your mother Urgle. You are a great boy. You have so much going for you. You can be whatever you want to be in life. Remember, Death isn't a rehearsal, it's a play." What did he know? My mother was right. Oh how I missed the way she used to cook dumplings and criticise my trousers.

As my mind raced underneath that open window I looked down at the Osmonds. Osmond Three had his paw over his eyes. Osmond Two was trying to circle my leg. Osmond One and Osmond Four were asleep.

Louisa's voice jolted me back to life.

"And that's not all," she said in a firm tone leading up to what was obviously going to be the high point in her speech. The hall went silent as though suddenly emptied of people. Forty-seven bottoms shuffled to the edge of their seats. I braced myself for the next gut-wrenching punch.

"I saw him steal a torch from the Little Pitty Torch Museum."

The audience gasped as one. It was a good job they did because I gasped with them, only louder. Osmonds One and Four woke up with a start and ran into the wall. Louisa must have seen the torch I was holding when we met on my birthday by the burger bar. It was *my* torch. I hadn't stolen it. But with so much bile for me in one group of people there was no point in protesting. I was now not just a stupidly named idiot. I was also a torch thief. Another glance down at the Osmonds saw them drenched in sweat. I had to get them back to their refrigerated hutch. I turned on my heels and headed home. But I was different now. Before tonight I was resigned to being unlikable. Now I was confirmed as being unliked. Urgle Protap lives in Little Pitty. He has a triangular garden, four African weasels, a job in a toothbrush factory, a 300 metre hydraulic arm in a vast underground bunker, every Ordnance Survey map except for the Venezuelan town of Elorza *and* he's a torch thief. I was determined to do something. The only question was what and to whom?

I slept for two days and nights.

On the third day I woke up. From the deepest of comas I had surfaced in an instant. I lay motionless in my triple bunk bed. (I'm in the middle bunk. No one sleeps above me and no one sleeps below me.) I climbed starkers down the little wooden ladder and once safely on my blue carpet I pulled on a pair of sheepskin pants. They normally tickled me and made me giggle but this morning the laughter wasn't there. I would like to say at this point that I began to ponder and muse at length on what course of action I should take. That I paced back and forth deliberating for hours, before coming up with a way ahead. However, the truth was different. From the second I opened my eyes and greeted the new day I was already sure of what to do. Come to think of it, maybe that's what woke me. The plan was coming together in my subconscious and once fully formed it was as though I had been activated to make it real.

A dead uncle of mine once said 'meet force with force'. This would be my mantra for the day ahead. I say the day because that is all it would take. Twenty-four hours hence Urgle Protap would have set the record straight once and for all.

This is what I planned. I would decimate the town of Little Pitty with a nuclear device made from the plutonium of toothbrush bristles. You see, reader? Maybe my job isn't so laughable after all. There *is* a point to it. Now I know this is a very selfish plan and yes, I'm aware it's illegal and tantamount to terrorism, but I was a desperate man and who am I accountable to? Who have I got to behave correctly for? Reader I'm speaking to you. I see you have no answer. Well, I'll tell you. I am only answerable to the Osmonds. If I look after them my duty is fulfilled. And besides, the resulting nuclear winter will mean that they are no longer restricted to the refrigerated hutch. They can run free.

Most people feel they owe a decent life to themselves, their family and their friends. Well, the Osmonds are my family and friends and as my wonderful mother often said to me, "Don't respect yourself, Urgle. You are an idiot with a triangular lawn." She was right. My father was wrong. That's why I threw him into a hole on his 50th birthday and fed him goat's cheese and cardboard until his ears fell off. The Osmonds are my one concern and I feared what would happen to them if I was driven out of town by an angry mob of torch thief haters.

Before continuing I feel the need to reassure you. I am no murderer. While I was now committed to turning little Pitty into a freezing weasel haven, I was also determined to make the current residents leave. Out of harm's way, away from danger, beyond the blast zone. This is where providence, if it had let me down before, came up trumps beyond my wildest dreams.

When I was twelve years old I found an ants' nest under a rock. Upon lifting the rock the ants ran around each other in blind panic. Returning to the same nest an hour later I saw it was totally deserted. I took this as my inspiration. If I could metaphorically lift the roof off Little Pitty, everyone should flee.

Now as I said earlier, hydraulics is my passion, or more specifically the 300 metre arm in my underground football stadium is my passion. That unseen miracle of technology which had been half built for so many years was now totally built. It was, as they say, finished and functional. Surely this was the moment it had been built for. Yes it was time to test this monstrous mechanical arm that gleamed at me from inside my candlelit bunker. It was time for this severed limb off a robot King Kong to flex his muscles. To herald a triumph over the chattering Little Pittiers. The gang that couldn't exist without consuming the blood of the loner through the drip of gossip and prejudice. Yes alright, I'll tell you what I did. You've come this far with me. I will tell you. I am Hitler! I am Stalin! I am your pillow! I am the local man you never speak to! You know, the one who sits on a bench on the high street and does absolutely nothing for hours and hours! That's me! You never make eye contact with me but I see you! When you walk away I study your back! I see your back! Aarrgh! I see you! I'm unimportant! Do you hear me? I'm behind you! I'm your floor! Hey look out! I'm your shoes!

Sorry about that.

The town of Little Pitty is similar to San Francisco in one way. It sits on a giant tectonic plate. The right-hand edge of this plate, I worked out from my Ordnance Survey map collection, sits directly above my underground football stadium. Are you catching on? It's directly above the hydraulic arm of justice. Everything was going my way. This was meant to be. The town of Little Pitty is like a trophy and it's about to be held aloft in victory. Tipped up in the air like one end of an ants' nest.

Once in position next to the control panel my hand didn't bother to hover hesitantly over the button like it would if this was a Hollywood film. There was no point in being overdramatic or showy because I was alone.

I stood over the gold button and thumped my clenched fist on it. The hydraulic arm, all 300 metres of it, began to rise in total well-oiled silence. Moving with it, like its own ghost, was an enormous black shadow slowly scaling the steep grey walls of the bunker. I was petrified and I was elated. Two tears trickled down my face. One from each eye. (The left one was slightly in the lead.) Still the arm continued its gradual salute. Nothing I had ever seen looked as unstoppably strong. It was the arm of God and I, its creator, was humbled in its presence.

Perfectly balanced and with the smoothness of a dolphin swimming upwards from the depths it reached its first destination; the ceiling. Without a fuss it calmly clamped into place like a royal butler placing his hands beneath a silver tray. Then after the smallest of pauses it ripped upwards.

Immediately the silence was shattered by the roar of devastation. The roots of a thousand trees were torn apart in the same second. The arm did not even shudder. Onwards it continued like a giant talon shredding mere tissue paper. Above me, as showers of mud and rock fell around my slippers, the right-hand edge of Little Pitty was lifting off. It was like witnessing the sinking of ten Titanics. Daylight poured in through the widening gap. Blue sky and bright sunlight seemed to shout with celebration at this astonishing sight.

Then I heard the cries of panic. Forty-seven different voices attached to forty-seven different bodies that were probably running in forty-seven different directions. My plan was coming to a gorgeous fruition. There was no mistaking it. The ants were fleeing.

After two minutes of mayhem, during which I breathed twice, it was all over. The arm had completed its ascent.

I now found myself standing in broad daylight at one end of my deserted football stadium. At the other end the mighty arm hailed me. I stared at the corpse in its grasp. A towering cliff face of mud and rock. Little Pitty was suspended in a vertical position. A dead pheasant strung up. I watched unable to move as earth, stones and whole trees continued to fall away in large chunks like suicides jumping from a clay skyscraper.

After cautiously pressing the button for a second time my hydraulic Frankenstein obediently began to reverse slowly to its starting place. Gradually it lowered the now empty Little Pitty, the land groaning under its awesome grip like a dying whale being laid on the ocean bed by the thing that killed it. Then I felt my face breaking into half a smile. Was it my imagination or was the arm being deliberately gentle with its fallen prey? The battle was over. It was no contest but there were no hard feelings. The dark curtain closed and the last strip of blue sky disappeared.

I detonated my toothbrush bristle nuclear device on the ground where the town hall used to be. All remaining vegetation was consumed in half a second. The blast that pulsated out from the epicentre in the following second flattened everything else.

In life it's a lot easier to be destructive than constructive and so I suppose I took the easy route. I sense that is what you are thinking. Well, maybe I did but I doubt it. Hydraulics is not an easy science. Hiring two thousand workers and training them to work in total darkness is not simple. Plate tectonics is not a piece of cake and extracting plutonium from toothbrush bristles is tortuous beyond belief. Yes, I take the point that punching a stranger in the face is an easy way to make him unhappy and making him happy is a much subtler art. Frankly though, I don't care about strangers. I care about the Osmonds and preserving the memory of my beloved mother.

Today I opened some post that I should have opened last week. Osmond Three had obviously intercepted the postman before I could get it. He often does that, the cheeky fellow.

It was an invitation to a meeting at the town hall to discuss the behaviour of Macwhip Scramblepot, my other next door neighbour. So the 'strangely named twit', that Louisa spoke of, wasn't me after all. Scramblepot works at the Italian burger bar. He was the torch thief. It's funny how things turn out, isn't it?

I'm just looking out of the window now at where my triangular garden used to be. Outside a nuclear winter rages and the Osmonds are merrily playing in the snow and the ash. Hopefully today will be the day I get the map of Elorza.

One of the most familiar faces in British comedy, Stephen has been a regular guest on TV: Whose Line Is It Anyway? *radio:* Just a Minute; *and stage: the* Comedy Store Players. *He started as one half of The Oblivion Boys appearing in a famed series of lager ads and regularly appearing in* The Young Ones, Blackadder, Mr Bean, Saturday Live, Friday Night Live *and in his own TV police series* Lazarus and Dingwall. *Ever-versatile, he toured with Eddie Izzard in* One Word Impro, *had a nine-week West End run at The Albery Theatre and even appeared in the BBC production of* Vanity Fair.

stephen frost

hippy trippy

"Have you got a corkscrew?" Queuing up for food on a film set. Booze not usually served. A wagon up a side street in Bristol. I'm dressed in a heavy blue wool suit and black brogues. My own. I'm knackered and bored. Shooting a film for a bloke I met in a pub who said I'd be perfect for the part. No money; bring your own cozzie.

"You get a Hoover put on your knob in a posh hotel," he'd said to encourage me.

"I'll do it!"

Food on a film set is like gold dust – if you're not getting paid then food is the next best thing. Take whatever you can get. Booze is usually forbidden for obvious reasons, but these two girls behind the mobile counter were different. Wild look in their eyes. All I wanted was shepherd's pie and peas. They were trying to open a bottle of rather good wine. Now, I'm not a smart dresser but for the part I was 'playing' in the 'film' I had to be well dressed. So my hair was short and shiny. Suit smart but big, bought off a builder in Greenwich who did my kitchen 'cos he knew an Irish bloke who had just died and he was the same size as me. He was right – it was a perfect fit. In my pocket was a Swiss Army knife. Why? Because I always carry one. I've got three. Had them for years. But this was the first time I'd been called upon to use one. The two pairs of eyes look up. These eyes are deep. These eyes have seen things. They are not bored eyes. They are eyes of interest, of character, of fun. Long hair, steaming pots. They don't look like they belong where they are right now.

"Come round the back," one tells me.

"I'll have the fish, no potatoes please," says the man queuing up behind me. A small actor dressed as a bell hop. Too late. They've gone. I follow them. Round the back.

"Would you like a glass of wine?" one asks me.

A glass! It's always paper cups.

"Yeah. I'll do that." Corkscrew in.

"Where's my fish?" cries the bellhop.

Plop! Cork out. Here we go, cheers! "This is nice."

"Do you want some food?"

"Yeah."

"Here you go, this is our stuff."

"*Fish please!*" comes the voice from back round the front.

The journey begins.

Out back, squatting peeling potatoes, wearing nothing but a pair of green shiny shorts and a black trilby is ....

"Bernie!"

"What?"

Splosh! Peeler and potato drop in the bucket.

"Yeah! Hey, geezer." Wet potato handshake.

"I'll have the fish please!" Sounds like Buttons is starting to get desperate.

"Someone give him his fish! ... More wine, Steve?"

"*Stephen,*" I say. "How do you know my name? Yes please."

"Seen you around Bristol, geezer," explains Bernie. It doesn't answer my question, but I accept it.

"*I just want some fish! We start filming in five minutes!*" He's hopping mad now.

I'm an actor. I feel sorry for him, I know what he's going through.

"I'll give him some fish," I say, standing and launching myself into the back of the chuck wagon. My head pops back out: "Which one's the fish?"

"The white stuff!" comes back at me in unison accompanied by a giggle.

Right, here I am. Blue suit, six foot six, slicked back hair, standing behind the steaming food counter, spoon erect.

"Now, who wants the fish?"

A tired voice replies, "Me."

Splosh! Biggest portion he's ever had. He's happy. I'm an actor, I understand. Back round the back: "I've got to go. Nice to meet you."

"What about your corkscrew?"

"Keep it, I've got three of them. Cheers."

"What are you doing tonight? Meet up for some more wine?"

"I'm driving home tonight; this is my last day on set."

"Pop into our cottage," she says. I smile, hands outstretched. "First exit off the motorway out of town. You can't miss it. There's a row of them next to a farm on a hill."

"OK. See you there later," I say.

OK. See you there later? With directions like those?

But I did.

After the final scene of the day, I left straight away, still in costume. Big blue suit, black leather shoes and still wearing my slowly smudging make-up. Big red Volvo zooming towards London. First exit appears. I turn off and drive and drive and drive. Why? I'll tell you. Three days working on a film for no money, which is going straight to video, then straight to the bargain bin basement bucket thing. These people had more oomph, more *whatever* in meeting them for two minutes than the script, actors, director, all put together. I'm going. And there it is! In the pitch black, night stars shining. A row of cottages on a hill, next to a farm. I pull up. Put on my battered old Barbour, unwaxed since it was bought. Bought for standing around on cold, wet draughty film locations in the middle of nowhere.

The gravel crunches outrageously loud under my leather shoes. I feel like a gentleman farmer going to collect the rent off the workers. Which cottage? Easy. The one with all the lights on and some groovy sounds pouring out on the light beams. Knock knock. Nervous. Why? I'm a grown up. If it's not them I've made a mistake, so what? Knock knock. Door opens immediately.

"Geezer! I knew you would come." Turns back into the hallway. "I told you he would come. The geezer's here." Trust, trust, trust, trust. The potato peeler is wearing a trilby. "Come in, come in."

I walk in. Big grin on my face. I'm happy. I'm comfortable. I feel safe. Small cottage, front room, smiling faces.

"Come in, come in."

More people there than I thought.

"This is Steve."

"*Stephen*."

"He was working on the film."

"Hello. Come in, come in. Wine and cider?"

"Yes please." I had brought nothing; about to explain.

Big, broad guy wearing a trilby comes out of an adjoining room, bearded, moustache: "The kids are asleep. Hello, nice to meet you."

"This is Roughy," says another bloke wearing another trilby: "He used to play drums with us."

"That's Seggs," says Roughy, nodding his trilby towards Seggs' trilby.

"This is Sue, this is George, this is Vickie." George, big smile. Sue I'd met at the catering wagon. Vickie, short, short blonde hair, short tartan skirt.

"Sit down, we're going out tonight. Do you want to come?"

"Going out? It's midnight in the middle of nowhere!"

"No Steve, we're ..." Vickie stops, looks at me very seriously, but still smiling. "... We're *going out*! Who's gonna drive?"

I don't know where I am, who I'm with, where they are going or what they are going to do, so I don't think I should offer my driving services. "So where are we going?" Coats being put on, bottles in pockets, bags over shoulders, Vickie whispering to people going round the room handing something out.

"Are you going?"

"Yeah."

"Here you go then." Into the palm of the hand. To Seggs, "Do you want to go?"

"Not tonight thanks," he whispers back, but still gets up and puts his coat on. He's not going but he is going. Nothing slipped into the palm.

Vickie smiles again. "You're gonna go, aren't you, Steve?" her arm outstretched towards me, fist closed, palm down.

"*Stephen*," I say shyly. I position my hand under hers and ask. "Where are we going?"

Seggs brushes past, "Couldn't carry one of these could ya?" He hands me a bottle of wine, I take hold of it; he doesn't let go. I'm holding a bottle of wine in one hand and my other is outstretched under Vickie's. Seggs continues all in one breath: "It's Llamastide, so we've got to go to where the first rays of the sun hit the hill. Set light to a corn wheel, roll it down the hill and make wishes for the future."

"I'm going."

Seggs releases the bottle, Vickie unclenches her fist, something soft falls into my hand.

A voice from the hallway "Come on, let's go. We'll take Seggs' car and George's ... Sue, Bernie, come on!" Hang on, there's more names than people here or is it the other way around?

Out in the cold, cold courtyard, crystal clear sky and bodies disappearing into cars.

"I'm just going to get a hat from me car," I shout at no one in particular.

Open the door of my big red Volvo and sit behind the wheel. Pull on a big black woollen hat and catch myself in the rear view mirror. Big orange made-up face, black hat, suit, shirt and black tie, big grin. This is great, I don't know these people but they've taken me on. What was that? Something fell out of my hand, onto the floor of my car or onto the dark gravel. I try and look for it, but I don't know what I'm looking for. Leave it, shove the bottle of wine in the poacher's pocket of my jacket and join the others. Crunch, crunch, crunch across the gravel, get into the passenger seat of a white, beat-up old car next to Seggs. Right, here we go. Tape on – old Ska stuff.

"We're going to see if we can find old Arthur first, Steve."

"*Stephen*. Oh yeah, where does he live?"

"Up Glastonbury Tor."

"Oh. People live up there?"

Bernie and Sue in the back, canoodling. "King Arthur, ruler of Avalon, he might be about tonight," laughs Bernie.

I stare straight ahead.

"OK."

Driving through the night, twisting down country lanes, Bernie and Sue singing in the back; she's got a great voice. Me and Seggs talking about music, punk mostly. He tells me about a single he had out once and it turns out I've got it. "Never made a penny out of it," he grins. I give him three quid: it's all I've got.

"What's this for?"

"I bought it. I played it. You have it."

"Cheers. Do you like plums?"

"Yes, I do actually."

What a pleasant conversation I'm having at one o'clock in the morning, travelling to I don't know where with three people I hardly know.

Marvellous.

"Where are they, Bernie?" Now, I'm expecting a brown paper bag to be produced from somewhere and told to help myself. Bernie, arm around Sue, leans forward poking his head between mine and Seggs' shoulders and points at the road ahead.

"Down here, down here, down here, left, down here … Bingo!" We pull up in a cul-de-sac of what looks like council houses. In front of us a big tree caught in the headlights, laden with big ripe plums. Hand brake on.

"Help yourself," smiles Seggs.

Everyone gets out, pulls the fruit off the trees and stuffs them in their mouths. They are gorgeous. A lot of pip-spitting going on. Me being slightly concerned. "Won't they mind?" – Spit – "They never pick them" – Spit – "Yeah, but they're not ours" – Slurp – They look at me, plum juice dripping from their mouths – Spit – "Yes they are!" They all spit in unison. Of course they are. They're right. Everything is ours. More plums. Then off in the motorcade of two.

We hit a track where loads of other vehicles are parked and, as I get out, I bump into a bloke with long blond hair and a combat jacket. "Sorry."

"That's alright, that's why the army use them."

"Eh?"

"It's a good night tonight," he says in all seriousness.

"Go through there," he points to a hole in the hedge.

"Is Arthur about?" hisses Bernie in a stage whisper.

"No not tonight," and off he walks down the hill.

We pile through the gap. Halfway up the hill, we stop and sit on what can only be described as a park bench. I open the first bottle of wine with my second Swiss Army knife. We all stare at the fantastic night sky.

Vickie sighs and says, "Look at the size of that star. It's massive. It's either very close or very big and a long way away."

I take a swig of wine. "Actually, it's not a star. It's a planet." I feel like a schoolteacher, I'm certainly dressed like one.

"Really?"

They all gather round.

"Yeah, it's reflecting the light of the sun not producing light by itself, not sparkling like the stars are. It's either Venus or Saturn or Jupiter – I'm not sure. If you look closely, you can see it's got a crescent shape, like the moon."

Silence.

I had them with the planet bit but lost them very quickly with the loose astronomy stuff.

OOOOOOH, OOOOOOOH!

A low moan comes from the top of the tor, sounds like a cow stuck in mud.

"Lets go."

After a few minutes, we reach the top of the tor. Underneath its arches a young girl, dressed in a long white see-through cotton gown, dances to the sound of a didgeridoo, played by a bloke sitting on the floor. Jokingly I say "Is Arthur here?" She stops; he stops.

"No," they reply together.

We look at each other.

"Right" says Seggs.

"Off to the hill. Thanks."

The music starts up; she starts dancing.

"Goodnight."

We slide very quickly back down the hill and back into the cars.

"Who's going to drive now?" asks Seggs.

Bernie pops up from the back now wearing a red headband and rose-tinted sunglasses. "Me," he says with a big roar of laughter. "I'm a really good trippy driver. Ha ha ha ha!"

Now I know what I dropped in the farmyard.

"What about traffic lights?" I joke with a lump in my throat.

"They're great. Ha ha ha ha ha!"

"It's all right, I'll drive," says Seggs. "I'm not tripping tonight."

Thank fuck for that.

Dark lanes, more ska music, lots of laughing, zoom. We stop. Seggs stares out of my passenger window. "Yeah, this is it, come on." I get out and, strangely, he follows me out of my door climbing over the gear stick and hand break. "Yeah, this is it."

Vickie opens the boot of George's car. "We're here. Moon cake?" She opens a tea cloth full of what look like scones. I'm starving.

"Yes please." I take two and eat them immediately.

"Whoa!" says George "You're brave, Steve."

"Eh? It's *Stephen*. Why?"

He just laughs and walks away.

Seggs is off; he's dead keen: "Come on this way."

We all stumble, single file, down a narrow, muddy, bumpy, unlit track, through the middle of what looks like large bunches of broccoli, but I know are trees. Seggs lurching down the path clutching an acoustic guitar. "There's a pub up there but we'll come back and torch it later."

"Why?"

"They refused to serve me five years ago."

He didn't realise I was thinking out aloud about the guitar, not asking why he wanted to burn down a country pub and, anyway, the severity of his answer was outweighed by my growing concern at having to keep my balance on the back of this huge silver, slippery serpent which the track had recently transformed into. I stopped, looked up. Broccoli. I looked down. Snake. I looked ahead. "Why the guitar?"

"You never know. You never know."

"Of course."

You take *two* moon cakes into the forest? Always check the ingredients. We're walking upwards now, dodging low branches, but keeping up a fair pace. It's more like an army route march than a pagan ritual promenade and I'm dressed for neither. After a good hour of wheezing and paranoia, I hear a beautiful cliché from behind me. It's Sue: "I've twisted my ankle, you go on without me." The sky is beginning to lighten. We all stop, look at each other and then slump in a circle around Sue, who is lying in a foetal position in a small muddy alcove awash with tree roots on the side of the hill. I pass the wine around, Bernie rolls a number and Seggs sings one. On his guitar. *Love Train* by the OJs. Sue smiles and opens a small locket, takes out a white pill and swallows it with a gulp of wine. Bernie and Seggs are singing in harmony now. I notice George fiddling with an old cinecamera.

"What's that for? Does it work?"

"Yeah, I need it to film the clouds."

"Of course."

The song has finished, Sue is smiling and it's getting lighter by the minute. We break through the trees, which now look like trees, into a steep clearing. Everyone dashes to the summit as best they can and sits facing the ever-lightening eastern horizon. My black brogues are covered in mud and my hands and face are covered in bramble scratches. Bernie takes a battered corn circle out of a plastic bag, squirts some lighter fuel on to it. I don't know where we are but we are very high up and from behind the hills in the distance here comes the sun and its rays. The corn wheel is lit – *whoosh!* – and is rolled down the hill. It makes it about half way down and then falls on to one side. The sun gets higher and warmer. George starts filming the clouds, which I must say are magnificent this morn.

"Did you make a wish?" whispers Vickie. I turn my head and smile and nod. I didn't make a wish. I didn't need to. What a view! The sun was revealing where we had just trekked for the past couple of hours or so. It was a giant bowl shape, filled with trees … and we had been down it, around it and up it. I stand up and stretch my arms out.

"Hey!" I shout. "We've licked the bowl!"

Seggs nods in agreement. "Yes, yes, we did and now we've got to go back."

I drop my arms and the elation turns into aching limbs. I know now what I should have wished for. Without the aid of moon cakes, this is going to be a bit of a trek. I notice further along the top of the hill we are on is a bench. Obviously put there so you can sit and take in this view properly. As the others start to walk back down, I head toward the bench for one last sit and look. As I get nearer, I notice that behind the bench is a sort of flat area, a sort of flat carpark area, with two cars parked in it. Our cars.

"Hey!" I call after the others. "We're here! We're here already!" and start laughing quite hysterically. I'm joined by the others, who are now all pointing at the cars and laughing. Beyond the cars, I recognise the giant broccoli we disappeared into hours earlier. "We got out of the cars the wrong side! We went that way when we should have come this way," I laughed at the others.

"I thought it took longer than it should have," says Seggs. "Come on – breakfast."

I sit next to Seggs in the car, shaking my head: "The wrong side, the wrong side."

Lovely people but no sense of direction.

"Well, at least we get something hot to eat quicker," he says with a big grin on his face.

"Look," I say, "I've got to get back to my car ... go home."

"You can if you want but after brekkie we're gonna find a pub that's open and then have a look at Acker Bilk's viaduct. It's that way I think. Are you coming Steve?"

"*Stephen*."

I didn't get home for three days.

Marvellous.

Perrier Award-nominated back in 1998, Ed's performance career in the UK and Ireland includes, in just the last few years, two sitcoms – Sam's Game *(ITV) and* The Cassidys *(RTÉ), feature film* RAT *with Pete Postlethwaite and Imelda Staunton and radio comedy play* The Pig's Back. *He's also performed at comedy festivals all over the world from Kilkenny to Melbourne and hosted a series from the Montreal* Just for Laughs *festival called, imaginatively enough,* Ed Byrne's Just for Laughs. *In the US, he has made an incredible five appearances on NBC's* Late Night with Conan O'Brien. *Ed recently spent far too much on one of Prince's old guitars that was custom-made for his* Purple Rain *tour.*

ed byrne

what i don't tell journalists

I've often been asked what my most embarrassing moment has been. It's one of those questions journalists from local papers like to ask when they interview you. It's not the most common question they ask comedians. The most common questions are, in this order: *What made you want to be a comedian? Where do you get your material from?* and *What was your worst gig?* Strangely enough your best gig is something they're not particularly interested in. When they ask me for my most embarrassing moment I normally tell them about the time I bought a girl a bunch of flowers without realising they were fake. It was only after I suggested she put them in water for the third time that she realised I wasn't joking and informed me as tactfully as she could that they were plastic. Boy, was my face red! It's not really the most embarrassing moment I've ever had but it's a short enough anecdote and seems to do the job. My most embarrassing moment is too long to go into in any detail in an interview that's supposed to last just a few minutes; however, it's the perfect length for my contribution to this book, so here goes …

Some time ago I was in the early stages of a relationship with a young woman. It was around that point, a few months in, when the giddy feelings of infatuation start to subside, replaced by something deeper and the heady whirlwind romance starts to develop into something more serious and all the fun starts to leech out of the situation. It's proof that God has a sense of humour, that falling in love is more fun than being in love.

We'd reached that stage where a deeper commitment was required and all the standard relationship protocols were coming into play. A drawer was set aside in my flat. A second lot of contact lens accoutrements were purchased to take up residence in my bathroom. Things that were once referred to as 'mine' were not yet being referred to as 'ours' but were passing through the transitionary phase by being referred to as 'the'. Not *my* leather jacket any more, not yet *our* leather jacket, merely *the* leather jacket.

But, with things getting a little more serious, there were fringe benefits. We no longer had to pretend to like stuff we hated just to impress or please the other person. I was able to come clean about not having seen all the plays and art house movies I claimed to be so au fait with. She, in turn, could finally admit she didn't really like heavy rock music at all. Our separate lies, having served their single purpose could now be revealed.

We had also reached that stage where it was accepted and understood that we were monogamous now. To be honest, I'm not sure exactly when that occurred, I only hope it didn't occur before I realised it had. Monogamy, of course, is the keystone of commitment. You can be as supportive of a person's career as you like, as caring about someone's problems as you want and as attentive to their needs as is humanly possible but if you're fucking somebody else none of the above is worth a damn. It's something that people can have great difficulty with, but if you're a man there is one upside. No condoms.

Yes. We had reached the point where membrane contraception was no longer going to be necessary. My girlfriend (I think I had started calling her that by now) was already on the pill so the rubber balloons we'd been using were purely our way of protecting ourselves from each other and each other from ourselves. My girl-friend's selfless hormonal pollution of her own body for the sake of our sex life coupled with the new period of fidelity and faithfulness we were embarking upon meant I didn't have to worry myself with keeping a stock of frangers by the bed and the strife of maintaining an erection made precarious by alcohol whilst performing the whole unwrapping and unrolling palaver was now behind me. There was only one thing standing in my way, one task that had to be performed before we could enter this new world of sexual spontaneity and slightly more premature ejaculations. We both had to be 'tested'. This was the nervous Nineties, after all and, in fairness I did have a chequered sexual past so it was off to my local clinic to get the all clear. A simple blood test, a few days wait, no sweat, or so I thought.

The way I see it, AIDS is a disease that can be detected in the blood and, therefore, you should be able to go to the haematology department of your local hospital to get your blood tested, simple as that. There are other ways to contract HIV than simply having sex. There's drug use, blood transfusion or you can be assaulted by one of these needle wielding muggers that apparently exist outside the realm of urban legend. But the health service still deems it a sexually transmitted disease so in order to be tested for it, you have to go to the nearest clap clinic. I've been tested for AIDS since, for insurance purposes. It's a piece of piss. They can detect it in your saliva instantly, in the comfort of your own home. It's a truly bizarre experience, sitting at your own kitchen table with a wad of cotton wool in your mouth, about to find out if you have a terminal illness or not. But on this occasion, because there wasn't a big insurance company paying for the procedure I had to drag myself off to my local hospital and, once inside, find 'the clinic'.

Now here's the problem. I embarrass easily. That may seem strange for someone who gets on stage and talks openly about being shit in bed, crap at fighting and having a small cock, but it's true. Like many comics I developed my humour to cover up insecurities and deflect embarrassment. All somebody has to say to me is, "Is your face going red?" and my head will instantly heat the room. I'm not so bad with friends but strangers, one-on-one, are a problem for me. Also, as a man, I don't like to ask directions. I don't know why we're like that, but we are. We feel it threatens our masculinity if we show that we don't know where something is or where we are. If a married couple pull up next to me and the man says, "Sorry, mate. How do we get back onto the North Circular from here?" I know he'd rather be saying, "S'cuse me. Would you mind fucking my wife for me? I'm shit at it." Men are supposed to know where things are and if they don't know where things are they're supposed to be able to find them anyway. The only exception to this is in their own homes. Then it is acceptable for a man to be clueless regarding the whereabouts of anything from his slippers to his children. I think the thinking behind this goes something like: *I've been out all day, knowing where everything is. Now I'm home I don't even have to know where the replacement toilet rolls are.*

I'm not a very manly man but there are some traits I have which are decidedly masculine. One is my ability to fart loudly, another is my aversion to asking directions. I'd gladly swap the two of these useless masculine traits for just one useful masculine trait like being good with tools but, alas, this is how I am. So, dig if you will the picture: I'm wandering round a hospital in Tooting trying desperately to find a sexual health clinic that appears to have been hidden deliberately and I don't want to ask anybody how to get there for fear they may think me foolish for not being able to find it and disgusting and sinful for needing to find it in the first place.

What struck me at this stage was just how difficult the sexual health clinic was to find. There was no sign of it anywhere, and I literally mean *no sign*. There were signs pointing out everything else.

There was even a sign for the staff canteen. Why? Surely anyone who needs to know where the staff canteen is knows by now. In retrospect, maybe I should have gone to the staff canteen and then, by listening in on their conversations, found somebody who worked in the clap clinic and followed them back to work. The best ideas always come too late.

Amazing. Signs for everything but the sexual health clinic. It was as if even the hospital was embarrassed about it, and you'd expect a hospital to be a bit more mature about things like that.

I wandered and wandered, not as lonely as a cloud but just as eager to wet the floor, for what felt like an age before finally deciding I'd had enough. "Pull yourself together, you pathetic arsehole," I said to myself. Actually I just thought it to myself. If I'd actually said it out loud to myself that would have been just as embarrassing as the scene I'd been trying to avoid. No, what I mean is I finally decided that I was being silly and there was no reason not to ask somebody the way to the clinic. I figured, what does it matter what these people think of me, I'll never see them again. Anyway, they're medical folk. It doesn't even occur to them to get embarrassed about this sort of thing. I can ask somebody easily. No problem. Here I go. I'll ask the next member of staff I meet … provided it's a bloke. I'm not asking a girl.

No sooner had I made this resolve, a doctor of the male variety came pacing round the corner. He was slim, quite good-looking I suppose, slightly taller than me, slightly older and though you wouldn't exactly describe him as dashing he was at least quite brisk. This looks like my man, I thought. He's a man of the world, he's educated, he's been around, looks like a bit of a lad, probably caught a thing or two off the odd student nurse when he was in medical school. No reason why I shouldn't get directions off him. Certainly no reason to be shy about where I need to be. Not with him. He was probably a filthy bastard in medical school. Most medical students are filthy bastards. He probably spent his time at college filling syringes with his own sperm and squirting people with it at parties. Dirty fucker. I'll ask him.

"S'cuse me. Can you tell me where the—"

"I'm sorry. I'm very busy, ask someone else."

"Oh yeah? I bet you weren't too busy at Uni to drink a shot glass of menstrual blood for a bet! Eh?"

I didn't say that. I didn't even think it until much later. All I said was, "Righto. Sorry to bother you." And all he probably heard was, "Right". It's bad enough being ignored by Dr Who-the-fuck-does-he-think-he-is but, to add further awkwardness, the whole exchange was noticed by an extremely attractive young nurse who was in the vicinity at the time. Even her noticing my being body-swerved by the Noah Wyle wannabee wouldn't have been so bad but the deep-seated desire in her to care for people, mixed with the lost little puppy look on my face compelled her to ask me, "Is there something I can help you with?"

"Is there something you can help me with?" I thought to myself. Then I thought:

"Oh, you could have helped me, but I couldn't possibly ask you what I need to ask you. Sure, if you were a man, or maybe if you weren't so pretty or maybe if you were much older, but not that much older because I'd be embarrassed in another way then. You're so very attractive and even though I'm going out with someone and we've reached that level of commitment that requires I go for an AIDS test I still have that male, in-built wish for you to not think ill of me and to find me as attractive as I find you but you probably like that ever-so-busy young doctor with his handsomeness and his tallness and, yes, he can be rude but, godammit, he saves lives everyday and his rude-ness strangely makes him more human which makes you like him even more, in fact you're secretly in love with him but he's so hard to get close to because he doesn't have any time for a relationship because all he cares about are his patients and it's exactly that sort of dedication which makes you love him more. God, if only he could see the real you, get to know the person behind the uniform and then you could be together and devote your life to caring for the sick and maimed as a couple and just manage to find enough time to care for each other as well. If only."

"Was there something you needed to ask?" she pressed

"I was just wondering what time visiting hours finished," I said, displaying the sort of quick thinking that has led to so many guest appearances on some of the lesser known TV panel games.

"Not for another two hours. You've plenty of time left. Who are you visiting?"

"Nobody," I said, displaying the sort of slow thinking that has kept me off *Have I Got News for You*. I then beat a hasty retreat and thought to myself, "Well, at least she thinks I'm odd which is just one step away from being interesting."

I was now thoroughly lost. Having scarpered from Florence Nightingale's bemused stare I now knew neither where I was going nor where I was coming from. I was just about to call it a day, go home and break up with my girlfriend and tell her our relationship wasn't worth the hassle when I came upon the machine that I thought could be my saviour. Sitting against a wall about halfway along the corridor was a computerised information point. My heart leapt with joy. This was the reason machines were invented. To limit human interaction. Cashpoints not only mean you can access your money 24 hours a day, they also mean you don't have to be told how little money you have by somebody half your age. Now, that's better living through technology.

Normally I hate technology. Actually, that's not fair. I love technology but it seems to have a problem with me. I'm writing this tale of woe on my girlfriend's laptop because the screen on mine is broken. The reason it broke is simple. It's the same thing that caused two Psion organisers to break and a Nakamichi DVD player to stop playing DVDs. The same thing has rendered the soundcard on my desktop unable to make a peep and caused said desktop to actually break, yes break, any Palm Pilot I try to synchronise with it. What is it that's wrong with all these machines? As I say, it's simple. They belong to me. I have never owned a gadget that didn't come complete with its own bag of gremlins thrown in free of charge like some kind of special offer.

"Mr Byrne. I could sell you a zip drive like the ones I sell to all my other customers but for you I have something a little bit special. How about a zip drive that needs to be reinstalled every time the computer is turned on? Yeah? Exciting, isn't it?"

Nothing in my house works properly. The only reason the computer I'm using now hasn't crashed is because it hasn't yet realised that I'm not my girlfriend.

Sometimes it's my fault that stuff doesn't work. I'll admit that. As much as I have bad luck with machines I also bring a certain amount of dumb luck on myself. I'm the guy who bought himself a brand-new mini dv camera, 20 hours worth of battery power and 15 hours worth of tape for a two-week trip to the Grand Canyon only to spill a bottle of Gatorade on it on the first day, effectively turning it into a lemon and lime flavoured, silver coloured brick. It's very easy to break a video camera on a rafting trip but only I would break it with a bottle of Gatorade before we even got to the river.

Murphy's Law states that anything that can go wrong will go wrong. When it comes to my interaction with the world of electronics, Murphy's Law is a pretty hard and fast rule. There is another law, however, that states that if Murphy's Law can go wrong, it will. Murphy's Law, like Sod's Law, cannot be depended upon. Where Sod's Law states that the bus you've been waiting on will come the moment you light a cigarette, you can't actually make the bus come by deliberately lighting a cigarette. Similarly you can't actually make it rain by deliberately washing your car. The way this effects me is that all of the electrical appliances in my house can be relied upon to break or malfunction whenever I want to use them but will work perfectly the moment a repair man gets within four feet of them. As soon as I get connected to a BT engineer, the crackle on the line mysteriously clears up. This is my plight. Any machine I use will calculate how best to irritate, infuriate or embarrass me by either not working properly or by working too well.

But the machine in the hospital, this was the answer to my prayers. I could ask the machine for directions. I don't care what a machine thinks of me. It probably hates me. Most machines do. Who cares? The great thing about this machine is that I don't own it so there's a good chance it'll work, at least until it twigs who's using it.

I sidled up to my new silicone-based pal and pressed the touch sensitive screen where it said 'DIRECTIONS'. The screen then asked what letter the ward I was looking for started with and displayed all 26 letters of the alphabet for me to choose from. I was tempted for a moment to touch the Z just to find out what branch of medicine begins with Z but I had more pressing matters to attend to. I selected G for Genito-urinary medicine, the latest user-friendly term for the clap clinic. It's gone through a few name changes over the years. First it was a social disease which made it sound quite friendly. Then it was VD. Personally I always liked venereal disease, from the goddess Venus. It gave it such a romantic connotation; but that was dumped and replaced with Sexually Transmitted Disease which I find rather cold and devoid of any romance whatsoever. Now it's a 'Genito-urinary infection' which leaves nothing to the imagination and manages, through its more clinical title, to somehow conjure up a more vivid mental picture of the affected area. I don't know why they kept changing its name. It's not like it's a product that has to be marketed to its public. This isn't the same as bringing us into line with the American market by turning Marathon into Snickers. You can change its name as much as you like. People hate Sellafield just as much as they hated Windscale.

Having pressed the letter G, I was given the choice of Genito-urinary medicine, Geriatric ward and Gynaecology. You know what it's like. You go into a big department store for one thing and then you end up being tempted by the bargains elsewhere in the shop. I resisted the urge to browse and hit Genito-urinary medicine and got ready to memorise the detailed map that I expected to see displayed on the screen. That was when the machine sprang into life.

Remember how I said that, with me, machines will always either fail to function or will manage to function better depending on which will cause me the most grief? Well, based on that axiom, there was no way this machine was going to function at anything less than full capacity at that precise moment. *I didn't know the fucker spoke to you!* Not just spoke to you, but bellowed in the loudest Received Pronunciation voice you've ever heard. This thing was so loud, people near me jumped. Everybody stopped what they were doing and turned to look at the ever-reddening man who thought he could avoid embarrassment by asking a machine for directions. Sounding like the BBC World Service played through The Who's stage amps, this bastard machine explained to me – and everybody else within a half mile radius – how to get to the Genito-urinary Medicine Clinic and it must have said the phrase Genito-urinary medicine at least three times in the process. Nobody was in any doubt as to where I was going now. None of the 30 or so people on the corridor could ignore what was going on. None of them. I put my face in my hands and sighed. Rubbing my eyes and reflecting on what an arsehole I now looked I heard another voice from behind me, to my left.

"You could have just asked me," she said.

I turned around and there she was. The pretty young nurse had made an encore appearance in my life for one final time just to make my humiliation complete and, with that, she was gone. That was the most embarrassing moment of my life.

It seems strange that I considered that moment so embarrassing because after being directed to the clinic by the machine I was put through a number of procedures both medical and bureaucratic that others would have found far worse. I had to answer a huge list of questions about my sexual history that most people would find far more embarrassing but I didn't really mind. It was just one man asking them so it wasn't a bother and the only shame I derived from it was that by answering the questions truthfully I kind of felt like I was bragging. I felt like I should have asked, out of politeness, what foreign countries he had had sex in. Having completed the interview they deemed me worthy of a full barrage of tests of a very intimate nature that involved scraping the inside of my cock with an implement that looked like one of those things they give you in service stations to stir coffee. As painful and humiliating as these procedures were, they were nothing compared to the sheer ground-please-swallow-me awkwardness and shame I suffered at the cruel hands of the machine. I will never forget it as long as I live. The only good thing to come out of it is I have a better story to tell if I feel like coming out with something more interesting than the time I bought fake flowers.

Incidentally, the tests were all negative which was a relief, but strangely annoying as it makes me feel I went through it all for nothing!

A stand-up, writer and actor, Owen made his TV debut on Saturday
Live *in 1986 and has since performed on numerous shows including his
own special for BBC TV. He wrote the film,* Arise and Go Now,
screened in BBC2's Screenplay *series.* Shooting to Stardom *(Channel
4), won the Irish Short Film Award at the Cork and Chicago film festivals. He is an annual visitor to the Edinburgh Festival where his one-
man plays have won awards including a Perrier nomination and the
LWT Comedy Writing Award for his one-man play* Off My Face *which
is currently being adapted for radio. His first book of poetry* Volcano
Dancing *was published in August 2003.*

owen o'neill

the basketcase

Ambrose Cassidy parked his white Ford pickup truck across the road from Sweeney's Hardware and Building Merchants and walked at a steady unhindered pace through the rain which was coming at him from all sides. This was bad-tempered, bastard angry Northern Irish rain, rain not to be messed with. Blowy rain that ambushed him, skelping him across the mouth and whipping round the backs of his legs and head. Ambrose held his face up to the battering of the liquid pins and needles. He was calm and serene, he embraced this rain, saw it as a cool shower sent from heaven to wash away the smell of death that had been hanging around him all day. Other people ran in all directions, diving into doorways, fighting with umbrellas. Ambrose saw a man struggling to make a makeshift raincoat out of a black bin-liner; all that effort to protect himself from the rain. Ambrose noticed the man's fingers were badly stained with nicotine; he had a lit cigarette in his mouth and pulled small heavy clouds of smoke into his lungs. Ambrose thought that was funny and smiled to himself.

Dell Sweeney was testing the new collection of doorbells just in from Belfast, with his big podgy, beefy sausage fingers. "That's the third friggin' Big Ben chime in a row, have they no imagination these people? Hold on, what's this? That sounds like *God Save The Queen*." He pressed the bell again. Ding dong ding dong dong

dong. "It is! Imelda!" He shouted for his wife. "These fuckers are taking the fucking piss altogether. *God Save The* fucking *Queen* on a doorbell around here. Who the fuck am I supposed to sell that to? Imelda!" Imelda appeared up from the trapdoor in the floor wearing a baseball cap, peak to the back, and holding a paint brush. Dell raised his index finger. "Listen to this. Is this *God Save The Queen* or am I going mad?" Dell pressed the bell. Ding dong ding dong dong dong. Imelda stared at him. She had a way of pursing her lips when she was both angry and puzzled. "I'm not sure, press it again." Dell pressed it again. Imelda cocked her head like a dog and hummed the first bars of *God Save The Queen* just to remind herself what it was like: "Hmm Hmm he hum da dum dee dee dee da da dum dee dee da dum Da da da…" "For fuck's sake, woman I didn't ask you to hum the whole thing just tell me if you think it's *God Save The Queen*." Imelda gave a long sigh: "Press it again." Dell slung it back in the box. "No I will not. It's clearly *God Save The Queen*, any eegit can tell that and I'm sending it back." Imelda huffed at him: "Please yourself. I think it's *Greensleeves*." "*Green*shite!" he shouted at her as her head disappeared into the hole in the floor. Dell stared at the bell in silence and for the first time became aware of the rain rattling on the roof and windows. When he looked up, he was startled to see Ambrose Cassidy standing in front of him. He hadn't noticed Ambrose come into the shop and made a mental note to get a louder hinge-bell on the front door. Ambrose could not have been wetter had he been swimming in the river. His tee-shirt and brown corduroy trousers clung to his bony frame like a wet flag around a pole, rivulets of water ran down his body and formed a pool around his saturated plimsolls. Dell stared at him: "Listen to this and tell me what you think it is." Dell pressed the bell. Ding dong ding dong dong dong. Ambrose lifted the front of his tee-shirt and rung water out of it: "It's *God Save The Queen*." "Fuckin' right it is and it's going back; who am I going to sell that to?" Dell slung the bell back into the box. Ambrose stared blankly at him and then Dell suddenly remembered who this man was and the terrible tragic circumstances that had befallen him and he became embarrassed at having asked such a frivolous question. "I'm sorry, son. I'm not thinking straight. I'm damned sure that doorbells aren't the uppermost thing in your mind at the moment. I was sorry to hear about your trouble."

"Trouble?" Ambrose lifted his tee-shirt over his head like he was celebrating scoring the winner in the Cup Final. Then dried his hair. "I'm not in any trouble, Mr Sweeney."

Dell knew he shouldn't have started this conversation. "No, no of course not. I was referring to your wife. Terrible sorry to hear about that ... it can't be easy."

"Nothing to be sorry about, Mr Sweeney. It's hardly your fault."

Dell folded and refolded some invoices on the counter and coughed politely into his fat fingers. "How is she?" Dell immediately gritted his teeth and wished he could keep his mouth shut.

"She's dying, Mr Sweeney. She has seventy-two hours and twenty-five minutes left to live. They can pinpoint death so accurately these days. Is that a step forwards or backwards, what do you think?"

At this point Dell guessed that Ambrose was probably slightly unhinged. Grief could do that to you. He remembered the time his Grandfather shot the cows after he lost all his savings on a horse. 'Paddy's Delight' fell at the second last at Cheltenham.

"I try not to think of it really," Dell said. "Just plough on you know. Get on with business. So what can I do for you?"

Ambrose stepped nearer the counter and took a deep breath. "Twelve eight foot lengths of six by two, nine four inch bolts, three kilos of six inch nails, sixteen feet of half inch wire cable, six four foot lengths of half inch metal rods. One sheet of steel, four foot square and an inch thick. Two tins of Swarfega—"

Dell suddenly raised his hand. "Wow, wow, young fellah, steady on there; let me write all this down. My God, is it the Ark you're building? We might need it if this rain keeps up eh?"

Ambrose gave Dell a searching look. "The Ark? No it's not the Ark, it's a present for Josephine, a surprise."

Dell looked away quickly and began scribbling on a pad breaking the lead on the pencil. He pulled another from his top pocket. "Righty ho, fine. Three kilos of what?"

* * *

Josephine was floating again. She didn't mind it now. She had gotten used to it. It wasn't so much an out-of-body experience as an out-of-bed experience. She spread her arms in the crucifix position and wafted towards the ceiling. It needed painting and she laughed because it wasn't important any more. The blood hummed loudly through her veins. The cancer seemed to have magnified every sound inside her body. All her gurgles and swallows and burps had become volcanic. The boom-boom of her heartbeat. Sometimes she could even hear the squelch of the marrow in her brittle bones. She thought about Ambrose driving the pickup in the rain. She loved him more than ever. Her illness and imminent death had brought them closer together. She could see inside of him. See the love he had for her which was blazing out of control. It diminished everything around them. She realised that the Universe was tiny and insignificant. This love was bigger than all of it. Larger than life. It was the most powerful thing she had ever experienced.

* * *

Dell wrapped a piece of string around the brown bag containing the six inch nails, snapped the string expertly with his porky fingers, tied a neat bow on the side and placed it on top of Ambrose's large order. "Righty ho! I'll have this lot delivered to you after lunch."

Ambrose shook his head. "No. That's no good. I've got to take this stuff with me now. I have a deadline. I'm a man of my word, Mr Sweeney."

"Of course. No bother. Is that everything?"

Ambrose thought for a moment, then reached into the box of doorbells and picked up the *God Save The Queen* doorbell. "I'll have this."

"What?" Dell gaped at him. That's the *God Save The Queen* one. Why would you want that on your door?"

Ambrose frowned. "I could do with a laugh, Mr Sweeney."

Dell nodded and let a little half smile creep across his mouth. "Oh I see. Irony. I'm not big on it myself now, but I see where you're coming from. I'll throw it in free of charge, glad to get rid of it."

Dell furrowed his brow in concentration as he totted up on his calculator and did that breathy whispering thing accompanied by little whistles. He did the same thing in church when he prayed and it always drove Imelda mad. He slapped the calculator on the counter. "Two hundred and seventy pounds nineteen pence. Let's call it two seven 0." Ambrose squinted at the numbers on the calculator. "Would it be okay if I dropped the cheque in tomorrow, Mr Sweeney? I just didn't think to take any money with me." Dell held his breath for a few seconds. "You can't give me anything at all, some kind of deposit?" Ambrose leaned in close enough to kiss Dell on the lips. "If you don't trust me, Mr Sweeney, I'll drive all the way back to the house immediately and get my cheque book. I'll be a couple of hours because I'll have to give Josephine her morphine, carry her to the toilet, feed the dog and take him for a walk. I haven't taken him out for three days, I just haven't had the time." Dell took a step back, tucked his shirt in all the way around his massive stomach and hitched up his trousers.

"No problem. Drop it in tomorrow or whenever you're passing. Bring your truck around the back and I'll help you load her up. You'll need a hand with that sheet of steel." Dell turned and walked out of the back door kicking it open as he went.

* * *

It was the one where Laurel and Hardy were trying to get the piano down the flight of steps. The outcome was inevitable, disaster wasn't far away: disaster and laughter. Laurel and Hardy had always made Josephine laugh no matter how many times she saw their films. Ollie stopped talking to Stan and looked straight at her. "Huh!" he said. "Ya think you got problems, look what I'm lumbered with." Josephine smiled, lay back on the pillow, put the oxygen mask over her face and breathed deeply. Downstairs, Ambrose was hard at work constructing his surprise for Josephine. She drifted in and out of sleep as he hammered and sawed and whistled long into the night.

* * *

The coughing fit woke her up, she tried to move and then realised she was being held, someone's arm around her back. Ambrose was speaking but he was too far away. Something cold on her forehead. She thought she must be in the sea and had swallowed some of it. Ambrose was probably teaching her to swim. She could see him above her, wavering and distorted. "You're okay, Jo, relax. I've got you." His voice was faint and muffled through the drone of deep water. Josephine's coughing subsided. Ambrose wiped the sweat from her brow with a flannel. He was grinning at her. "Wow, I thought you were going to croak then. All my hard work for nothing." He positioned the straw between her lips and she sucked at the cold pineapple juice which was delicious.

When she spoke it was a whisper, "No way. I've got hours left. Is it finished?" Ambrose pulled a splinter from the palm of his hand. "Almost, I just have to test it before I unveil it to you. You're going to love it, Jo. Just the two of us, gliding along, quiet and peaceful, no doctors or oxygen, or morphine, or pineapple juice." Josephine drooped her lip. "I like pineapple juice." Ambrose laughed. "Fine, you can have gallons of it." "It sounds wonderful, Ambrose." He stroked her forehead. "It will be. I have to go and get some big cheese; will you be okay?" She eased herself up in the bed. "Put on *Sons of the*

Desert – that'll keep me amused till you get back." Ambrose found the tape and slotted it into the VCR and before he left did his best Oliver Hardy impression. "Oh my little Jeany Weany."

* * *

Belinda Turner was very happy with the display in the window of her cheese shop. She thought the railway sleeper had been a stroke of genius on her part. She stood on the pavement admiring it and nodded contentedly. Yes, the round cheeses placed alongside the sleeper definitely looked like train wheels. She knew that the whole steam-train motif was a good idea. It was classic and traditional and homely and that's what people wanted these days. Ambrose walked past her into the shop. She recognised him straight away. Everybody in the town was talking about it, so sad, and his wife only in her late thirties. Ambrose was at the back of the store studying the big cheeses hanging on hooks from the ceiling, covered in muslin cloths like shrouds around the dead. Ambrose noted it was always the same in cheese shops, initially the smell was very powerful, overwhelming sometimes, and then after only a few minutes, it almost ceased to exist. Belinda stood behind him, her arms folded, rocking slowly on her heels and subconsciously trying out all her most sympathetic smiles.

"Anything in particular you wanted, Mr Cassidy?" Ambrose answered her without turning around. "Edam, I think. I like the red skin and the rubbery consistency. Nice." Ambrose turned and faced her and thought she had a real cheesy smile. This made him laugh out loud. Belinda was slightly taken aback by his laugh but decided to ignore it. "Yes that's a very popular choice. How much would you like?" Ambrose made a big circular motion with his hands, "I'll have all of it." "Oh my goodness, are you having a large cheese party?" "No. It's ... sort of ... going towards a present for Josephine." Belinda was relieved that it was him who had mentioned his wife's name. This handed her the opportunity to offer her condolences without seeming to pry. "I see, that's nice." She gave him her best gentle smile. "I was really sorry to hear about your wife ... It's so sad. How is she at the mo—"

Belinda never got time to finish her sentence before Ambrose cut in loudly. "Dying!" He popped a piece of Swiss Gruyere into his mouth and then checked his watch. "She has about four hours left so we better get a move on eh?" Belinda felt herself flush and was starting to feel genuinely uncomfortable. She reasoned that Ambrose's peculiar behaviour was his way of dealing with his wife's death. "If I can have your address, Mr Cassidy I'll have this delivered to you straight—" "I'll take it with me." The tone of Ambrose's interruption was weary and impatient. Belinda smiled nervously. "It's quite large, are you sure you'll be able to manage?" Ambrose sighed loudly. "I'll roll it home. It's not a problem." Belinda stared at him for a second, expecting him to start laughing again. He didn't. She walked to the back of the shop, got a small sack-barrow, eased the blade under the large roll of cheese, tipped it back and wheeled it to the front door. "You can have a lend of this sack-barrow if you like; it'll make things easier; rolling the cheese will certainly damage it." "Sack-barrow?" Ambrose raised his eyebrows. "I always thought they were called porters' trolleys, you know like they used to have in railway stations in the olden days." Ambrose picked up the roll of cheese and balanced it on his shoulder. "I'll drop by tomorrow and pay you if that's okay?" Ambrose was out of the door before she could answer. He walked for a few yards and then Belinda watched as Ambrose rolled the cheese along the pavement like it was something he did every day of his life. Then it suddenly occurred to her that he was right. After lunch she would position the sack-barrow in the shop window, put an old-fashioned suitcase on it with the lid half open showing the cheese inside. She smiled at the thought.

* * *

Ambrose saw the sparks dancing past his sunglasses as he cut through the steel in the living room. The angle grinder roared like a motorbike and the energy surged through him. He felt good, mentally, spiritually and physically. This was the last piece of work he had to do and then he would test it. He was confident that nothing could go wrong; he knew it was going to be perfect.

* * *

Josephine watched Stan Laurel light up his thumb by flicking it like a Zippo and never doubted that it was real. Then she saw herself aged twelve walk into the bedroom with her friend Lucinda Hamilton. They had a skipping rope and asked to her to sing along. Josephine nodded and began the chant: "In and out through stocky bluebells stocky bluebells stocky bluebells. In and out through stocky bluebells, I'll be your mas-ter. Rappa tappa tappa on your shoulder rappa tappa tappa on your shoulder." Ambrose entered the room – the girls ran off giggling.

He came and took her hand. "What is it?" She smiled and rubbed a bit of dirt from his cheek: "Nothing, I was just skipping." Ambrose kissed her hands. "I've tested it out and it works like a dream. I'm going to pick you up and carry you downstairs; you must promise to keep your eyes shut until I tell you to open them."

She nodded: "I promise."

Ambrose picked her up, feeling all of her fragility against his chest. It was like holding a fledgling that had fallen from the nest, his baby bird, he would teach her to fly.

Ambrose laid Josephine gently on the sofa. "No peeking." She laughed, "I'm not." Josephine could hear what sounded like a sheet flapping, something being removed. A moment passed and then Ambrose said, "Okay, you can look."

Josephine opened her eyes and, with a sharp intake of breath, clasped both hands over her mouth. "Oh my God, Ambrose! It's … it's wonderful, it's absolutely amazing. I was trying to figure out what it would be but ... I would never have guessed. Will it work, will it stay upright?" Ambrose handed her a piece of Edam cheese. "It works, believe me." They sat for a long time together on the sofa, not saying anything, just looking at it, absorbing the full meaning of it and what it meant to both of them. It was Ambrose who spoke first. "Do you think, I mean if you're feeling up to it, could we make love?" Josephine took his hands. "Yes, yes please, it'll be okay, don't worry, I'll be gentle with you."

* * *

To say that Dell Sweeney was arguing with his wife wasn't entirely true. Dell was really arguing with himself. He followed Imelda around the shop. She had a price gun in her hand and moved quickly from aisle to aisle shooting things like a mad sniper. Dell struggled to keep up with her. "I mean," he panted, "Just because his wife is dying doesn't cut any ice! I need to be paid. Undertakers don't work for nothing why the fuck should I? Two hundred and seventy pounds is a substantial amount of money. He said he was going to pay me straight away: that was nearly three days ago and I gave him that fucking *God Save The Queen* doorbell for free and this is all the thanks I get." Imelda stopped abruptly and pointed the gun at him. With her free hand she tightened the bun in her hair and skewered it expertly with a clip. "You know your trouble, Dell? You're far too trusting. If I was you I'd go and ask him for it straight away. He might be thinking of leaving the country." Even though Dell had lived with Imelda for twenty-eight years, he was still not sure when she was being sarcastic. On this occasion, he didn't care; this was the opening that he was looking for. Dell slapped his thigh. "I will! I'll go first thing in the morning!" He had been told to go and he would go. "Life goes on. People have to be paid!" After Dell stormed out of the shop Imelda picked up the phone and made an appointment with THE HEADMASTER. It was the new place on the high street. She had wanted to be blonde all her life, now she was going to do it and it made her feel reckless and invigorated.

* * *

The first ray of the late morning sun found its way through the opening in the curtains and warmed his face. Ambrose had been awake for some time. He knew that Josephine was dead because her feet were cold and she hated having cold feet. Ambrose got up, found a pair of woollen socks in her sock drawer, put them on her and straightened the hair away from her eyes.

"We don't want you getting cold feet at this stage of the game. That would never do." He slid one arm gently under her legs, the other around her back, picked her up and carried her downstairs; he noticed she was heavier than the day before. He sat her on the sofa and propped her up with cushions. "It's going to be the biggest adventure we've ever been on, Jo. You just wait and see." Josephine's eyes were open, the look on her face was calm and contented. Ambrose spent the next few minutes shuffling around, moving things about: "I haven't been this excited for ages." Ambrose finally settled himself into position and was ready.

"Okay, Jo, this is it! Bon voyage!" Ambrose raised the sharp pliers in his right hand and snipped through the wire. The steel blade of the guillotine hurtled from its moorings and sliced clean through his neck. His head dropped into the wicker basket which contained two large lumps of Edam cheese and blood spurted onto Josephine's white woollen socks. At that precise moment the tune of *God Save The Queen* echoed throughout the house.

Dell pushed his big finger into the doorbell and shuffled impatiently. "God Save The Queen – Jesus." He tried peering through the window but could only see some sort of wooden contraption that he couldn't quite make out. *I'll be back,* he thought to himself. *Can't stand people who don't pay their debts, no backbone.* Dell began to climb up the small hill away from Ambrose's cottage and, just for a fleeting moment, he thought he saw them on the river. He was sure it was them. Ambrose and his wife in a boat drinking wine. Dell ran as quickly as he could in his overweight circumstances to the stone bridge and was positive he saw them disappear around the bend in the river. "Christ!" he shouted, "some people have no shame. No shame at all."

Dominic continues to tour the UK despite the distractions of an increasingly heavy literary workload. His best-selling first novel Only in America *was published in 2002 and is currently being scripted for a feature film; his second* The Ripple Effect *was published in 2003. His Radio 4 series* The Small World of Dominic Holland *is still remembered with fondness by those who heard it and he says his worst gig was at Stringfellows nightclub.*

dominic holland

hobbs' journey

Hobbs ambled idly along London's Park Lane. It was a warm June evening and he was proudly wearing the dinner suit which had served him so well over the years and most likely was older than himself. As usual, he was excited as he made this familiar journey up the illustrious 'Lane'. Where would he be eating tonight and as whom? He didn't know yet.

Two peculiar things should be noted about Park Lane. Given that it is arguably the poshest road on Earth, it is odd then that it is in actual fact a very busy dual carriageway and, regardless of its wealth and prestigious location bisecting Hyde Park and fashionable Mayfair, Park Lane will always be most famous for occupying the number two position on the board game of Monopoly, something which must irk its residents but probably doesn't keep them from sleeping.

It is a road like no other. Poncy-named estate agents employing lots of Emmas and Sophies; car showrooms for the insecure; five-star luxury hotels; and that's about it.

Its hotels are suitably few and reassuringly expensive but in actual fact offer a 'Park Lane' gateway to the common man because, each evening and most lunchtimes, these hotels throw open their ball-room doors to the world of corporate dinners and industry award ceremonies. Coming up from Marble Arch, first up on one's left is the veritable 'daddy' of the corporate lunch, the Grosvenor House Hotel, followed by the smaller but more illustrious and choosy Dorchester, giving way to the Intercontinental and finally the Hilton standing tall and proud on Hyde Park Corner, smugly keeping watch over London's congestion.

Until the industry lunch, most people's personal association with Park Lane hotels didn't extend beyond playing the famous board game. But now every self-respecting profession or association has a 'dinner' there and, each evening, many thousands of businessmen squeeze themselves into ill-fitting hired dinner suits attending anything from the Garage Forecourt Trader Awards to the British Direct Mail Gala Evening. Ceremonies which others might scoff at; but, to those involved, these are their Oscars and respect is due. Normally, a certain Joe Schmo might just be a petrol garage owner from Cleethorpes, but tonight he's at the Dorchester Hotel and nominated in the 'best crisp display' category and if he wins, the photo of him receiving his award from some newsreader will be displayed proudly in his garage shop, one presumes by the crisps.

There's no such thing as a free lunch applies particularly well to just such occasions because, whether it's an industry jolly or a firm do, somewhere down the line, no matter how indirectly, people are paying for their fare. Not in Hobbs' case, however, because in his simple life the 'free lunch' really was free because, of all the Park Lane dinners that he'd scoffed, he hadn't been invited to any of them.

Hobbs preferred the term *tramp* to *vagrant*. He'd joined the ranks of Britain's homeless long before *Trainspotting* and *grunge* had given sleeping rough some bizarre form of cachet and he had spent the last twenty years of his life living on London's streets with only short winter bursts in hostels keeping him alive. Over the years, countless people had hurried by him anxious to avoid costly eye contact whilst asking themselves the same question: "How the hell could things have gotten so bad for this poor wretch. And there's me wanting a bigger garden on a quieter road …"

No explanation of how people descend society's social strata is ever the same and, in Hobbs' case, not even he was aware of how he had come to prop up the league table of human life. Everything had been fine, until he woke up one morning next to his cold, grey and stiffening wife and he simply hadn't ever recovered. It was probably the shock as well as his sense of loss. He'd fallen to sleep with everything and woken up with nothing. His life had changed irrevocably and, as he cuddled his dead wife with tears stinging his eyes, it was clear that most of him had died in the night as well. There had been no warnings; she'd had no aches, no pains, nothing; she just simply died and Hobbs was desolate. That morning, quite literally, his life imploded and, most sad of all, he wasn't important enough for anyone to notice. Nobody was available to grab him and stop him slipping through the net. The final warning letter from work about absenteeism arrived shortly before his final pay cheque and things spiralled downwards from there until, one day, he wandered into a hostel complaining about frost-bitten hands. That was twenty years ago and now he owned nothing more than his fading memories of his wife, oh and a dinner suit. Almost everything else was a distant blur. Whether he was deliberately blocking them out, he didn't know, but his old more successful life remained firmly locked away.

Hobbs was now what they refer to as institutionalised 'street' which means that he wasn't ever going to make it back indoors. Give him a penthouse on the Thames (with concierge and the use of a gym!) and he would inevitably gravitate back outside to the massive house without a roof. And so it was ironic that Hobbs could still conceive of and in fact relish certain luxuries that life had to offer, like for instance, black tie dinners on Park Lane.

He kept his dinner suit at the Salvation Army Head Quarters. He was well known there and much liked. Nobody bothered him about his occasional need for a shower and a blow dry. He scrubbed up pretty well. *I'm a London tramp but tonight, Matthew, I'm going to be a dashing sixty-year-old corporate professional.*

Hobbs mooched around the Dorchester's lobby.

"Can I help you, sir?" a suitably servile lady enquired.

Hobbs smiled and gestured confidently that he was fine as he moved past her towards the ballroom to establish what function would be taking place this evening. Hobbs depended on three things for his supper. First the correct attire of course, secondly an assured swagger that said he was indeed a fully paid up member of the Association of British Sausage and Saveloy Manufacturers but, most importantly of all, Hobbs relied on *No shows*. Invited guests, who for whatever reason couldn't make an appearance. *No shows* were Hobbs' ticket and the seating plans were his directions.

He wasn't very hopeful about the Dorchester this evening. The place was packed with Indians and Hobbs suspected that a wealthy young couple were about to tie the knot. Not even Hobbs felt confident about gatecrashing an Indian wedding. To start with, he wasn't dressed for it but that was the least of his concerns. Within seconds, he was back on Park Lane making his way to the good old trustworthy Grosvenor House Hotel.

On a good night, Hobbs would select his hotel based on the menus that were on offer but this evening his options were running out. The Hilton, the Intercontinental and now the Dorchester had all let him down, but he wasn't unduly concerned. It was rare indeed that he ever went home hungry and the Grosvenor was always his best bet. Hobbs called it his *banker*.

The Grosvenor could not have been designed with any more consideration for the plight of the hungry and cold gatecrasher. It is enormous, with more entrances than can ever be manned. The cavernous and aptly known Great Room can uncomfortably seat 1,500 people and has seen so many stand-up comedians die that it really should erect a monument to them. Two great big staircases fan their way down into the plush ballroom from a balcony where Hobbs could spy the empty seats of the people generous enough not to have shown up.

Tonight's occasion was the 8th Bloom Ball, a charitable foundation established by the famous financier Gerald Bloom. This was less than ideal for Hobbs because he'd an idea that he had attended the 7th Bloom Ball held here last year and, if so, then he certainly couldn't remember as whom.

"Champagne, sir?"

Hobbs thanked the waiter and replaced his empty flute on the tray and then took another. Underpaid staff flurried about with bottles of Bollinger wrapped in serviettes to keep them cool but crucially so that the brand wasn't obscured. Skimping with Cava wasn't Mr Bloom's style, which probably accounted for the alarmingly low number of spare seats as the dining room below steadily began to fill up.

"Once again, please … if you could all kindly take your seats, ladies and gentlemen please. Thank you very much," the master of ceremonies bellowed at the assembled ranks of London's elite. Hobbs peered down from his familiar position at all his options evaporating before him.

…table 38 has got two spaces left … Hobbs sighed as he noticed a man haring down the staircase with his wife hobbling angrily in tow *… table 32's full … table 8's gone. One space each at table 13 and 15 …*

Hobbs walked along the balcony so that he could see the other half of the room. He noticed another couple of latecomers running down the steps, no doubt heading for tables 13 and 15. He had to be mindful before he approached a table too early. He had to satisfy himself absolutely that the spare seat represented a *no show* rather than a *very late show*. Try explaining to someone delayed on the tube that you're them with a mouthful of their fillet steak. Hobbs shuddered at the thought.

They were halfway through their starters now and Hobbs could see that there were only two spaces free in the entire room, both on table 13 – unlucky for some, he thought. It had to be a couple who hadn't shown up and that suited him perfectly. He started to get anxious as he studied the seating plan to try and establish the names of the two *no shows,* and therefore his own identity. Female names were the first to go, followed by any overtly foreign names. Hobbs had more sense than to pretend that he was a Mr Mohamed Ibrahim Iqbuar Illamain for the whole evening.

His knobbled finger slid shakily down the list of people at table 13. The signs were good. Most of them were straight off *NO*s. Mr and Mrs Michael Foster of Micro Systems, *could be* – Mr and Mrs Chris Raith of Barclays, *could be* – Mr Saurabh Mussala, *nope* – Mr and Mrs Chris Best of Heath Group, *possible* – and … Hobbs' finger suddenly froze at the last name on the seating plan. Imperceptibly, he shook his head and actually felt unsteady on his feet. *Mr and Mrs William Hobston.* The plug deep within his mind blocking out his old self had just been jolted heavily and it was unnerving.

Hobbs quickly turned around to see if anyone was aware of him before staring back at the name again. *William Hobston.* His mind began to race. It was a name he hadn't heard for over fifty years, not since he was at school, and even then it was only his teachers who had ever called him *William.* At home, he'd been known as Billy until he was fourteen or so and since he left school, he had simply been known as *Hobbs.*

He wondered whether it wasn't a sign telling him to get the hell out of there but he knew that he couldn't. Not now; how could he? What if it was Mr William Hobston and his wife who hadn't turned up? It would mean he would have to pretend to be himself for the whole evening.

"Hello. Sorry I'm late ladies, gentlemen." Hobbs smiled broadly at table 13 but crucially didn't announce who he was. Well he couldn't yet, could he? People at the table peered at the new arrival curiously. There was something about him that wasn't quite right; peculiar, almost, but none of them knew why.

"Chris Raith – Barclays – and this is my wife, Maureen."

Hobbs shook his hand. So, he wasn't going to be Mr and Mrs Raith then.

"And you are ...?" Raith asked.

"... nice to meet you," Hobbs shut him down before stretching his hand out to a portly man who was doing his best to not stand up without appearing to be rude.

"Michael Foster – Micro Systems – and you are?"

Sorry. I've no idea yet, not until I've met this next bloke.

"Hello, Chris Best ..."

Chris Best did go on to say who he worked for but Hobbs didn't hear him because he now knew that William Hobston was indeed the *no show*. Taking his seat, he had a good feeling about the night ahead. Tonight was going to be special. He could feel it.

"I'm Bill Hobston ... sorry I'm late, bloody tubes."

Mrs Raith was aghast because her social circle didn't often bring her into contact with people who used the underground.

"The very thought of those trains makes me shudder," she began. "Being all cooped up in a tunnel with people one doesn't know." It was obvious that in her day Mrs Raith had been a very striking woman, beautiful even, but it was also equally apparent that she hadn't accepted the onset of old age with any grace at all. She couldn't have smiled if she wanted to which was appropriate somehow, because happiness was the last thing that she reminded Hobbs of.

"Who did you say you worked for?" Raith asked.

Hobbs coolly poured himself another large glass of red. If Mr Bloom had chosen the wine, then he had excellent taste.

"Erm, Hobbs & Major: we're a stone masons. We specialise in gravestones."

Hobbs watched the familiar sight of faces falling around the table. He'd learnt through bitter experience that, at these dinners, he needed a job that people wouldn't want to dwell on. And one they wouldn't be familiar with either, thereby avoiding the inane, *Oh, do you know* ... conversation. In the early days, Hobbs had gone with banking and spent the whole evening floundering.

"Do you do kitchen worktops?" another lady sitting opposite asked.

"Oh yes, we're having our kitchen done, aren't we darling," Mrs Raith added.

"Yes, dear, you are," Raith joked but his wife wasn't amused and glared at him angrily. Her plastic surgery hadn't done anything to suppress her anger expressions.

"No. We pretty much just do headstones," Hobbs answered, quite literally cutting the enquiry stone dead. "So, if any of you are planning to die, then I've got some lovely Arabian marble." No one at the table quite knew what to say, which was exactly what Hobbs had intended. He just wanted his nosh and to be left alone.

"Is your wife coming?" another gentlemen asked. It was the portly man, Mr Foster perhaps.

"No, she's dead," Hobbs answered instinctively because, after all, he was being himself. However, it was a foolish answer to give.

Until five minutes ago, this had been a typical charitable ball dinner table but Hobbs' arrival had changed all that now. Until he pitched up, everyone had been quite happy playing the subtle unofficial party game to establish the table's most successful couple. Although Hobbs felt guilty having caused such an atmosphere, it actually served him perfectly well because he now fully expected to be left alone to fill his stomach like some giant snake that only eats once a season. One man, though, had been staring at Hobbs curiously since he'd sat down. Hobbs had noticed it and it was becoming uncomfortable.

"Bill Hobston?" the man said inquisitively as if the name meant something to him. Hobbs looked worried and raised one of his bushy eyebrows at him. This was hardly being left alone.

"Not William Hobston?"

Hobbs nodded and immediately regretted it. His memory plug was being kicked at again. Perhaps his bone-idle subconscious was now assuming control. The man was clearly delighted. "I can't believe it. William bloody Hobston. I haven't seen you for ... Does the name Chris Best mean anything to you?"

Hobbs was now panicking.

"Veg-e-tables sir?" a waiter asked him.

"Er yes please. Everything." *And make it quick please.*

"Chris Best." The man was now pointing to his chest as if that might help Hobbs remember him.

"Erm ..."

"We were at school together."

Were we? Hobbs could hardly remember even going to school. He lobbed another lump of beef into his mouth and swallowed whole. There was no time for chewing.

"Cardinal Vaughan. We were both at Cardinal Vaughan."

Hobbs had no idea what his school was called but now, though, the name Cardinal Vaughan did ring some faint and very distant bell with him and probably accounted for Hobbs' hesitant nod of the head. Chris laughed raucously.

"I knew it was you. How the devil have you been?"

"Oh, you know..." Hobbs fumbled. He still didn't know whether he was the Bill Hobston whom this bloke had gone to school with, but the bell in his head was definitely getting louder and, at the moment, Hobbs was slightly more intrigued than he was scared.

"Are you old school friends?" someone enquired incredulously.

"Yes, I can't believe it. I haven't seen Bill since he left school –

and Bill here didn't leave in the way that we all left school, did you Bill?" Chris smiled ruefully. Hobbs looked puzzled and was aware that everyone was waiting for an explanation about how he came to leave school.

"Er, yes that's right ..." Hobbs faltered blindly, hoping people might let it go but it didn't look as if anyone would, not least Chris himself who was still smiling broadly. Hobbs was now really panicking.

"... erm, my family moved away ... abroad," Hobbs offered noticing the smile on Chris' face growing even bigger.

"Oh really, where?" Raith asked.

"I'm sorry." Hobbs stalled.

"Where did you emigrate to?" Raith repeated.

. Hobbs now felt very vulnerable. "Er ... France." Chris was now shaking his head and chuckling to himself. Hobbs glanced over to the staircase and considered just making a run for it. A toilet break from which he would never return.

"We've got a place in France," Raith announced and suddenly the table's wealth and happiness game was back on and he clearly wanted to win.

"Where? The south?" Foster asked, taking up the challenge.

"Yes, St Tropez," Raith answered proudly.

"We looked at France didn't we darling? But we ended up in Portugal for the year-round sun." Game on then.

Chris Best was happy to let Foster and Raith fight it out and then he would challenge the winner with his three boys at Harrow and his place in Tuscany but, for now, he was fascinated by his old friend.

"Do you know Bill here was the best football player I have ever seen," Chris announced, much to Hobbs' relief. He owed Raith a big thank you because it appeared the circumstances of his leaving school and his life in France had been forgotten.

"And I can still remember the game when you broke your leg.

God it was awful. Just at the ankle; it was almost snapped clean in half. Even the ref was in tears."

Hobbs' heart skipped a beat and then began to race. Under the table, he slowly moved his right foot until it cracked. His ankle still occasionally hurt him to this day. He swivelled his foot round again and dutifully it clicked again like it was telling him something else that he'd forgotten.

"You must speak French then?" Mrs Raith asked. For the first time she seemed almost impressed by him. Hobbs felt like he had been hooked again.

"Erm ... no, not any more ... I used to."

Any hint of admiration now vanished from her cold face and, not for the first time, people looked at Hobbs oddly. Isn't speaking a language like riding a bike, something that can't be forgotten?

Hobbs whimpered. *Couldn't we have stayed with the football?*

"He never went to France," Chris Best chuckled. "Well, he might have done, but it wasn't why he left our school I can tell you that now. Not the William Hobston I knew anyway." Hobbs didn't respond. He knew that his toilet break was now the sensible course of action, but he couldn't leave now, not yet anyway. Once again, the table were all waiting for an explanation, and it seemed that Chris would have to provide it.

"Bill, are you going to tell them or should I, because it's nothing to be ashamed of. You were a bloody legend at school after you got expelled."

Expelled! Suddenly another bell chimed away as his dusty old mind increasingly started coming to life.

"Can I?" Chris asked politely.

Hobbs nodded. *Please do.* He was now as intrigued as the rest of them.

Hobbs had no chance of ever winning the table's success game or hierarchy game but for now he was the table's alpha male and his fellow diners were more than happy to pick bugs out of his coat.

"Okay then …" Chris began. "I can honestly say that it was the funniest thing that I've ever seen. We were on this geography field trip to Ireland for a week, on a farm in Tipperary, and down the road from our hostel was this place that we were told we weren't allowed to visit."

Everyone around the table laughed, anticipating exactly what all inquisitive children would do in such circumstances.

"So, of course, William here and a few others go straight down there. And it's just the most beautiful farm any of us had ever seen. Honestly, you've never seen grass like it."

"What, green you mean?" No one laughed at Raith's comment, not even politely.

"This place was stunning, with paddocks and stables you could eat in they were so clean. Do you remember, Bill?"

Hobbs nodded politely.

"It was beautiful …" Chris went on, "and it had the most elegant-looking horses we'd ever seen. Great big beautiful looking things, you know, it was obvious even to us city boys that these were no ordinary horses."

"A stud farm?" a lady ventured.

"Hang on," Chris answered.

The proverbial bell boys must have been exhausted by now because Hobbs' head was now a cacophony of noise. Slowly the fog that had obscured his mind was clearing, memories of his old forgotten life were re-emerging and currently one image that was most prominent in his mind was an old beaten-up black and white horse. The rapt table hung on every one of Chris' words.

"… anyway, one night, none of us can sleep because of this awful moaning coming from way off in the fields. It was pretty bloody scary actually but Bill here went to investigate and, anyway, it turns out to be some knackered old pony tethered to a tree down the lane. It was a real old workhorse; it wasn't even one colour. It was black and white, as I remember." Chris looked over at Hobbs for confirmation.

Another *Ding Dong*.

Hobbs nodded, his eyes now wide open. Like an old rusted screw that eventually gives up the fight and starts to turn, Hobbs' closed mind had finally burst open. Lucid and clear images came rushing at him all at once. The faces of his family; of his older brother going off to the war and his mum standing in their tiny garden looking at his dad sitting proudly on his bike. And his wife Mary on her wedding day looking beautiful. What an evening this was turning out to be. He'd been expecting to get well fed and hadn't considered the notion of getting his marbles back.

Hobbs chuckled because he was now in a position to finish off the rest of his expulsion story for himself and Chris had been right, it was bloody funny. The plush premises up the road were indeed an exclusive stud farm and temporary home to highly valuable mares waiting to be sired by a stud that was on its way from another farm. As it turned out, the travelling stud would be too late because Bill Hobston decided to give the old black and white workhorse the best night of its life. He led the braying beast up to the stud and watched as it literally wreaked hundreds of thousands of pounds of damage with the thoroughbred race horses. Not that the mares appeared to mind. After all, to a horse, a horse is a horse and this old fellah nearly killed himself servicing every last one of them with his heavily polluted seed.

Understandably, there was hell to pay. These mares had come from all over the world to get impregnated with future Kentucky Derby winners but, after Dobbin's efforts, they were now nurturing future tubes of glue. Hobbs laughed even more than the people at his table. He remembered the cheer his classmates had given him when he had returned from the police station, without charge he noted. There had been some heated debate about exactly what crime had been committed and the lawyers reluctantly concluded that there was no legal precedent for forcing two animals to copulate. Michael Hobston was released but promptly expelled from school and so a school legend was born and now almost fifty years later a hero of table 13 at the Grosvenor House Hotel.

"Port, sir?"

"Yes please." *Why not?* Hobbs asked himself. He deserved a glass of port.

It was now well after 11.30 pm and the charity auction was thankfully drawing to a close. Currently up for grabs were two first-class tickets anywhere on the British Airways route map and Mr Jonathan Ross no less was appealing for another paltry five hundred pounds:

"... is that it then, ladies and gentlemen? Six fousand pounds ... anywhere in the world. Just imagine. To experience the wonder of getting on a plane and turning ... left...."

The charity auction is where the hierarchy competition played at tables is now thrown open to the whole gala dinner, a chance then to establish who is the wealthiest and most benevolent of them all. Raith had eventually prevailed on his table and he was now a serious contender for outright winner, having already purchased a pair of Kylie Minogue's signed hot pants for ten grand. He gestured with his cigar.

"Oh yes, thank you very much, on table 13, I have six and half fousand pounds."

No one in the room bothered to clap the flash bastard any more. They all just wanted the blasted thing to end so that they could stretch their legs before the inevitable tribute band launched into Abba and Queen.

"Is that it then? Six and half thousand pounds ... going to the kids wemember ..."

Raith grimaced. *Never mind the bloody kids. Just bang the fucking hammer down.*

"Sold."

Thank God. Raith looked relieved. The price of his ego had cost him considerably but, looking around the room at the number of people he'd beaten, it had probably been worth it. The urbane television presenter was nearly through with his night's work.

"And so finally, ladies and gentlemen, we now come to the pwize dwor of the evening, which as ticket holders of course you are all automatically entered for. Last year, if you recall, a BMW was won and then promptly sold I should imagine, which is why this year the organiser Mr Bloom has decided to go straight and award a cash pwize."

For the first time since the auction had begun, the room fell absolutely silent, something which Ross was quick to seize upon.

"That's shut you all up, hasn't it? The chance of winning some cash eh? … But how much? That's the question, isn't it? I can almost hear you all thinking it …" Ross paused, enjoying the power he suddenly had over the room.

"Ladies and gentlemen, it's only … *twenty fousand pounds …*"

The room burst into excited applause and then fell absolutely silent as quickly again as Mr Ross plunged his arm into the tombola. Hushed anticipation enveloped everyone. Raith had quickly calculated that it was his chance to possibly break even.

Jonathan Ross looked at the ticket and smiled.

"Table 13…"

A sigh of disappointment rung out across the room which quickly became excitement for the lucky people on table 13 where all attention was now focused. Raith clenched his teeth. The Chrises held their breath but Hobbs didn't react at all. It was most peculiar and strange but he didn't need to react because he already knew what was coming next. He couldn't explain it but it was obvious. He was already the biggest winner in the room anyway by having reclaimed his life, but still he felt there was more to come.

"The winner is ... William Hobston."

Of course it is. Hobbs smiled. What else could he do?